STEPHANIE FAZIO

CAPTAIN HARKIBEL

BOOK IV OF THE BISECTER SERIES

Syafant Press

Syafant Press

New York, New York

Cover designed by Teodora Chinde

This book is a work of fiction. Names, characters, places, and incidents either are the product of the author's imagination or are used fictionally, and any resemblance to actual persons, living or dead, business establishments, events, or locales is entirely coincidental.

Stephanie Fazio

Visit www.StephanieFazio.com

Printed in the United States of America
First Printing: January 2020

Library of Congress Control Number: 2019916031

ISBN 978-1-7335929-7-0

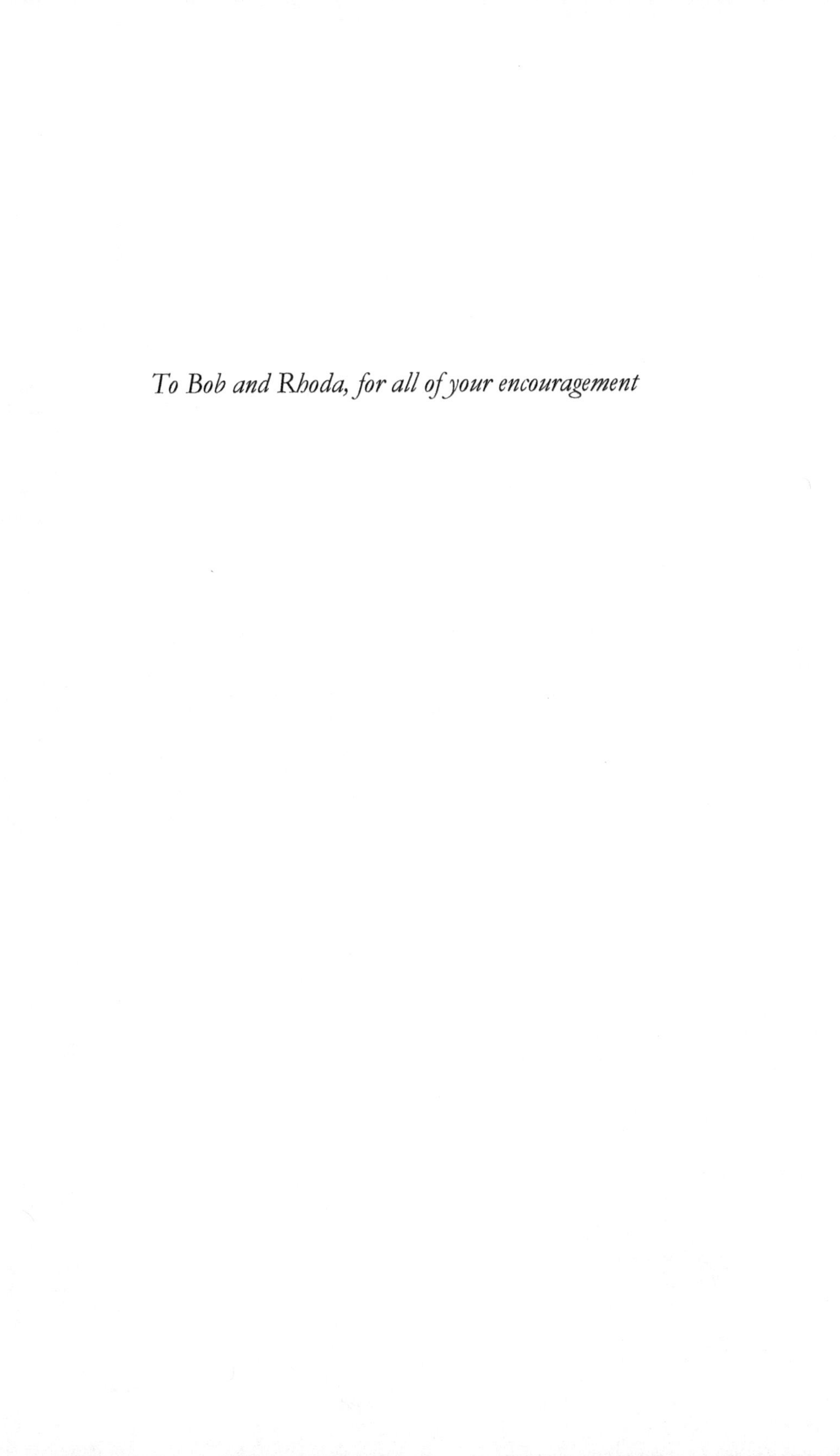

To Bob and Rhoda, for all of your encouragement

PROLOGUE

SIX MONTHS EARLIER

The sun is gone…just gone. After a lifetime of high and low day, when darkness could only be found deep in an underground cave, I can't process what I'm seeing.

Thick waves of black smoke are billowing up from the embers of the darkness tree logs. They're spreading across the sky in all directions. My eyes water and my throat burns from the horrible, cloying smell of the smoke.

The Duskers' chant of "Go in darkness," repeated over and over again by hundreds of voices all speaking in unison, has turned into an ominous drone. The sound makes me almost as uncomfortable as the smell.

I turn to Wade, who is standing beside me. His cloak is in a pile on the ground by his feet, and his neck is craned back as he stares at the mass of dark smoke rolling across the sky.

He glances at me, his eyes full of wonder, before turning his attention down to his bare arms. He's rolled up the sleeves of his shirt, and we both stare at his bronze skin…skin that doesn't show even the hint of a Burn blister.

"So, what now?" Wade asks.

I look across the expanse of molten, poisonous darkness tree sap that has flooded the area between the Solguard army and the Duskers. Nothing remains of the scaffold that held Crowe and Hendrix in the moments before the fire. Nothing remains of Hendrix.

I shudder as the memory of his tortured screams echo in my mind. I see the twin pinpricks of his green eyes, which were the only color in a sea of black flames, before they were extinguished.

"Bring me the Bisecter!"

Crowe's voice, filled with fury and hatred, makes the cries of *Go in darkness* cut off mid-chant.

The Duskers clutch their weapons as their gazes seek me in the dense knot of Solguards.

Hide, the panicked voice from my childhood urges inside my head. *Don't let them find you!*

I look at Wade. I look at the organized columns of Duskers, still armed and battle-ready. And then I look at our soldiers…beaten, bloody, and too few to take on such an army.

"Retreat!" Wade shouts.

No one hesitates. We all run.

We have a short reprieve because the Duskers will need to run around the section of sap-covered ground, but they have crossbows and hundreds of soldiers. We have no more than a third of that number, and all of our archers' arrows are spent.

Our army—what's left of it, anyway—is racing for the splintered remains of the iron gate. I slow my pace.

"Hemera, come on," Wade yells when he realizes I'm no longer beside him.

I look back at the Duskers. Their crossbows are raised, and the Banished stragglers at the back of our fleeing tide have begun to fall.

Even though I can no longer see them, I know Crowe and Jadem are somewhere in the midst of their soldiers, driving what is about to be a slaughter.

I tamp down my fury before it consumes all logic and reason.

"Make sure Wokee gets out," I tell Wade before racing back through the crowd, toward the Duskers and their crossbows. I stop beside a Northerner, who must have twisted his ankle in the muddy ground. He's clutching it, and I can see it's swollen.

"I can't run," he chokes. Tears stream down his cheeks.

I bend down and lift him up. Since the Zeroes were ripped away from me, everything feels harder. I struggle under the man's weight, but I manage to run back through the crowd at a speed faster than any of the Banished are managing without extra burdens.

I deposit the injured man on the other side of the iron gate. Then, I go back for another injured Banished. And another.

I duck out of the way of the crossbow bolts that fly through the increasingly short distance between us until there are too many for me to avoid any longer. I carry the last person I can save—a Westerner with a broken arm and a gash across her stomach. The wound is deep enough that she might die even if I can get her out of here. I couldn't stand the thought of her dying on this side of the iron gate, though.

I run with the woman bouncing in my arms as arrows slam into the ground all around us.

Solguards on the other side of the fractured iron gate are working furiously to use the bent and torn pieces of metal to construct a makeshift barrier. Hopefully it will slow the Duskers down long enough for us to get away. As I sprint for the opening that's been left for me, I see Liglette riding on the only stag that is still alive. She's racing toward us with her hands on her bow and arrow. I can see the quiver on her back is full of a dozen mismatched arrows and recovered crossbow bolts.

"Go back!" I shout to her.

I can sense the Duskers gaining behind me, and the air is filled with the whine of their crossbow bolts flying through the air. I duck on instinct as one of them lands in front of me.

Liglette ignores me. She positions her stag to shield me from the Duskers' arrows.

"Liglette—"

"Go!" she commands, releasing arrow after arrow with a speed and precision that would make Ry proud.

The Westerner in my arms has gone quiet. I adjust my grip on her and keep going, because at this point, it's all I can do. As I get to the gate, I pass her through the narrow opening the Solguards left in the tangled pile of metal.

The makeshift barrier won't keep the Duskers from chasing us for long. I turn and look back at Liglette.

I call her name.

Her stag bellows and lurches as an arrow strikes its shoulder. Dark blood coats its tawny fur. Another arrow brings the stag onto its knees and throws Liglette over its head.

She scrambles to her feet, abandoning her empty quiver and bow, and runs.

Come on. Come on. Come on!

"Hemera, don't you dare—" Ry starts, but I'm already going back for the Western leader.

I won't leave her.

I bite back a cry as an arrow glances off my thigh. Fire races down my leg, and I stumble.

I feel Ry's arms around me, dragging me back.

"No!" I yell, tearing free from her grip.

Liglette is still out there. She needs me.

When an arrow impales my arm, I can't hold back my scream. It feels like fire has filled my veins.

"You'll get yourself killed," Ry grunts, hauling me back out of the Duskers' range.

This time, I don't have the strength to fight her.

Ry doesn't let go of me even once we've reached the rest of the Solguards. Duskers are everywhere now, and all I can do is watch as Liglette tries to get to us.

Hurry up, I want to scream, even though I know she can't go any faster.

Liglette doesn't make a sound when the first arrow pierces her. She stops running. She arches her back as though to rid it of the missile now lodged between her shoulder blades. Then, she stumbles forward.

One step. Two. She's almost close enough to grab my hand.

The next arrow wedges itself into her side, pulling a short cry from her. Her sweat- and blood-slicked hand reaches in my direction, even though she's still several paces away.

"Liglette," I call, desperate now.

My fingers dig into my palms until I feel the sticky heat of blood.

The next arrow strikes her chest. Liglette goes rigid. She just stands there, her eyes wide and her mouth open in surprise. And then, she falls.

I shout her name, but she doesn't get up. She doesn't cry out or scrabble to regain her footing.

"No!" a Westerner beside me wails.

He tries to run to Liglette, but I grab his arm and pull him back. There's nothing we can do.

The beloved leader of the Western Banished…my friend…is dead.

Tears wetting my cheeks, I stay where I am. I don't want to leave her, but I know that if I step out from behind the safety of the rock, I'll end up just like her.

"Mer, come on!"

Ry grabs my hand. I yank the arrow free from my arm, clenching my teeth against the raw agony. I press my hand over the wound to stem the flow of my brown blood. With Ry helping to support me, I turn my back on Malarusk and limp after the rest of our army.

The dark haze of smoke is stretching across the sky. It turns color and sunlight to a cloudy gray that makes it look like a sickness is devouring the land and chasing after our fleeing army.

Far in the distance, on land still bathed in sunlight, my father is leading the one-hundred Zeroes away from me.

CHAPTER 1

NOW

I cough into my arm, trying to muffle the sound. I pull my arm away and find my sleeve spotted in blood.

My eyes are watering from the darkness ash particles that are now a permanent fixture in our air. There is no escaping them.

The coughing, and a dozen far more unpleasant effects of Darkness, have become so familiar I barely notice them anymore. I squint into the heavy gray fog of Gloom.

Gloom is the twelve hours of each day when the sun had previously been too strong for any but I to withstand. During these hours, the air is coated in a dense, gray haze. But as the day wanes and the now-shielded sun lowers on the horizon, Gloom is replaced by Dark.

Dark is so dense it is no different from standing inside a cave without any light. Except, for some reason, it feels more impenetrable.

Even though it's still several hours away from Dark, visibility is poor. The sky is polluted with the particles of darkness ash that never dissipate, no matter how ferociously the wind blows. It's not like there's anything to see around here, anyway. The land is barren and colorless. All life has fled or died, and the earth is blanketed in the same gray ash that has blocked out the sun.

If only the ash was edible, I think, as my stomach grumbles.

I brought enough waterskins for Dayne and I to make it a couple of weeks, but I didn't bring any food. I couldn't bear to raid the fortress's meager stores…not when everyone is starving. Instead, I told the Solguards in charge of allocating the daily rations to give my and Dayne's portions to Wokee and Everlyn.

We've been foraging along our journey, but our prospects have been pitiful. Dayne speared a hare that was skin and bones yesterday, and we haven't come across anything edible since.

It's been six months since Crowe lowered her torch to the mountainous pile of darkness tree logs. Six months since the first layer of ash clouded over the sun.

That day marked the beginning of what is now known as Darkness.

"Come on," I tell Dayne, who is a silent, unnerving presence at my side.

The Zeroes we've been tracking for the last week won't rest, and neither can we.

A Solguard scout caught sight of the Zeroes hunting in the mountains. It was the first hint I'd gotten about the army that had once belonged to me, before my father stole them away. Dayne and I immediately set off to follow the Zeroes in the hopes that they would lead us back to wherever Zeidan has been hiding for the last six months.

The sound of footsteps makes me go still. Dayne copies my movements without me needing to say anything. The invisible blood bond that now exists between us makes words unnecessary.

I motion for Dayne to stay where he is as I creep forward. The footsteps are too erratic and close to be the Zeroes. From the footprints in the ground we've been using to track them, the Zeroes are still half a day ahead of us.

Duskers?

It's unlikely, since there isn't a grove of darkness trees in this area…or anything else, for that matter.

I pull my sling out from my belt, put a stone in the leather pouch, and begin winding it by my side as I squint into the poor lighting.

A small group of people appears through the fog. I let out the breath I was holding, since I can tell from their stooped posture that they're not a threat to us. The poor visibility makes it difficult to make out much, but I can see they're stumbling from exhaustion, and I hear the whimpering of children.

I step forward slowly to avoid startling them.

When they catch sight of me, hoarse cries of fear send them into a fit of rasping coughs.

"It's okay," I say quickly. "I'm not going to hurt you."

I have no doubt that, wherever these people came from, they've seen plenty to terrify them. These days, there are all kinds of deadly threats the Duskers didn't bother to mention when they told us all to pray for Darkness.

There are the monstrous wormkill, which have brought their homes closer to the surface and have an insatiable appetite for human flesh. There's the risk of cold rot…the opposite of the Burn but just as deadly. And of course, there's always the lingering fear of starvation that hovers over all of us.

"Please. Help us."

The ragged cry comes from a dirty, starving woman holding what looks like a filthy blanket around her in place of a cloak. She clutches two children against her sides—a boy and a girl. They look as emaciated as the woman I assume is their mother. Their cloaks are travel-worn, and they're all covered in a layer of the darkness ash. They stink of unwashed bodies, but after a week of travel, I can't pretend like I smell much better.

"I'll help you in any way I can," I tell them in what I intended to be a soothing voice. It turns into more of a croak as the darkness particles tickle my throat and set off another round of coughing.

While I struggle to regain my voice, I stare at the woman and her two children, trying to guess at who they are and where they came from.

We're on the border between the Dusker territory and the Subterrane territory, so my best guess is that these travelers are Dwellers, although I have no idea why they would have wandered so far away from their Subterrane.

Probably searching for food, if their skeletal frames are any indication.

Before I can ask them where they're going, heavy footsteps pound the ground. This time, I instantly recognize the sound. The beast chasing this ragged group of Dwellers is a Zero.

I don't know if it's one of the ones Dayne and I have been tracking or another. It doesn't matter.

"Get back!" I tell the mother and her children.

The little girl screams, and her mother hurries to hush her.

Dayne takes his position by my side and grips the sword he's favored since he became a Zero himself. I have my sling in one hand and my own sword in the other.

A resentment that's been building in me since the Battle of the Iron Gate, when I watched Liglette and so many others fall, quickens my pulse. These Zeroes are the reason why, for months, all I felt was anger and an unquenchable need for more.

Raising my sword, I go to meet the Zero.

Our blades crash together, shattering the unnatural quiet around us. The force is enough to splinter each of our weapons, and the shards of metal burst into the air. I barely manage to avoid the deadly pieces as they drop back to the ground.

I let my useless hilt fall from my hand. With a feral cry more animal than human, Dayne comes at the Zero with his own sword. The Zero ducks out of the way of Dayne's strike.

Dayne stumbles back, and I reach out a hand to keep him from falling to the ground.

The Zero is strong, but it's no match for me and the anger that's been building in me these last months. I've been so helpless...so useless.

Not anymore.

I throw all of my weight at the creature, and we topple to the ground. We roll twice, and I feel the bite of stones and debris cutting through my clothes. I manage to wrap my limbs around the Zero. It's graceless, even for me, but it's enough to immobilizing the creature.

Dayne, I think, pulling on the invisible tether between us.

As the Zero writhes in my grip, I lock my arms around its torso and my legs around its stomach. I can feel the creature's unnatural muscles bulging as it struggles.

"Kill it!" I yell.

Dayne thrusts his sword into the Zero with such force I'm afraid it will go right through the Zero and lodge itself in my chest. And then, with the pain that follows, I'm convinced that's exactly what has happened.

Every breath I take is a burning agony.

Dayne reaches forward and pulls the dead Zero out of my grip and shoves it to the side. I look down, only to see that there's no blood coming out of my chest. There isn't even a slash mark in the fabric of my cloak.

The pain fades as quickly as it had come, and I recognize it as the result of the whisper of connection I still have with the Zero. The one-hundred might belong to my father, but that doesn't undo the fact that my blood runs in their veins.

"You did it." The woman's voice is hoarse. "I didn't believe they could be killed." She drops her hand, and there's an awed expression on her face. "Who are you?"

The better question would have been *What are you?* But I'm not going to tell her that.

"My name's Hemera," I tell her, before accepting the hand Dayne holds out to me and letting him pull me to my feet. I smile and nod my thanks.

As expected, Dayne says nothing. He hasn't said so much as a word in the six months since I turned him into a Zero to save his life.

Limping a little from a twisted ankle that is already beginning to heal, I make my way back to the mother and her children.

"That was…*wow*." The little boy's eyes bug out from his filthy and emaciated face. The sight of him reminds me of the first time I met Wokee. The memory tugs at my heart.

"We're safe now, right?" the girl asks, clutching her mother's cloak.

An ache of sympathy goes through me when I notice the girl's fingers are black with cold rot.

From seeing so many others perish from the disease, I know that her toes, wedged into her cracked and damp boots, are probably rotting, too. It won't be long before the disease is in her blood. Once that happens, there will be no way to save her.

Pity, followed by helpless fury, holds me in a tight embrace I've become overly-familiar with these last six months.

"Thank you," the woman tells me, her fearful gaze shifting to Dayne.

"Don't worry, he's not like them," I reassure her, even though I'm not sure whether that's true.

She gives Dayne another wary look before asking, "You don't have anything to eat, do you? We've been on the run for two days and have barely had a morsel."

My own stomach clenches in response as I shake my head. "I'm sorry," I say, feeling overcome by helplessness again, but she waves away my apology.

I hand over my water, knowing it will do nothing for the ache in their bellies. Still, the children guzzle it down and smack their lips in satisfaction.

"I'm just glad we got away from him," the woman says, watching her children tap the last drops from the waterskin. She shudders, and I don't think it's from the cold.

"Him?" I ask, even though I already have a good idea who she's talking about.

"Captain Harkibel."

There's so much loathing in the way the woman says that name that it makes me flinch.

Even though some of the Banished use that title to refer to me, I know this woman is talking about my father. For once, I'm glad for the gray fog of Gloom, which will make it harder for this woman to notice any resemblance between Zeidan and me.

"What happened?" I ask. "What did he do to you?"

"He's going to turn all of us into those…creatures." Her gaze slides to Dayne again.

Understanding strikes me like a blow to the chest. I even stagger back a step.

"My…" I stop myself before I say *father* and correct, "Captain Harkibel is making more Zeroes?"

The woman nods.

"Death or Zeroes. That's the choice he's giving to every Dweller in the Subterrane territory."

My mind reels from this piece of news. The last time I saw Zeidan, he had one-hundred Zeroes under his command. Now, if what this woman is saying is true, he'll soon have double…even triple that number….

"Please," the woman begs. "I don't want my children to turn into those creatures."

Before I can say anything, the ground shakes beneath my feet. The children cry out and cling to their mother. Dayne lets out a low, rumbling growl as he moves to stand at my side.

A giant's shadow appears out of the haze. And it's headed straight for us.

CHAPTER 2

My sling is whipping in a circle by my side before my brain catches up to my instincts, and I recognize the hairy beast sprinting across the barren ground toward us.

It's Vlaz.

The hyenair comes to a sliding stop only a few paces away from me. He whimpers in excitement as he pads over to me.

"What are you doing here?" I ask, my heart growing light in my chest as I recognize the two people on Vlaz's back as Wade and Ry. Vlaz swipes his giant, purple tongue over my face in greeting.

"Thank you," I tell him, laughing. "I needed a bath."

That feeling of lightness transforms to dread as soon as I consider what reasons the Solguard leader and his second-in-command would have for tracking me here all the way from Tanguro.

It's been more than a week since I've seen either of them, and yet Ry's first words to me are, "My butt is numb."

"My face is numb," Wade replies, sliding off Vlaz's back.

"Trade you," Ry offers.

Wade cocks his head at her. "I'm not sure how that would work."

"Fine." Ry sighs, following him onto the ground. "No trade. My butt's cuter, anyway."

I take their banter to mean there isn't too great of an emergency back at the fortress.

"What are you doing here?" I ask again, needing to raise my voice above the argument that's heating up…about whose butt is more attractive.

"Hiya, Mer!" Ry's stride is bow-legged as she comes over to give me a hug.

"You took off without bringing any Solguards to have your back," Wade says, his expression far less amused than Ry's. "So, we came after you to make sure you didn't do anything…rash."

"I have Dayne," I point out.

Wade and Ry both look at the motionless and silent Zero beside me with suspicion.

"Um, yeah," Wade says, making it clear he doesn't trust Dayne now any more than he did a week ago.

When Ry lets go of me, Wade steps forward with his arms raised partway, like he's going to put them around me. Then, at the last moment, he steps back and drops his arms to his side.

An unpleasant stinging sensation goes through my chest before I silently tell myself to snap out of it.

Wade wouldn't be here if he didn't care about me.

"You really came here just to have my back?" I ask, the thought warming me in spite of the chill wind that is making the mother and her two children tremble.

Wade gives me a short nod before going to retrieve the weapons and supplies tied onto Vlaz's back. Ry goes over to talk to the Dwellers, who are staring up at Vlaz with a combination of terror and awe. I stay to greet the hyenair.

After my father stole the Zero army, Vlaz stopped growling at me. He still won't come near me if Dayne is too close, but otherwise, he's back to his friendly self. During those first few weeks when I craved the lost connection with the Zeroes like I might have missed a lost limb, Vlaz's renewed affection was like a bright spot in a sea of darkness.

Vlaz lowers his head so I can scratch his flopped ear, which is easily the length of my forearm. I reach all the way up with both hands to pet him to his satisfaction.

He drools in contentment as I coo to him. Soon, there's a puddle of sticky slobber on the ground between us.

My chest squeezes at the sight of the hyenair's too-thin frame. His ribs are visible even through his shaggy coat, and his black fur has lost its sheen. I can feel the gritty particles of the darkness tree ash in his fur as I continue to scratch his ear.

When Dayne takes a step closer, Vlaz's upper lip curls, revealing his long fangs.

"Vlaz," I say in the soft-but-dominant tone Wokee always uses with him.

Vlaz lowers his head, but his hackles are still raised as his yellow eyes hold Dayne in their unblinking stare. Dayne, for his part, seems entirely uninterested in the hyenair, which could kill a human with a single snap of his fangs.

"So, dear old Daddy is back to wreaking havoc in the Subterrane territory?" Ry asks, taking the spare cloak Wade hands her and giving it to the Dweller woman.

"So it would seem," I reply, pushing down the tide of anger that threatens to surface at the mere mention of my father.

"Captain Harkibel is your *father*?" the mother, who has been tucking the cloak around her daughter, jerks her head up like she's just scented an enemy.

Ry looks at me and mouths *oops*.

"I—" I falter, not quite knowing how to begin to apologize on behalf of my monstrous father.

"So, what's the plan for when we catch up with the Zeroes?" Wade asks before I have to stutter over some kind of explanation.

"You don't have to help me," I tell Wade and Ry, still a little overwhelmed by the fact that they're here, when I had expected not to have any company aside from Dayne's.

Wade reaches out and taps the Solguard tattoo on the back of my right hand.

"You're one of mine," Wade says, his voice low. His index finger traces the inked rays of the sun across my hand, sending a very different kind of chill through me. "I'll never abandon one of mine."

Before I can let myself replay his words to search for hidden meaning, I take a breath and tell him my plan.

"Once I find out where Zeidan's hiding, I'm going to wait for him to come out when he isn't surrounded by all his Zeroes," I say.

"And then you'll kill him?" Ry rubs her hands together in anticipation.

"And then I'll kill him."

That thought has kept me company on this long and lonely journey. It's warmed me during the hours of Dark and given me strength when my legs would have collapsed from exhaustion.

"Sounds like a reasonable plan to me," Ry says, running a hand over the curved wood of her bow.

"We'll have to leave Vlaz here so the Zeroes don't smell him," I say, giving the hyenair one more scratch for good measure.

Ry stands in front of Vlaz's face. She points her finger to the north and tells the hyenair, "Go. Wait." She follows these commands with two more hand gestures I remember seeing Wokee teach Vlaz.

Even though I've seen Wokee's training sessions with the hyenair, it still amazes me to see Vlaz actually obey. We all watch as he gets a running head start and then rises into the air, his black feathered wings churning up darkness ash and dust.

Once Vlaz is gone, we turn to the mother and her two children.

"What should we do with them?" Ry asks.

I turn to the Dwellers. "You're free to go."

It's a stupid thing to say. *Where are they going to go?*

I'm still contemplating this problem when I catch movement out of the corner of my eye. I feel Dayne's emotions spike through the bond that links us. He's tense, prepared for any threat.

Before I have a clear view, I sense them. It's lighter than the brush of a feather, but it's there…a barely-perceptible thrum deep inside me. I open my mouth to warn the others, but Ry beats me to it.

"Zeroes!" she yells.

CHAPTER 3

Figures a shade darker than the backdrop of the gray sky converge on us. They're everywhere, and they're closing in fast.

Ry backs up and nocks an arrow in her bow. Wade draws his sword from its sheath.

The Zeroes are all around us. And now, because of me, Wade and Ry are in danger.

No, I think, drawing my dagger from my belt. *You won't touch my friends.*

I leap forward, slashing out at the first Zero I reach.

The Zero raises its scythe to block rather than cut. I duck away in a single, practiced move before plunging my dagger into the weak spot in its armor.

The Zero lets out a shriek that raises the hair on the back of my neck. My own cry rips from my throat at the burst of pain across my side in the same place I cut the Zero.

Not real, I tell myself. *The pain isn't real.*

I grasp the blood-slicked hilt of my dagger and move to thrust it in again. Before the blade makes contact, hands with inhuman strength are pulling me back…Zero hands. Their nails, more like claws, dig into my skin. Fresh blood speckles the already-filthy sleeve of my cloak.

I twist and kick, but a second Zero grabs my arms and pins them against my sides. The cold metal of its armor is like a solid wall at my back. The first Zero hooks its leg around mine. I would have toppled backward if it hadn't been for the Zero at my back.

I almost knock myself out when my forehead cracks against the metal plating of its armored chest. I try to use my dagger, but my arms are locked at my sides.

"Stop struggling, Daughter."

That voice.

How could my father be here?

I was supposed to sneak up on him, not the other way around.

"I've been waiting for you for hours," my father interrupts my thoughts in that infuriatingly smug way of his. "I assumed you would be here sooner, but I suppose I overestimated your speed, since you no longer have the added strength of the Zeroes."

I can hear the superiority and triumph in his voice.

Kill him. Kill him!

A voice that isn't entirely my own pulses inside my chest, and I know the thought is coming from Dayne through our blood bond.

"I sent those two Zeroes to Tanguro," Zeidan continues, his voice taunting me all the more because I can't see him. "I expected you would take the bait and come for me. I'm pleased to see I was correct in my assumptions.

"Zeidan, get away from her!" Wade calls out from somewhere behind me.

I can hear Ry cursing and the Dweller children whimpering, but my view is blocked by the two Zeroes sandwiching me.

I renew my struggle against my captors.

Ever since my father stole the Zeroes from me by feeding them meat laced with his own blood, I've felt weak, even though I know I'm still stronger and faster than any human or Halve.

Still, it's a relief to be rid of them. It was only after our bond was severed that I realized how the Zeroes had changed me. Their aggression, anger, and need for violence also became mine.

I'll never be able to erase the look of betrayal Ekil gave me when I banished the Halves from the settlement. I'll never forget what Jarosh said to me.

We'll die. You know that, right?

I had listened to my father and ignored my friends. And my father deceived me. Now, once again, I'm in my current position because it's precisely where he wanted me to be.

My own stupidity hits me like a blow to the chest. I had been so intent on finding Zeidan, and so wrapped up in my need to kill him, that I hadn't bothered to consider that he might have wanted the scouts to discover those Zeroes.

Zeidan knew what would happen when I heard the scouts' report. He knew I would track the Zeroes.

He wanted me to track them.

Like a fool, I walked right into his waiting arms.

Again.

The Zero in front of me moves just enough that my view is no longer blocked. As soon as I look, my heart sinks. Our situation is worse than I thought. At a quick glance, I can see all of the Zeroes are here. They've made a two-Zero thick circular ring around us. Dayne, Ry, and Wade are also being restrained by Zeroes. The Dweller woman and her two children are free from the iron grips of any Zeroes, but given that they're inside the circle with us, there's nowhere for them to run.

The Zeroes standing in front of me step to the side, and my father walks into the circle. He has a hand held to his side in the same place where I stabbed the Zero. He's limping like he's wounded, but I see no evidence of blood.

"Let the others go," I command, even though I have nothing to bargain with right now.

"I understand you're angry that the Zeroes belong to me now," Zeidan says, "but I took possession of them for your own good."

My laughter is harsh and without humor.

"Are you really keeping up with that line of *doing it all for me?*" I ask, derision dripping from every word.

"Everything I do is for you, and for the sake of making this pathetic excuse for a world better," Zeidan replies. "My offer for you to join me still stands. Think about it, Hemera. Think of all the good we could accomplish."

"I don't know where you got these delusions about doing all of this for me, but I'm going to pass," I reply, my voice full of acid.

Zeidan stays far enough back that, even if I were able to escape from my captors, he'd have time to retreat behind his shield of Zeroes.

Coward, I think.

He inclines his head like he's considering what to say to convince me.

Save your breath.

"Do you recall the Dark God festival when you were twelve years old, and you ran in the races against my express instructions to stay hidden?" Zeidan asks.

I hadn't expected that question, and it throws me off guard.

"The one where you accused me of cheating in front of everyone?" I reply. "How could I forget?"

Even all these years later, my cheeks turn hot at the memory of being booed out of the winner's circle.

"Do you know why I accused you of cheating?"

I sigh. I don't have any interest in my father's games and manipulations right now. All I want is to get away from these Zeroes and stick my knife in his chest.

"Because you didn't want the Dwellers to think anyone had the strength to challenge your authority...not even your daughter," I say.

He shakes his head. "There was a Dusker at the festival, and he saw the race. He was going to arrest you and take you to Malarusk."

That revelation is enough to make me stop struggling against the Zeroes. I hadn't seen the Dusker...hadn't known how close I'd come to being dragged to the Malarusk dungeon.

"Mer, don't listen to him," Ry snarls. To Zeidan, she says, "Go bother someone else with your little stories."

"I convinced the Dusker to come back to the Subterrane under the pretense of discussing some urgent matter," Zeidan continues, as though he hadn't even heard Ry. "As soon as we were alone, I killed him. While everyone else was at the feast, I buried his corpse."

My jaw goes slack. I've killed plenty of Duskers in the last year, but during my time as a Dweller in Subterrane Harkibel, it was unheard of to attack a Dusker.

If anyone discovered what my father had done, he would have been tortured and killed. All of his plans and experiments would have died with him. I can't imagine him risking all of that…for me.

"Why are you telling me this?" I ask.

"You assumed the worst about me on that day—that I wished to humiliate you—when the truth was that I was saving you. I have dozens of other stories just like that one." He pauses, considering his next words. "It is true that I wish for greater power, which these Zeroes provide. But it's also true that I've spent every day since you were born safeguarding you from those who would seek to do you harm. I got my hands bloody long ago so you would stay safe."

"Hemera," Wade says through gritted teeth. "Don't listen to him."

Wade's right. I don't want to feel anything toward my father except hatred for everything he's done…all he's taken.

I think about my mother. She's dead because Zeidan was controlling the Halves. I think about all the humans and Halves in Tanguro who were killed in his experiments to create the first Zeroes. I think about how I betrayed the people who matter most to me because I believed my father was helping me.

I snarl and twist, but the Zeroes' grasp is unyielding. Overcome by a rush of petty fury, I spit at Zeidan. The harmless glob lands on the ground in front of him.

My father raises an eyebrow at me. His expression is tolerant.

"Fight me," I demand, furious and humiliated at the same time.

My father shakes his head. "I have no desire to fight with you."

"Then, let us go." I hate how the anger in my voice has turned to pleading.

"I can't do that, Hemera," my father replies, stepping closer to me. "Not until I get what I need from you."

He's so close. If I could just get away from these Zeroes….

I give my arm an experimental yank. The Zeroes react immediately, tightening their grip until I can do little more than move my eyes in their sockets.

Zeidan prowls closer. He knows there's nothing I can do to him.

Now that there isn't any distance separating us, I get my first good look at my father in six months.

He's changed. His hair and beard, which used to be a tangle of salt-and-pepper, are now neatly trimmed and fully white. I can't decide if it makes him look older or younger. He doesn't have the wasted, sunken appearance like so many of the people in our fortress. If anything, my father looks filled out in a way I've never seen him before. He's taller, too…almost as tall as Dayne. His brown eyes also seem darker, although that might just be some trick of the Gloom.

"If you won't join me, then I will have to take what I need," Zeidan says.

He turns away from me, but not before I see disappointment pinching the corners of his mouth.

"And what's that?" I ask.

I didn't think it was possible to loathe him any more, but I feel my resentment growing with each passing second.

My father smiles at me.

"Your blood, of course."

CHAPTER 4

I don't have a chance to react before the Zeroes shove me onto the ground, making it even easier for them to restrain me.

"Hemera!" Wade yells.

"Get your hands off her!" Ry screams.

I feel Dayne's fury and desperate urge to protect me propelling him forward.

"No," I tell Dayne, my own emotions rising to match his. "Stay where you are."

My father won't hesitate to kill him, and there are too many Zeroes for Dayne to take on. Zeidan might be able to bleed me dry, but I'll never let him near Dayne.

I feel a burst of resentment from Dayne at the control I'm exerting over him. The emotion is like a slap to the face, since it's the first time in months I've felt anything from him aside from rage.

My father stalks up to me. I twist my head enough so I'm looking at his face instead of his boots.

"Let the others go," I say through gritted teeth. "Then, I'll give you what you want."

"That's not how this is going to work," Zeidan replies. "I gave you a chance to cooperate, and you spit in my face…quite literally, I might add."

He smirks at me before motioning one of the Zeroes forward. The Zero produces a glass jar and a dagger.

"Don't touch her," Wade snarls as he struggles against the two Zeroes holding him.

My father ignores Wade, Ry, and Dayne as they continue to fight ineffectually against the Zeroes restraining them.

"Hold out your arm," Zeidan commands me.

"Or what?" I shoot back, knowing full well I'm in no position to deny him anything.

My father sighs. "Either do as I say, or my Zeroes will slaughter each and every one of your friends."

"I'd like to see you try, you piece of—" Ry's voice cuts off as her Zero captor wraps a hand around her throat.

My blood runs cold, and it has nothing to do with the temperature outside. I know my father. I know he wouldn't hesitate to make good on his word to force me into compliance.

"Okay." I hear the resignation in my voice and feel my body curl in on itself in defeat.

"Hemera, no!" Wade shouts.

I hold out my wrist, allowing my father to make a small incision. Brown blood immediately wells to the surface. My father holds up the jar to capture the droplets.

"Up to your old tricks, aren't you, Zeidan?" I ask, trying to distract myself from the jar filling with my blood.

"I answer to Captain Harkibel again these days," my father replies. His gaze tracks the blood as it gathers at the base of the jar. "It seemed appropriate given that I've reclaimed Subterrane Harkibel."

He glances up from the blood to look at me. "Being back there feels a bit like everything is coming full circle."

"Sentimental," I murmur, feeling a little dizzy as my blood continues to fill the jar.

"That's enough," Wade yells, still straining against the Zeroes holding him captive.

My father doesn't so much as glance his way.

The jar is more than halfway full, and still, my father keeps the glass pressed against my wrist.

"The Dwellers are dying of starvation and poison from the darkness ash," Zeidan tells me. "I'm doing them a service by transforming them from their weak human forms into something far more durable."

"Liar!" the Dweller woman shrieks as she clutches her children. "You're a monster!"

I don't even know if my father has heard her. His gaze is fixed on the jar.

He continues, "At this moment, I have a more pressing use for your blood."

My father reaches into his pocket and pulls out a roll of script tree bark. I recognize it before I even see the writing covering both sides.

My mother's letter. The one she left for me in the Crystal Caves explaining what she'd done to me…the recipe she'd written down for how she made me into a Bisecter.

My hand reaches unconsciously for the key necklace I still wear. Since I learned about what my mother did to me, I've thought about getting rid of the necklace a hundred times. I've just never been able to do it.

"My transformation is nearly complete," Zeidan replies.

That's when I understand. My father's altered appearance…his height, muscles, and darker eyes….

My breathing hitches. I shouldn't be surprised by the realization of what my father's been up to for the past six months. I knew he had my mother's letter, and I knew he desired to become like me. Still, I hadn't believed he would ever manage to successfully replicate my mother's creation.

"There's one more ingredient I need to take the final step of becoming just like you," he says, squinting at the script tree bark.

Like he hasn't already memorized every line of it, I think bitterly.

Holding the jar in one hand, Zeidan takes a vial of dark liquid out of his pocket with the other. He unscrews the lid on the vial, adds it to the jar of my blood, and swirls around the contents.

"I needed to make some adjustments to your mother's formula, since her procedure was for an unborn child," Zeidan tells me.

His patient explanation reminds me of when I was young and he was telling me about a new breed of plant he'd discovered.

"So, that's it." I rub away the dried blood from my wrist as the Zeroes form a tight knot around me, keeping me blocked off from my father. "You have what you want. Tell the Zeroes to let my friends go."

Ignoring me, Zeidan gestures to one of the Zeroes standing by. It comes forward and hands him a narrow length of tubing and a bone needle. My father takes the dagger he used on my wrist and makes a gash beneath his collarbone. I watch in fascinated horror as he uses the bone needle and tube to siphon the blood out of the jar and inject it straight into himself.

For several seconds, nothing happens. Everyone is silent and motionless as we wait to see what will happen.

My father begins to change. At first, it's just a slight pulling of the skin around his eyes and mouth. His eyes roll back in his head, and his back bows.

His shoulders twitch. He doubles over even as his torso seems to lengthen. Bare ankles appear where his pants are now several inches too short. When he jerks again and his spine snaps back with such force I think it might be breaking, I see the expression of sheer agony on my father's face. His skin is bloodless, and spider web-thin black veins have appeared all over his neck.

There is a ripping sound—loud in the otherwise silent enclosure of Zeroes—and my father's shirt splits down the middle. The black veins shiver down his skin, crisscrossing and overlapping until there is more of the black than his flesh.

His breathing comes in short, erratic gasps. He starts to moan, but the sound cuts off as he collapses to the ground, his whole body convulsing.

He writhes. The Zeroes holding onto me drag me back, their claws digging into my skin, to give my father room.

He screams. It's the kind of scream that would have me covering my ears if I had the freedom to move my arms. The sound has me clenching my jaw until I think it will break. I smell burning, but I no longer know whether it's some part of my father's transformation or a figment of my own imagination.

Zeidan's thrashing stops so abruptly he must have passed out. Unless.... *Could he be dead?*

I don't even have a chance to react to that possibility before he's sitting up.

The motion is fluid and graceful. It's nothing like his erratic movements from a few seconds ago.

He doesn't look like one of the Zeroes. He's larger and more muscled than he was before, but compared to the Zero now crouching by his side, he still looks human.

"Lantern," he commands, and his voice sounds the same as it did before.

One of the Zeroes approaches and holds out the light. My father stands motionless for several seconds. Then, he lifts up the lantern. His gaze locks on mine. My breath catches.

My father's eyes are black…black as the Zeroes surrounding us…black as mine.

My father isn't one of the Zeroes, though. Aside from the black eyes, and some extra height and muscle, he looks exactly the same as he did before.

He glances at me before striding several paces away. He squats down beside a large, flat boulder that is half-buried in the dirt.

Without a moment of struggle or hesitation, he lifts the boulder from the ground and thrusts it over all of our heads the way a child might toss a small wooden disc.

The boulder sails through the air, and I lose sight of it in the darkness. A faraway thud comes several seconds later when the boulder hits the ground.

Someone—one of the children—lets out a muffled cry. The sound is drowned out as Zeidan raises his hands up to the dark sky and lets out a victorious shout.

"Mer, what did he do?" Ry demands.

What have I done?

My blood. My mother's note. Black eyes and inhuman strength.

I stare at the man…who is no longer just a man. My father is a Bisecter.

CHAPTER 5

I stand before the only other Bisecter in existence.

I can't make my mouth form a single word. The knowledge of the strength that lies behind his deceptively human body is almost too much to comprehend.

He's like me.

"Finally, Daughter. Finally, we are equals."

A thousand thoughts pass through my mind, but I can't find the words to voice even one of them. With a jolt of surprise, I realize it's because I'm afraid of him. I'm afraid of my father…of what he's become…of what he's now capable of.

He looks at me in expectation. When I still don't say anything, he sighs and turns to the Zeroes.

"Kill the humans," he says.

"No," I begin. "You said if I gave you my blood—"

My words are cut off by the wails of the two children as the Zero raises its scythe. The curved blade slices through the air, and then their mother falls to the ground.

"Mama," the little girl sobs.

The boy's hands are covered with blood as he tries in vain to staunch his mother's wound.

The Zero's movements are slow…predatory…as it turns on the little girl.

My screams combine with others as a cacophony of anguish and terror fills the air. My muscles tear as I writhe against the Zeroes.

My father wouldn't. He can't.

"Please!"

My legs give out as the little girl's lifeless body hits the ground.

Vomit fills my throat. A third Zero has come to restrain me. I'm barely aware of the blood leaking from the places where their nails dig into my flesh. One of the Zeroes slaps a hand over my mouth to drown out my cries. Its hand is big enough to cover my nose and mouth. I can't breathe.

The Zero drops its hand, only to close it around my throat. Its grip is tight enough that every breath feels like inhaling darkness smoke. My face is locked in place, so I have no choice but to watch the horror playing out before my eyes.

The little boy, crouching beside his sister's lifeless body, forces himself to his feet as the Zero stalks closer. He stands his ground. The boy is impossibly tiny compared to the towering Zero. He has nothing but his balled fists to defend himself against the Zero's scythe.

There's nothing I can do to help him. I can't even open my mouth to plead with my father. I'm useless.

The little boy starts to back away, but he trips over a rock on the ground and goes down onto his hands and knees. He crawls to the edge of the circle of Zeroes, trying to scoot between their legs.

For one, hope-filled second, I think he might make it. The Zeroes standing in the circle are motionless and staring straight ahead. But as soon as my heart begins to beat again, I see the flash of a blood-stained scythe. I hear a thud as the blade connects with its target.

The child doesn't make a sound. He just collapses in a small heap.

The air fills with screams. I can't see through the tears pouring from my eyes. One of the Zeroes adjusts its grip, bringing its forearm within reach of my mouth. I shift my head and bite down on the creature's arm as hard as I can.

The Zero lets out a startled a growl and lets go of me. I don't hesitate before wrenching myself free from the others.

My knife is still in my belt, and I lash out with it at anything I can reach.

My father. Kill my father.

It's all I can think about…all that matters.

"Hemera, no."

The sound of Dayne's voice—lower and gruffer than the brother I remember, but still recognizable—shocks me enough to make me hesitate.

A Zero's scythe cuts through the air in the place I would have been if Dayne's voice hadn't stopped me.

The fact that I would be dead right now if not for Dayne's voice is less of a surprise than the fact that he can speak. But there's no time to talk to him or try to understand.

The Zeroes still have Dayne, Ry, and Wade, and the only way I'm getting them back is if I kill my father.

I twist away from two Zeroes that try to grab me. I'm almost within reach of Zeidan, who is watching me with an expression that is more amused than angry.

I grip my dagger and run toward him. My father might be a Bisecter now, but I have an advantage he doesn't…a lifetime of being what I am.

A slight patter of something on the ground isn't enough to draw my attention away from my father. It's only when I look up and am pelted in the face by droplets of searing rain that I realize what's happening.

Gloomy rain—rain that burns and scalds, much like the Burn blisters in the days of sunlight. The rain, polluted with darkness tree ash in the air, erodes skin on contact. If a person stays out in it for too long, their skin melts away in a slower version of contact with the poisonous darkness tree sap.

"Hemera!" Wade yells.

I turn to see that the Zeroes have let go of their prisoners. They're ducking their heads and roaring as the searing rain finds its way through their armor and burns their skin. Their perfect formation dissolves as they rush toward my father. In their haste, they step on top of the lifeless bodies of the mother and children.

My vision goes red with rage.

I won't let my father get away with this. I won't let him hurt anyone else.

Already, there's a thick shield of Zeroes surrounding Zeidan, and they're herding him away from me.

A howl of fury escapes me.

"Zeidan!" I shout.

The wind and rain tear the word away from me, and my father retreats without so much as a backward glance.

"Mer, come on!" Ry gasps, trying to shield her face from the pelting rain.

I barely feel the gloomy rain. Even as the droplets fall into the puncture wounds all over my arms and legs left by the Zeroes' claws, all I can see is the sickle blade slicing into those children.

"Hemera, we have to go." Wade grabs my hand and pulls me away from the Zeroes...away from my father.

I fight him, desperate to go after Zeidan even though I know there's no point. With hundreds of Zeroes whose only purpose in life is to safeguard him, I won't even get close enough to use my dagger. But logic isn't a priority right now. All that matters is getting to my father. Making him pay....

I'm swept off my feet and slung over Dayne's back as though I weigh no more than an empty flour sack. He ignores my shouts and curses. I pound on his back and scream until my vocal cords are shattered, but he doesn't put me down.

Too many Zeroes, is his silent reply to my furious commands.

Dayne begins to run in the opposite direction...away from my father and vengeance.

CHAPTER 6

Dayne doesn't put me down until we're too far away for me to see the Zeroes. With the rain washing out their footsteps, I won't be able to track them down.

I had my chance to kill my father. Now, it's gone. He's gone.

If it wasn't for Ry and Wade, I would have gone after him and probably gotten myself killed. But Ry's whimpers are enough to keep my attention on finding some kind of shelter. I'm the reason they're out in the gloomy rain right now, and they've already come close enough to death for my sake today.

We run across the barren land of the Subterrane territory. I squint through the gloomy rain for a grove of dead script trees or anything else that will offer some refuge.

A tightening of the bond inside me is the first sign that Dayne is no longer running beside me. I turn to look for him, biting back a cry as the rain falls into my eyes.

I follow the invisible tug of our bond, trusting in it since I can't see more than a foot or two in front of me.

"Hemera?" Wade asks, his shoulders hunched as he tries to shield himself beneath his cloak.

"This way," I gasp, hoping Dayne knows what he's doing.

I keep up a steady jog until I feel the tightness inside me begin to ease. It's only when I look down in an effort to protect my face from the brunt force of the rain that I see Dayne crouching on the ground.

He pushes aside a long, flat rock indicating the covering of a cave. I would have run right past it if Dayne hadn't been here. Once we're all inside the tunnel, I pull the covering back into place and enclose us in darkness.

The only sound is my friends' ragged breathing. It smells like rotting earth down here, but it doesn't have the foul stench I've come to associate with the wormkill. Instinct tells me this cave is abandoned, as nearly all of them have been since Darkness came and it no longer made sense to live below ground.

"Is everyone okay?" Wade asks.

"Yes," I say.

"Alive…I think," Ry replies.

"Dayne's fine, too," I add.

I don't need to see him to know he's alive and uninjured.

There's the sound of fumbling, and then sparks light the air as Wade strikes a flint to the blade of his dagger. He holds up a small candle, the flame emitting a weak glow. I swallow my gasp at the sight of Wade's face. It's speckled with red burn marks from the rain.

"That bad, huh?" he asks me.

"I've seen worse," I reply with a forced smile, trying to distract us both from the pain he must be feeling.

"And I thought women found me attractive." Wade gives me a wry look.

"Well, now you know better," Ry tells him. She puts a hand to her cheek and winces. "Lucky we got down here before my whole face burned off."

"How did you know this cave was here?" Wade asks me.

"I didn't," I reply. "Dayne did."

My friends go quiet. Neither of them approved of my choice to turn Dayne into a Zero, and none of us know quite how to behave around him anymore.

On the day I transformed him into a Zero, my brother's eyes turned from blue to black, and the soft-spoken, loyal, and protective man he used to be was gone. That man was replaced by a creature made of muscle and primal rage. Everything that made him the brother I knew had vanished.

I still don't know if I made the right choice by turning Dayne into a Zero. He would have died if I hadn't, but there's a persistent voice in my head that says Dayne would rather be dead than living like this. It all comes down to one truth. As selfish as it is, I could never have let my brother go. Having him like this is nothing like the way it was before, but it's something.

Until today, I had thought he was as mute and devoid of humanity as the other Zeroes.

I don't know if the words were forced from him because of some desperate need to save my life, or if it's an ability he's held back until now.

Time to find out.

My pulse speeds up in anticipation…in hope.

Talk to me, I think to Dayne.

A distant sort of anger takes hold of me that I know isn't my own. A few moments later, I hear his rumbling voice.

"Kill him."

The voice is deeper and raspier…more devoid of emotion…than the one belonging to the brother I remember. But that doesn't matter. *Dayne can talk.*

Excitement makes thoughts jumble inside my head. Maybe Dayne is coming back to himself. Maybe he isn't the emotionless creature he seems.

Maybe the brother I remember isn't gone. Maybe he's just buried inside this Zero.

As for Dayne's words themselves, I don't need any explanation for the subject of his rage. I can feel the source of the anger radiating off Dayne as easily as I can interpret my own emotions. *My father.*

"Dayne can talk?" Ry asks, incredulous. "I thought I'd imagined his voice before, and that I was losing my mind."

"Your mind's still intact. For now, at least," Wade replies.

I tune out their light-hearted teasing as I focus my attention inward to the blood bond connecting Dayne and me.

Why have you kept silent for so long? What else do you remember from before you were changed? How much of my brother is buried inside this creature you've become?

No response.

"Dayne," I begin, my voice cracking on the sound of his name. "Do you remember me?"

"Yes." His voice has a harsh undertone that is so different from the soft-spoken brother I remember…the man I'm now afraid only exists in my memories.

"Dayne, is that really you?" Ry asks before my guilt can consume me entirely.

Dayne must have heard her, since the Zeroes have heightened senses, but he doesn't even glance her way.

"Do you remember Wokee?" I ask, still unwilling to give up on my brother, especially now that I know there's more going on inside him than any of us suspected.

"The child. Yes."

My heart sinks at the way he says those words. There isn't an ounce of warmth or feeling in them. Not even protectiveness.

"Do you remember what I did to you?" I ask, my voice no more than a hoarse whisper.

"Yes."

Dayne's resentment shoots through the bond again, and this time, I understand the source of the emotion: me. If I wasn't so certain that he wouldn't—couldn't—do anything to harm me, I might be afraid.

"You're angry with me."

Dayne doesn't say anything, but he doesn't need to. I can feel his answer through the tension radiating inside me.

You wish I was dead, don't you? I'm too much of a coward to ask the question out loud, so I say it through the silent bond Dayne and I share.

"No," Dayne says.

The word lets some hope sneak through the guilt and regret of my own emotions. But before I can form another question, Dayne speaks again.

"If you die, I die."

CHAPTER 7

As soon as the gloomy rain has passed, we're back on the Outside, trudging across ground that has turned into a thick muck.

"I hope Vlaz found somewhere safe and dry to hole up in during the rain," I say as the mud slurps at my boots.

"He'll be fine," Ry assures me. "He's—"

A Burn vulture's shriek cuts off her words. I look up and see it circling overhead. Its movements are haphazard and jerky, like it isn't in control of itself.

The creature's cry has a distinctly human quality, which makes it even more disturbing.

I look up in time to see the giant creature falling in a mass of feathers and talons. There's a sickening thud as the beast hits the ground a short distance in front of us. We all stop walking and stare.

The Burn vulture's orange feathers are coated in the same gray ash that has blanketed the sky and blocked out the sun.

I have no love for these beasts that survive by feeding off the weak and dead, but there is something disturbing about seeing such a powerful creature fall.

"Seeing something so big be taken down by the Darkness makes me feel—"

"Vulnerable?" Wade offers. "Like we're clinging to our own lives by threads?"

"Yeah."

We all go quiet, and I know we're sharing the same thought. If we can't push back the tide of Darkness that Crowe and Jadem brought on our world, we'll all be doomed.

I hear another flutter of wings overhead, but this time, it's Vlaz. He lands in front of us, his bony sides heaving.

"What do you think, boy?" Ry asks, giving the hyenair's flopped ear a scratch. "You strong enough to carry Wade and me back?"

Vlaz's dull yellow eyes brighten a little, and he lies down in the muck so Ry and Wade can clamber onto his back.

Before Darkness, Vlaz could have carried four adults without a thought. Now that he's starving along with the rest of us, he doesn't have the energy to carry more than two. Even if he was stronger, though, Dayne and I would still need to go on foot. Vlaz can barely suffer Dayne to be within his sight. If Dayne tried to ride him, I have no doubt someone would get killed.

"See you back at the fortress in a couple of days," Wade tells me.

"I haven't gotten that slow," I remind him. "Let's make it a day."

The ghost of a smile crosses his face. "See you then."

I wait until Vlaz is in the air and flying back in the direction of Tanguro before turning to Dayne.

"Ready to run?" I ask.

He doesn't answer, but the slits of his nose open and close as he scents the blood that binds us together.

"I'll take that as a yes," I mutter.

Knowing he'll match me step for step, I take off in the direction of the Wild Lands.

✳ ✳ ✳

After the first few weeks of Darkness, when the novelty of being able to go outside without fear of the Burn had worn off, we learned that survival in this new age would look very different from what it had been before.

Solguard scouts reported that the Wild Lands were less affected by the darkness trees, since the Duskers had been less attentive to planting the trees on land beyond the northern mountain range. Those of us who had taken refuge in Valior's settlement packed up our meager possessions and headed north.

We arrived in the Wild Lands to find that the reports about it being less impacted by the Darkness had been over-exaggerated. It was warmer and lighter than the territories closer to Malarusk, but not by much. The plants in Tanguro died more slowly, but they still died. And without the sun, there was no way to bring them back to life.

The more darkness trees the Duskers burned, the more the veil of ashy black thickened and spread.

As Dayne and I run, my stomach growls, reminding me that it's been more than a day since my last meal. I ignore the emptiness and run faster.

We've been tracking a straight path northward for hours. There hasn't been even a hint at anything aside from the shriveled remains of dead trees and animal skeletons. So, when I catch movement out of the corner of my eye, I pull up short. It's the time of day when Gloom turns to Dark, and the eerie color of the sky plays tricks on people's eyes. I peer into the distance, searching out that glimmer of movement.

There it is again.

"Did you see that?" I ask Dayne.

One short nod of his head.

I pull my sling out of my belt, letting the anxiety and tension rolling off me warn Dayne to be on his guard.

One flash of movement turns into another, which turns into two more.

Duskers?

The thought sends simultaneous shudders of anticipation and dread coursing through me. For six months, I've fantasized about killing Crowe almost as often as I've thought about killing my father.

I squint into the distance, searching for gray cloaks and crossbows to tell me I'm right. I get close enough to use my sling, but I don't release the stone I've readied in the leather pouch.

A strange sense of familiarity keeps bringing me closer step by step, even though it would be smarter just to give this company a wide berth. With the poor lighting, Dayne and I could probably slip past without anyone being the wiser.

The wind picks up, and for a few seconds, the fog lifts. It's just enough for me to get a clear glimpse of the camp in the distance. A surprised sound escapes me at the sight of the figures milling around the weak fire. It isn't a group of Duskers like I'd thought, or even the bandits that are known to wander in these parts.

It's the Halves.

CHAPTER 8

"Ekil?"

His name comes out of me in a barely-audible squeak.

The Halve is emaciated and more stooped than the last time I saw him. I clear my throat and try again.

"Ekil?"

He whips around to face me. At the same time, three other Halves leap to their feet, gripping their stone clubs and baring their teeth. I put away my sling and hold my hands out in front of me to show I mean them no harm.

"It's me. Hemera," I say, before thinking that announcing myself might encourage their hostility rather than calm them.

Whatever grief and hardships have befallen the Halves, it's my fault. I'm the one who banished them from the Eastern settlement in a fit of rage when Brogut attacked one of my Zeroes.

My friends begged me not to make the decision, but I'd been so consumed by my bond with the Zeroes that I couldn't see clearly.

Now that I'm myself again—fully in control of my thoughts and free from the all-consuming rage that flowed through the bond—I'm filled with shame. I can barely bring myself to look the Halves in the eye.

"I'm not here to hurt you," I tell them, taking slow, careful steps forward.

I search for Brogut and his tree trunk spear. Even though it isn't like him to be anywhere other than at Ekil's side, I don't see any sign of him among the dozens of Halves crowding around.

They all watch me with a wary distrust, but none of them make a move to attack me.

They're probably too exhausted and weak, I think. Another wave of guilt crashes over me.

Their faces are sunken, and the knobs of their spines stand out in harsh relief against their bowed backs. Many of the Halves are shirtless, and the rest are filthy and covered in rags. They look like the monsters from my childhood, back when I believed the Halves were senseless beasts who hungered only for violence.

"Hemera Harkibel, you've got some nerve showing up here."

Jarosh strides forward, a wooden club in one hand and his other clenched into a fist. My heart aches at the sight of my friend. When I exiled the Halves, he left with them to be with his mate, Camike. This is the first time I've seen him since.

Shame knocks the breath from my lungs as I take in Jarosh's altered appearance. Six months ago, he was all lean muscle and looked every bit the Solguard warrior he was. Now, his cheekbones protrude so sharply they looks like they're about to cut right through his skin. But unlike many of the Halves surrounding him, there's no hollow look of defeat in his eyes. His gaze is full of fire.

"I'm sorry," I say, not even sure how to begin apologizing for all the damage I've done, only knowing I have to try.

"Sorry." Jarosh scoffs. "Sorry your psychopath of a father duped you once again, or sorry that you turned your back on your friends in favor of your pets?"

I open my mouth to reply, but the words sound too useless and pathetic in my own head. So, I don't say anything at all.

Jarosh lifts his club and switches to the Halve language. "Well, come on then, Bisecter. Finish us off. If you can."

Before I can stutter out an explanation or another apology, Camike comes up behind Jarosh. She wraps her arms around him and whispers something in his ear. Jarosh grumbles out a reply, but the furious expression on his face softens.

Camike is thinner than she was, but it's obvious she still takes pride in her appearance. Her animal hide dress is threadbare, but each hole has been patched over with colorful squares of cloth. Her thin hair is still plaited with feathers and wooden beads. And her black eyes still hold kindness, even when she looks at me.

"Why are you here?" Ekil asks, his gravelly voice and black eyes revealing nothing of whatever emotions lie beneath.

"And why would you bring that *thing* here?" Jarosh demands, indicating Dayne.

"I—" I wilt under the glares of the Halves, and for a moment, I'm a little girl in Subterrane Harkibel again. Instead of the Halves, it's the Dwellers who are staring and muttering about me under their breath. The difference this time, though, is that I deserve the Halves' contempt.

I force myself to stand up straight and meet their gazes.

"We went to hunt down Zeidan and the Zeroes. But I couldn't do it."

"Yeah, shocker." Sarcasm drips from Jarosh's voice.

"It wasn't that I didn't want to," I clarify, feeling my temper rise in spite of the fact the Halves have every reason to hate me. "There were too many Zeroes and we were overpowered, and then the gloomy rain came."

"Why are you here?" Ekil asks again.

Fifty starving, furious Halves stand waiting for my answer.

I lick my parched lips. I grasp for the waterskin around my throat before remembering I gave it to the Dweller children.

The children my father's Zeroes cut down....

I swallow the bile that rises in my throat and force the memory to the back of my mind.

"I'm on my way back to Tanguro," I tell the Halves. "We're living in the building that wasn't destroyed in our battle with the Duskers."

"You using the catacombs to make more Zeroes with Daddy?" Jarosh asks me, his face twisting in disgust.

Some of the Halves snarl at the reminder of their imprisonment at my father's hands.

"No, I'm not." The last of my patience disappears in the face of my rising anger. "We're trying to survive the same as all of you."

"Well, good luck with that." Jarosh turns away from me.

"Come back with me," I say before I've even thought about whether the offer is a good idea. "All of you."

"Halves and humans hate each other. Kill each other," Ekil says.

"Maybe there's already been enough death," I reply, holding Ekil's stare. "Maybe we can put all of those differences aside for now and help each other survive."

When none of the Halves respond, I continue, "We have plenty of firewood from the destroyed building, and it isn't as cold there as it is here."

Even as I try to convince the Halves to return to the fortress with me, I think about our diminishing food supplies. I think about our already-crowded living space. I think about the last time the Halves and humans made an alliance, and how they wanted to kill each other almost as much as they had our enemies.

One look at the Halves' emaciated faces, though, and my decision is made.

"Come," I insist. "Maybe if we combine our strengths and resources, we'll figure out a way to end the Darkness." I give the Halves a wry smile. "Once we've done that, we can go back to being enemies if you want."

"You bet your Bisecter butt we will," Jarosh shoots back, but already, he's motioning for the Halves to gather their meager belongings.

Ekil takes two steps closer to me. He points a gnarled finger at me.

"Give your word."

"I swear I'll do everything I can to keep the Halves safe," I say without hesitation. "And I'll make sure you are given an equal share of whatever resources our fortress has to offer."

"Your word isn't worth a handful of Burn vulture feathers," Jarosh says in the Halve language, "but I'm ready for a change of scenery." He turns to regard the Halves milling around the camp. "How about all of you?"

Their harsh rumbles answer in agreement.

Now, I just have to make sure the rest of the Banished leaders will let the Halves stay. It shouldn't take too much convincing. As much as the Banished and Halves hate each other, I know none of the leaders approved of my decision to send the Halves away.

Still, no one in the fortress will be happy about the extra mouths to feed. I'll have to convince them the Halves' presence in the fortress won't just be an act of charity. The Halves can help us as much as we can help them. Combining our forces will benefit us all.

Even if Valior and Tut try to argue against letting the Halves coming back, I know Wade will support me. He begged me to go after the Halves and bring them back before the Battle of the Iron Gate.

"What about Brogut?" Camike asks Jarosh and Ekil, her voice hushed.

Ekil's usually-stoic face transforms into something that can't be interpreted as anything other than grief.

"What happened to Brogut?" I ask.

"Stay out of our business, Bisecter," Jarosh snarls.

"He's sick," Camike tells me, putting a calming hand on Jarosh's chest. "He needs warmth and food."

"We have both of those at the fortress," I tell her.

"He is too ill to walk." Camike bows her head in defeat.

The rest of the Halves are weak enough that they can barely carry their own weight, let alone support the largest of them all.

"Show me where he is," I tell Camike, ignoring the growls as I stride past Ekil and into the Halves' camp.

Camike leads me to Brogut, who is lying motionless on the cold ground. His bare torso is raw with scorch marks from the gloomy rain, and his every rib is visible. I bite down on my lip until I taste blood.

My fault. My fault. My fault.

The words echo in time with my thudding heart.

I can stand here and succumb to the tears that want to fall, or I can do something to try and fix the mess I've created. I bend down and, as gently as I can manage, lift Brogut.

Even as little more than skin and bones, he's still a giant. His bulk is awkward to hold, and it takes me several seconds to adjust my grip so no part of him is dragging on the ground.

"Take whatever you can carry," I tell the Halves as I find my footing with Brogut in my arms. "Let's get out of here."

CHAPTER 9

Even in their weakened state, the Halves move faster than any human. When we reach the Dusker territory, we have to go miles out of the way to avoid being seen by anyone in or around Malarusk. It takes us two days to reach the mountains that mark the southern border of the Wild Lands. I carry Brogut the whole way, and Dayne carries one of the other Halves who is especially weak.

In spite of everything that has happened between Brogut and me, now that my mind is clear, I have no interest in seeing him die. I'm especially not going to let him die in my arms.

As his breathing becomes increasingly labored, I find myself talking to him. At first, it's just mindless chatter about Tanguro and how we've transformed the building to suit our new needs as a result of Darkness. When that doesn't seem to interest him, I begin baiting him…asking him what kind of Halve allows himself to be conquered by a little cold and hunger. I manage to get a few weak growls out of him and a smile from Camike for my efforts.

None of the Halves are in good health, but I can't help but wonder why Brogut—the strongest of all of them—is so much worse. When I ask Ekil about it, he tells me that Brogut insists on giving up all of his food for the youngest and most vulnerable Halves.

And I almost murdered him.

The thought is enough to make me want to fall to my knees and beg for his forgiveness. The only thing that keeps me going now is the knowledge that Brogut won't survive another Dark without food and shelter.

By the time we are in sight of Tanguro, most of the Halves have stopped snarling at me whenever I get near them. The one exception is Jarosh.

We stop briefly for the Halves to rest and eat the pathetic remains of their food. I notice Jarosh slip his too-small portion into Camike's when she isn't paying attention.

Jarosh seems more concerned about a new hole in Camike's cloak than the fact that he's starving. When I try to talk to them, Jarosh leaps to his feet and grips his club, putting himself between Camike and me.

I can't blame him. I almost killed Brogut, and I put the rest of the Halves in danger. For that, Jarosh might never forgive me.

✳ ✳ ✳

The courtyard of Tanguro, which once teemed with luminescent plants and deadly animals, is now a wasteland. The fruit trees are shriveled, leafless skeletons. The ground is no longer covered with flowers and grasses in a hundred different colors. Now, the earth is barren, cracked, and coated with the inescapable gray ash.

I stop just inside the courtyard and put Brogut down on the ground. He's too weak to hold himself up, so I prop him against the waist-high stone wall that rings the courtyard and marks the borders of Tanguro.

"I think it would be best if you all wait here while I go explain things to the other leaders," I tell Ekil.

"Kind of you to spare us from their humiliating bigotry," Jarosh mutters none-too-quietly.

I don't say anything to that. I know Wade will welcome the Halves into the fortress, but I'm less sure about the other Banished leaders. They still haven't forgotten about all of their people who were killed by the Halves.

Liglette would have sided with Wade and me, but she's dead, and the Westerners decided to accept Valior as their leader.

A cold breeze stirs the darkness ash, and I catch the taste of it on my tongue. As the wind turns to more of a howl, I think I hear voices emerge. They're the voices of all the dead of Tanguro. There are the ones who have died since Darkness, as well as all the humans and Halves who died fighting against the Duskers beside me. I think I hear Brice's voice mixed in with the other ghosts.

The voices of the dead cry out to me, and all I can offer them are silent apologies and regret.

When I walk into the building, I'm surrounded by the familiar smell of woodsmoke. We keep one giant fire burning on the first floor at all times. It's a small comfort for the wounded and sick who lie on thin bedrolls in semi-orderly rows within the fire's warmth.

Fires are only lit on the building's other nineteen floors during the hours of Dark. To conserve our supply of firewood, Tut and the rest of the Northerners cut large windows on each floor of the building to allow light in during Gloom. After the fact, we realized the windows made it even colder during Dark. So, we'd stripped the specere tree leaves off the building's siding, since protection from the sun was no longer necessary, and built awnings over each window to keep the wind and gloomy rain at bay.

Everything in the building is tinged with a faint, pinkish-gold glow. The light comes from the enormous tree growing straight up through the center of the building. I stare up at the leafless branches and swear it's gotten taller since I've been gone. The trunk is now so thick around that two people can be standing on opposite sides and be hidden from each other. The bark shimmers, and when I press a hand against the tree's trunk, it's warm.

"Mer!"

Wokee appears from the other side of the tree and rushes toward me. At the last minute, he remembers his oath not to give any more hugs—on account of it being childlike, apparently—and replaces his smile with a more serious expression.

"I missed you," I tell him, pulling him to me in spite of his loud protests.

"Mer, you're squishing me," Wokee complains.

I earn another scowl when I kiss the top of his head.

"Tree's looking good," I say.

"'Course it is," Wokee agrees.

This tree is the one Wokee grew from the tiny golden seed Jadem left hidden in the Crystal Caves…the one she said would be the salvation of the Solguards. So far, it's been nothing but a nuisance, although I'd never dare say that out loud in Wokee's presence.

The tree has already grown up to the fifteenth story of the building, and the Northerners haven't been quiet about the extra labor of cutting holes for it to continue its upward journey.

The tree is the only living thing that seems to be flourishing in Darkness…aside from the darkness trees themselves. Still, in spite of all our early expectations, the tree hasn't produced fruit or anything else of value. The shimmery rose-gold color of its bark might be beautiful, but beauty doesn't fill bellies.

Vlaz is asleep by the foot of the tree. One of his enormous paws is stretched out over a tangle of roots. Everlyn is nestled in the crook of his other paw, fast asleep.

Wokee convinced a few of the kinder Northerners to build a special door in the back of the building that is big enough for Vlaz. The hyenair still has to crouch down when he's inside the building so his head doesn't scrape against the ceiling, but at least now he can come in away from the gloomy rain and wormkill.

The Banished are all less than pleased about having a hyenair sleeping in the same building, so Wokee and Everlyn usually wait until Dark before ushering Vlaz inside.

One of Vlaz's yellow eyes snaps open, but as soon as he sees it's me, he falls back asleep.

A few months ago, a group of Northerners tried to cut the tree down. Wokee sat in the tree's branches and refused to budge. Wade settled the matter by saying the tree was a symbol of hope and therefore would be under the Solguards' protection.

I don't think Wokee trusted the Northerners to keep their word, because he and Everlyn started guarding the tree at all hours of the day. Vlaz took up the cause soon after. Now, anyone who wants to do the tree harm will need to get past all three of them.

Personally, I think the Northerners have a point. The tree takes up precious space and even more precious resources without giving anything in return. Besides, every time I look at the tree, I'm reminded of Aunt Jadem's betrayal.

"Still not doing anything useful?" I ask Wokee as we stare up at the bare branches.

"It will," Wokee tells me with a confidence I wish I shared. "I know it will."

"Just don't get your hopes up too much," I tell him, even though it's too late for that.

"Hi, Dayne," Wokee says, tilting his head back to look up at the silent Zero standing next to me.

Just like every time when Dayne doesn't respond, I watch Wokee's posture wilt and his face fall. He goes back to tending the tree, but not before I see him swipe a hand across his eyes.

Before the Battle of the Iron Gate, Wokee snuck into a supply crate because he wanted to fight with the rest of the Solguards. Crowe's Duskers captured Wokee and Dayne to use against me, since Crowe was desperate to avenge her daughter, who was killed by my Zeroes.

Crowe forced me to choose whether to save Dayne or Wokee. I chose Wokee, and Crowe's guards stabbed Dayne before I could stop them. It was only because of Dellin that we got out alive.

Wokee still blames himself for what happened.

I clear my throat. "Dayne can talk," I blurt out. "And he remembers who he was before I changed him into a Zero."

Wokee jerks his head up, his gaze moving straight to Dayne.

"Really?" His eyes bug out of his too-skinny face. "Dayne, are you in there?"

The way he asks it, like the man we both remember is hiding just beneath the outer layers of skin, might have been humorous. If I didn't already know what would happen next.

Dayne doesn't react or even look at Wokee.

I can't stand to see Wokee's face fall, so I say, "Dayne, tell Wokee you remember him."

I feel a burst of resentment against the bond inside me. Then, in a too-deep, inflectionless voice, Dayne says, "I remember."

Wokee gets up from where he'd been crouching by the base of the tree and wipes his hands on his pants. He trots around the other side of the tree, and I lose sight of him behind the thick trunk. When he comes back and I see what he's carrying, I put a hand over my mouth to hold back a tidal wave of emotions. Wokee's holding a lute, the instrument Dayne had loved before he was turned into a Zero.

"One of the Northerners helped me make this for you," Wokee says, holding out the instrument. "I needed help attaching the strings since I couldn't get them tight enough, but I did the rest all by myself."

Even before Wokee offers it to Dayne, I know my brother won't react at the sight of it. Still, knowing what will happen does nothing to prepare me for Wokee's crushing disappointment, which he tries and fails to hide.

"That was really nice of you," I tell Wokee.

Wokee nods and sniffs. "I'll keep it safe for you until you want it," he tells Dayne, tucking the lute back under his arm.

"I'm sure he'll remember how much he loves it," I assure Wokee. "The real Dayne is in there. It'll just take time to bring him back."

I cringe at my own lie. When I first made my brother into what he is now, I transferred my blood to him through an artery in his leg rather than the one near his collarbone. My father said it might help him retain some shreds of his former self.

But just because Dayne kept his memories and isn't completely devoid of all emotions, I can't pretend that he'll ever be what he was before. That man is gone, as dead as if I'd left his body to rot along with all the others.

I bend down to kiss the top of Wokee's head and whisper, "What happened to Dayne isn't your fault."

"It is my fault." Wokee looks away from me, and I can tell he's trying not to cry. "If I had stayed behind like you told me, none of this would have happened."

"If you hadn't been there, Crowe would have done the same thing, except it would have been with Wade or Ry. You saved them."

Wokee looks up at me. The mournful expression on his face clears just a little.

"You're a good Solguard," I tell him. "And if old-Dayne was here, he'd tell you he was proud of you."

I sneak another quick hug before leaving Wokee to his ministrations of the tree.

I weave my way through the sleeping figures and discarded weapons strewn on the ground in search of the other Banished leaders. It isn't hard to find them. When they're not otherwise occupied by their duties, they have all begun congregating in the area we've designated for the sick and dying. Since we don't have any skilled healers in the fortress, the leaders' presence is the best medicine we have to offer.

And that's how I plan to convince the Banished that we need the Halves as much as they need us.

"Ah, Bisecter." Tut, the Northern Banished leader, stands up from where he's been talking in hushed tones with Valior. "What's the news?"

Wade, who has been kneeling beside a Solguard, gets to his feet. His golden eyes are haunted and rimmed in dark shadows.

Valior, the Eastern Banished leader, leans on his cane as he looks at me in expectation.

"I found a healer," I announce, deciding it's best to start with the good news.

Wade's eyes brighten.

"Well, bring him in." Valior looks around like someone might appear out of thin air.

"It isn't a *him*, and there's a small detail to work out before she can heal all of our injured."

Tut's eyes narrow in suspicion.

I don't even know if Camike has the skills to help all of our dying; the illnesses that plague us are different now than they were before Darkness. Still, this is the best chance I have of getting the Banished leaders to invite the Halves in without trying to kill them.

"Camike?" Wade asks, an incredulous smile curving his lips. "Did you find the Halves?"

I nod.

Wade takes two strides over to me. Before I know what's coming, he lifts me off the ground and spins me in a circle.

I can't remember the last time he held me. I wrap my arms around him and bury my face against his neck. So much has happened these past months to push us farther apart. As my obsession with the Zeroes grew, it drove a wedge between Wade and me. Then, after Wade became the Solguard leader, his duties became his only priority. Now, it seems like the only conversations Wade and I have are about food supplies and wormkill sightings.

"It was right of you to bring them back," he says into my ear when he puts me back down.

I give him a small smile and step away from him. It wasn't like I had actively been searching for the Halves. I don't deserve credit for saving the Halves from a fate I forced them into in the first place. But knowing all of that isn't enough to stop the flutter of pride I feel at bringing a smile to Wade's face.

The other Banished leaders are far less impressed. Valior is frowning, and Tut's face is starting to turn purple. A pang goes through me at the thought of Liglette. She would have supported me.

I swallow and turn my attention back on Tut.

Before he can unleash the fury I know is coming, I say, "The Halves can help us. They can hunt the wormkill better than any humans, and they can help the Westerners scavenge for food. They even offered to help Dayne and me destroy the darkness tree groves."

I'm making all of this up as I go along, and I realize belatedly I should have had a deeper conversation with Ekil before I started offering the Halves' services.

"Not going to happen." Tut shakes his head back and forth, making the gold threads braided into his goatee flicker in the firelight.

I cross my arms. "Are you going to let your hatred of the Halves be the reason all of our people die?"

Valior and Tut's gazes shift from me to the injured sprawled out on the ground.

"We can't," Valior says, although he looks less resolved than he did a moment ago. "The Halves are our enemies."

Tut nods in agreement.

"We need them," I say, sensing their emotions shift in my favor. "So, can I tell the Halves to come in without having to worry about your people attacking them?"

Tut lets out a growl, which I decide not to tell him sounds more Halve than human.

"The Solguards do the lion's share of the work around here," Wade says, coming to stand beside me. "My soldiers keep the wormkill away, and we've protected the Banished from thieves and looters who would have ransacked this place a hundred times over by now. And it's my scouts who bring us news from each of the territories."

"We are all very grateful for your people's contribution, young man," Valior says in his tremulous voice.

"I'm not looking for gratitude." Wade crosses his arms. "But if you don't agree to play nice with the Halves, you can find yourselves new accommodations."

My heart expands in my chest, and I feel a burst of appreciation for Wade.

"You wouldn't force us out," Valior says, looking wounded.

The expression is almost humorous on the old man's wrinkled face.

"Not so long as you keep your people in line," Wade replies, his face grim.

"Fine." Tut steps forward until he's nose-to-nose with Wade. "But let me promise you this. The moment my people don't need yours to survive, we're going to kill every last one of those beasts."

CHAPTER 10

The necessary agreements are made between the Halves and Banished, and Wade makes it clear to both sides what will happen to anyone who breaks the peace. Food is distributed, and after much grumbling from the Banished, living spaces are rearranged to make room for all of the Halves. All the while, the Halves and Banished mutter oaths about getting vengeance against the other at the first opportunity.

At least no one can argue with the immediate improvement Camike's presence has brought to the fortress. With herbs she brought with her, she has already cured several of the Banished who were suffering from cold rot.

"You feeling nice and absolved?" Tut asks me as we observe Camike's work.

I shrug. "I guess I am."

I'm still thinking about the moment I told Wade I'd found the Halves. It was the first real smile he's given me in…I can't even remember how long.

"I'm glad you're pleased." Tut gives me a bone-jarring pat on the back. "And since this was your grand plan, you can be the one to tell everyone that we're out of food."

My head whips around at that.

"What do you mean out of food?" I demand.

Tut just stares at me.

"All of it?" My voice is a whisper.

"We had a month's worth left, but after your little show of hospitality, we're down to a week." Tut scowls. "Probably less with the way these creatures eat." His grim expression tells me he isn't lying.

My mind races as I try to come up with a solution.

"The Westerners need to go on another hunt," I say. "They can go farther afield. There has to be some game somewhere—"

"That'll take weeks," Tut says. "What are we going to do in the meantime?"

He's right. Our people are already weak and scared, and if they find out there's only a week's worth of food left, there will be chaos. Everyone will forget about the bargain their leaders struck, and humans and Halves will fight to the death over a handful of dried berries. I shudder.

If only we had been able to prepare for the Darkness by stockpiling supplies like the Duskers.

I clench my fists as the injustice of it strikes me to my core.

From all of the scouts' reports, we learned that the Duskers had begun storing food and other supplies long before Crowe set the first darkness tree on fire. Their preparations have allowed them to live in abundance while the rest of us subsist day-to-day.

The scouts have reported that goods are regularly brought from the Dusker citadel at Malarusk to Darkness Peak, where Crowe and some of her closest advisors—my Aunt Jadem included—now reside.

That's when an idea occurs to me. It's daring…foolish. And yet….

"I'll fix this," I hear myself say as my mind sifts through details and logistics. It's a temporary solution, but if it can buy us a little more time to figure out something more permanent….

The thought of raiding the Duskers' supplies isn't a new one. It's just that we haven't been desperate enough to attempt it. Until now.

The Duskers know about the bandits who lie in wait along their travel paths, and they're always prepared with crossbows and swords to safeguard their goods. If we're going to manage to raid their supplies and survive long enough to bring the goods back to Tanguro, then we'll need to be smarter. Better.

I leave Tut without another word and go in search of Wade.

He's deep in a hushed conversation with Ry and a few other Solguards. From their worried expressions, I'm sure they're discussing the same problem Tut just relayed to me.

"I have a crazy idea," I say without preamble.

By the time I've finished explaining, Ry and the other Solguards are grinning.

"Food and revenge." Ry grins at me. "My favorite combination."

"Even if we're successful, we'll be right back in this same position in a few weeks' time," Wade says, sharing none of our enthusiasm.

His fists clench and unclench at his sides. I know him well enough to know he's trying to decide which Solguards to send on this mission…and how he's going to live with himself if they don't come back.

No one talks about how dangerous this raid will be. Even though everything we do these days is dangerous, attacking the Duskers' supply wagons is a bare step away from suicide.

"Dayne and I can take a small party," I say.

Bringing a large army of Solguards and Halves would give us a greater chance of success, but it would also lead to more deaths. We'd also run the risk of the Duskers spotting us from afar and turning back to Malarusk before we could overtake them. At least with a small group, we'll have the element of surprise.

"We can use those Dusker cloaks the scouts got," Ry says, her red curls bouncing as she rocks back and forth on her feet.

"Alright." Wade turns to one of the Solguards standing by. He says, "Get my sword and the Dusker cloaks, and bring me the scouts who were in the Dusker territory most recently."

"You can't come with us," I tell Wade as soon as it's just him, Ry, and me.

"The Solguards need their leader in one piece," Ry agrees.

Wade's jaw tightens. "The Solguards need a leader who isn't going to keep himself safe at the cost of more Solguards."

Ry keeps arguing with him, but I can tell from his set expression that he isn't going to budge.

We've all changed in these last six months, but no one has changed more than Wade. As the Solguard leader, he feels even more responsible for his people than the other leaders do. While everyone else grieves for those we've lost and accepts death as part of our new reality, Wade feels personally responsible. Every time a Solguard dies, part of Wade dies with them.

Every day, Wade takes on new burdens, risking himself to keep everyone else safe. He cares nothing for himself and is always the first to jump into danger if he thinks it will spare even a single Solguard life.

The few times I've tried talking to him about it, I've ended up doing more harm than good.

By the time the Solguard returns with the cloaks and Wade's weapon, Ry has thrown her hands in the air and stalked off to get Dellin, muttering about capy pig-headed Solguard leaders.

We've gotten good at quickly organizing ourselves—whether it's to face a wormkill that's come within our borders or to track down the rumor of food in some distant land—so only an hour has passed before we're ready to leave the fortress again.

After much deliberation, we settled on a group consisting of Wade, Ry, Dellin, Dayne, and me. We can't bring Vlaz because our only chance of success is if we can sneak up on the Duskers before they're aware of us. So, we'll need to cover the distance on foot.

With all the information the scouts have gathered about the Duskers' habits and movement, we have a solid idea of when the next delivery of supplies will be brought to Darkness Peak. If we move quickly, we should make it to the mountain before the Duskers start their climb to the summit.

We leave quietly without telling anyone except a few Solguards where we're going. We don't put on our Dusker cloaks while we're still in the fortress, because we don't want any questions about what we're up to. The only way to make sure everyone at the fortress isn't dead by the time we get back is to make sure no one knows how desperate our situation is.

I'm about to step out of the building when someone calls my name. I turn to see Jarosh, with Camike at his side, weaving his way through the Halves toward me.

I brace myself, knowing whatever Jarosh has to say to me can't be good.

I motion for the others to go ahead as I wait for Jarosh. Even once he's close enough to talk to me, though, he doesn't say anything. He shuffles his feet, looking uncomfortable in a very un-Jarosh-like way.

"What's up?" I glance pointedly at the door, making it clear I have other places to be.

Camike gives him a gentle nudge and murmurs something in his ear I don't catch.

"I wanted to say—"

The rest of his words are inaudible because he mutters them while looking down at the ground.

"What?" I step closer.

Jarosh lifts his gaze to mine. "I wanted to say thank you for what you've done for us," he says.

"Oh." Now it's my turn to feel awkward. "You don't have to thank me."

"I know, right?" Jarosh's lips quirk. "I kept trying to tell Camike how much you owed us, but she—"

At a sound of disapproval from his mate, Jarosh cuts himself off. He wraps one arm around Camike's shoulders, pulling her against him. "Really, Hemera. Thank you."

I offer Jarosh a tentative smile. "You're welcome."

CHAPTER 11

Two cold, miserable days pass before we reach the grove of darkness trees where we decided to wait out the Duskers. The horrible, acrid stink of the deadly sap has us all choking back coughs, but it's the only cover in this barren land.

After the start of Darkness, we learned the Duskers hadn't just been growing the darkness trees in the bowels of Malarusk; they'd been growing them in caves in all of the territories. They burned those trees, as well, and the layer of ash hovering in the sky expanded. After the sun disappeared, the Duskers began planting the darkness trees above ground.

The Solguards tried destroying the groves, but we quickly learned our efforts were pointless. The darkness trees don't die when they're chopped down. Instead, they regrow with an unnatural vigor. An entire grove of them can be burned to the ground, and within a few hours, they're regrowing from the pile of noxious ashes.

Even in places where the Duskers have stopped burning the trees, the shield of ash over the sun never goes away. The Duskers aren't satisfied with Gloom and Dark, though. They'll keep on burning the trees until there is only Dark.

We hunker down behind the thick trunks, careful to avoid contact with the sticky, lethal sap.

I had thought I couldn't get any more disgusted with these trees and the one who brought them into being. But as my throat burns and my eyes sting, I find my hatred for both reawakening.

Black sap oozes through the cracks in the bark. It looks like blood.

Many people who didn't witness Crowe's first burning of the darkness tree logs—and even some of the ones who did—believe these trees were sent by the Dark God to re-make our world. The truth is that they're nothing more than the result of a collusion between Crowe, the most ambitious Dusker Supreme in our history, and my Aunt Jadem.

This time, the burn at the back of my throat has nothing to do with the stink of the trees. I've promised myself that Crowe and Jadem will pay for what they've done to our world. It's more than a little gratifying to think that this raid will cause them some amount of grief.

We don't have to wait much longer before the Duskers' lanterns announce their arrival. We extinguished our own lights hours ago so we'd be less visible, but the Duskers aren't worried about being seen.

Now that their leader is being worshipped as the Dark God incarnate, the Duskers are as close to invincible as it's possible to be in this new world. Everyone knows that attacking or trying to steal from them is as good as begging for a painful, bloody death.

I open and close my hands, trying to work out the numbness brought on by the cold. Wade does the same beside me, although Dayne remains as motionless as he's been since we got here. The cold doesn't seem to bother him the way it does the rest of us.

Ry and Dellin are hidden behind some boulders a short way away. Our plan is for the two of them to use their archery skills to make the Duskers think there are more of us than there are. While the Duskers are distracted by the arrows coming at them from different directions, Dayne, Wade, and I will attack.

It's a flimsy plan that's liable to fall apart the minute the Duskers realize there are only five of us, but it's the only plan we have.

The Duskers have the benefit of being well-rested and well-fed. The five of us are just a pack of bone-weary, starving Solguards whose people won't last the month if we don't manage to get the supplies we need.

The Duskers draw closer. I count thirty of them, although with the way Gloom is turning to the ink blackness of Dark, there could be more.

Thirty of them against five of us are bad odds, even with Dayne and me being what we are. At least there's one advantage we have that the Duskers don't: we're desperate.

The only cause for optimism is that more Duskers means more food and better supplies. That means we'll have a better haul.

If we can kill them.

I place a stone in the leather pouch of my sling and crouch on the balls of my feet, getting ready to move.

My heart thuds against my chest as the Duskers come closer and closer. I can hear their muffled laughter and conversations, as well as the creak of the carts they're pushing.

I narrow my focus, listening for the sound of an arrow cutting through the air. I can't hear such a small noise over the ruckus the Duskers are making, but when a man screams and collapses with a feathered arrow embedded in his neck, I take that as my signal.

"Now!" Wade hisses, but I'm already on the move.

I release the stone in my sling, not bothering to watch as the Dusker falls to the ground.

Dayne moves in tandem with me. His enormous body, still unfamiliar to me, stalks forward with an almost feline grace. His steps don't falter on the uneven ground the way mine do.

I hear the Duskers' shouts and the click of arrows being fitted into crossbows. I move in a zig-zag pattern, keeping low to the ground, to make myself a smaller target and so our enemies won't be able to tell the direction my stones come from. I re-load my sling.

The benefit of the Duskers' lanterns is that they make it easy for us to see our enemies. The light must also be blinding them, because they're shooting wildly in every direction.

"Look out!" I yell to Dayne, who is standing in the path of the nearest crossbow.

My fear is replaced by fury. *No one threatens Dayne.*

I give up all pretenses at stealth and race for the Duskers. Using my momentum, I knock two of them to the ground.

My numb fingers fumble for the dagger at my belt. If it wasn't for Wade hacking through soldiers beside me, I would have a crossbow bolt through my chest by now.

I finally manage to free my blade and shove it into the nearest Dusker. He screams as he slashes at me with his sword. I hear the tear of fabric, but I manage to avoid the blade.

The Dusker continues to parry with me, but his strokes are getting more and more sluggish. I can see the life draining out of his eyes. With a final gasp, he falls.

I turn away, disquieted by the comforting warmth now slicked over my right hand. I slash at one Dusker with my knife and kick out at another. Four of them surround me. Even though they dwarf me, and their swords make my knife look like a child's toy, I'm not afraid. I dodge their swings and bring down my knife, slicing through flesh and bone with the force of my blows.

"Left!" Wade yells.

Without thinking, I slash my blade in that direction. A Dusker who had just been about to run me through with his sword cries out. Dayne kicks the man's legs out from under him, and I finish him with my dagger.

Hopeless shrieks come from the Duskers as they look into my brother's black eyes and glimpse his inhuman strength…right before he twists their necks.

I'm within sight of the carts. I glance at the stockpile of supplies that brought us here in the first place—food, blankets, and maybe even some medicine.

A hiss of pain escapes me. While I was ogling the supplies, a Dusker snuck up behind me and slashed the tip of his sword across my shoulder.

Dayne's furious roar comes at almost the same moment, and I know he's felt my injury as though it's his own.

One of Ry's arrows dispatches the Dusker before I can have my revenge, but there are plenty of others. I throw myself back into the fray, focusing completely on this task before I allow myself to get distracted by the supply carts.

When I turn around for my next opponent, I find only Wade. There are a few Duskers racing back the way they'd come, but Dellin and Ry will take care of them. The only ones left are the Dusker who were pushing the carts. I can tell they're new recruits. Their swollen and bruised faces bear the marks of the initiation ritual Duskers must undergo to prove their loyalty.

I can also tell from the way these recruits are trembling that they didn't become Duskers out of a desire to harm us. They did it out of necessity. Since the Duskers are the only ones with food to spare, joining their ranks is some people's only chance of surviving.

These recruits are weaponless and too scared to be any threat to us.

I turn my attention back to Wade, whose face is speckled with blood.

"Are you—" I reach up a hand to his face.

"Not my blood," he says, his chest still heaving from the fight. "You okay?"

"Fine," I begin, but a ripple of pain through the bond connecting me to Dayne distracts me. I rush over to him.

Dayne pulls his hand away from his shoulder, and I see that his palm is covered in brown blood. I hold up one of the Duskers' fallen lanterns to inspect the wound. It's deep—down to the bone—but that isn't the part that sends chills racing down my spine.

I reach back to my own left shoulder. The fabric of my cloak and shirt are gaping open and still damp from my blood. I trace my finger along the wound, which is already beginning to heal. My injury is identical to Dayne's.

When the Zeroes were under my control and one of them was injured, I felt its pain as acutely as if it was my own. But that pain was imagined. There hadn't been so much as a scratch on me, even though I was convinced I was bleeding out just like my Zero. The same has been true with Dayne. Whenever he's injured, I feel his pain, but I don't bleed.

But this gash across Dayne's shoulder proves that when the opposite occurs, when it's my injury, the actual wound appears on Dayne.

The realization makes my heart beat faster. Now, I don't just need to worry about my own survival. If I'm injured or killed, my brother will suffer the same fate.

CHAPTER 12

All of the sweat and blood from the fight have turned frigid against my skin, but I forget about that as soon as Ry and Dellin return and we head for the carts laden with supplies.

The Dusker recruits huddle in a group, shivering and weeping. They don't move to stop us as we examine the carts' contents.

My sense of achievement at our victory is tempered by anger as I look at the wealth of goods spread out before us.

There are hunks of dried meat and jars of preserved fruit, along with dried herbs I don't recognize but know Camike will. There are blankets, cloaks that are made for warmth rather than protection from the sun, and spare clothes.

I eye the cloaks. Wokee outgrew his months ago, and I've been desperate to get him a new one.

As unpleasant as the task is, we go around and collect the dead soldiers' boots and throw them into the carts along with everything else. They're too valuable to leave behind, and they might be enough to save some scout from losing his feet to the bitter cold rot.

We take the Duskers' cloaks, too, but none of us can stand the gruesome task of relieving the dead soldiers of their clothes.

Dellin and Ry collect the arrows and other weapons strewn across the ground.

"How many more times do you think we can do this before the Duskers wizen up and bring more reinforcements?" Ry asks, eyeing our haul.

"Probably none," Wade replies, dragging a hand down his stubbled cheek. "Crowe isn't going to be pleased about her supplies falling into the hands of Solguards."

"Good." Dellin smirks in satisfaction.

She and I exchange a knowing look.

After the Battle of the Iron Gate, when Dellin saved Dayne, Wokee, and me from Crowe, my distrust for her vanished. I know she still has secrets about herself, but after that, I stopped doubting her.

Ry bends over, hands on her knees, as a dry cough wracks her body.

"You alright?" Dellin asks, shooting Ry a worried look.

When she straightens back up, Ry glares at the darkness trees that are now almost invisible in the Dark.

"Why aren't the Duskers as sick of Darkness as the rest of us?" Ry grumbles. "Can't they just lay off the burnings so we can all go back to breathing normally again?"

Her questions are rhetorical. We all know the Duskers believe the gray fog of high day means they still haven't fully achieved the Dark God's prophecy. They won't stop until our whole world is blanketed by Dark at every hour.

"Duskers are better at taking orders than thinking for themselves," Dellin says. "Crowe has used their passion for Darkness and the Dark God to manipulate them into destroying what's left of our world." Her voice is filled with loathing for the Dusker Supreme.

It's an opinion I understand well.

I stamp the ground in an attempt to get some feeling back into my feet, which have gone numb in the wake of all the fighting.

"What are we going to do with the recruits?" I ask.

If we just let them leave, they'll go right back to Malarusk. But we can't bring them with us. We already have too many mouths to feed.

"The same thing we did to their masters," Wade replies, his voice grim.

I give Wade a sharp look. These men and women might be Duskers, but they don't pose a threat to any of us.

"Can't we just set them free?" Ry asks. She turns her attention on one of the recruits whose face is still covered in days' old blood. He's shaking, and his eyes are wide with terror. "You won't try anything stupid if we let you live, will you?"

"N-no," he stutters. "I p-promise. I'll serve you and only y-you."

"There you have it," Ry tells Wade.

Wade shakes his head. "For every one of them we kill, that's one more Solguard's life we'll save."

"Wade, this guy isn't capable of killing any of us," Ry argues.

"That's not a chance I can take." There's a hardness to Wade's expression I've never seen before. "They could have come to the Solguards for help. Instead, they gave their allegiance to the Duskers." He draws his sword and strides up to the recruit.

"Cap'n, no, please, I swear, I'll do anything—"

The man's words are cut off as his head is swept clean off his body. I watch it bounce on the hard ground and roll several feet before coming to rest against a rock. I'm too stunned to feel any of the emotions I know I should.

I manage a gasp before Wade move on to the next.

"Wade, stop," Ry says.

He ignores her as he slaughters the rest of the recruits. There's no other word for it. They cower and cry until their prayers to the Dark God are cut off. My feet have turned to lead weights, and I can't take a step. I can't speak. I can't do anything except watch the execution in muted horror.

Wade's sword slices across the final recruit's throat. Blood arcs up, splattering across Wade's face. He lets his sword fall to the ground, and for several seconds, he stands there staring at the dead. Then, he comes to stand before an open-mouthed Ry and me. His golden eyes are ablaze with challenge.

"Say it," he tells us. There's a harsh edge to his words I don't recognize. "Tell me I'm a monster."

I shake my head. Ry is crying, but my eyes are dry. After everything I've done—after all the pain I've caused—I don't have the right to judge Wade. Instead, I grieve for the easy-going man he'll never be again.

"My responsibility is to the Solguards, and I won't apologize for doing whatever I have to in order to keep the safe," he says when both Ry and I stay silent.

He walks away before I can find the breath to respond.

CHAPTER 13

The only sound is the creaking of the supply carts as we pull them along behind us on our way back to the fortress. I can't get the image of that recruit's head rolling across the ground out of my mind.

A rumble comes from nearby, making us all go still.

The ground underfoot begins to shake. A roar cuts through the silence.

Dellin screams as the ground only a few paces in front of us shatters.

A giant, slimy head covered in dirt rears up from the depths of its underground tunnel. The wormkill roars again as its head swivels in our direction.

Even though the beast has no eyes, it seems like it's looking at us. Its huge nostrils quiver as it searches for prey. Its mouth, which I happen to know is filled with countless poisonous fangs, curves upward in a ghastly grin.

I go still and hold my breath. The wormkill can't see, but personal experience has taught me that their hearing and sense of smell are exceptional.

It bellows out another roar, and I catch the rank stench of its breath. It's even worse than the smell of the darkness trees. I force myself to hold back my gagging before I give us all away.

The wormkill squeezes the rest of its bulk out of the tunnel.

Ry breathes out a quiet curse as the full length of the enormous beast slithers onto the Outside. Its head jerks in her direction. A giant strand of poisonous mucous drips down from the beast's neck and hits the ground with a *splat*.

"Start backing up," I whisper as I fit a stone in my sling.

I turn the ropes as slowly as I can, hoping the wormkill won't be able to hear the vibrations of the weapon cutting through the air. Then, I aim the stone in the opposite direction from where we are heading.

The wormkill's head jerks to attention at the sound of the rock hitting the ground, but it doesn't go after the stone as I'd hoped.

Moving in slow-motion, Ry pulls an arrow from her quiver and silently nocks it. I have another stone in my sling, but from my first encounter with the wormkill in the Malarusk dungeon, I know weapons don't hurt this beast the way they would most creatures. The wormkill have no bones, and their flesh just absorbs any impact. Our best chance against this creature is to get away without it ever knowing we were here.

Another roar echoes the first, and I turn to see a second wormkill appearing out of the same tunnel.

I clamp a hand over my mouth to keep my gasp from giving us away. Both of the beasts are inching toward us, although it's impossible to tell if they've sensed us or if they're simply coming in this direction.

Out of sheer desperation, I bend down to the ground and pick up another stone. This one is the size of my fist, and I'm hoping the weight of it will be enough to fool the wormkill into looking elsewhere for their dinner.

Moving as slowly and quietly as I can manage, I toss the stone into the distance.

It lands far out of sight, but the wormkill hear it. Both of their giant, slime-covered heads whip around. They snarl like they're two parts of the same whole. And then they start to slither off.

We all release our pent-up breaths at the same moment.

The wormkill stop, turn their heads back toward us, and bare their fangs. Then, in a movement so fast it shouldn't be possible for such enormous creatures, they attack.

Ry and Dellin's arrows fly through the air, embedding themselves in each wormkill's head. The beasts snarl, but the arrows only seem to incense them further.

"What do we do?" Dellin asks, her voice on the verge of panic.

"Run!" Wade and I yell at the same time.

I reach inside myself for the bond that connects me with Dayne. He's ready. I can feel his tension and simmering anger.

It takes about two seconds for me to figure out we can't outrun the wormkill. So, I stop.

"Keep going," I tell Wade when he starts to double back.

"Hey, uglies!" I call, stamping my feet and making a ruckus. "Over here!"

It occurs to me that Ry will give me hell for not coming up with a better insult than *uglies* later. Oh well.

I wait until the wormkills' attention is on me, and then I run toward them.

"Hemera!" Wade yells.

I ignore him.

The wormkill hurl themselves at me. I throw myself onto my stomach, hearing the satisfying thud and subsequent roar as the two wormkill launch straight into each other. I look up in time to see one of the wormkill open its giant maw. Its fangs snap shut on the other, ripping away a chunk of the other's fleshy neck.

The wounded wormkill lets out a bloodcurdling shriek.

A torrent of viscous, greenish fluid pours from its wound. The beast continues to screech, the sound raising the hair on the back of my neck.

Dayne and I split off as the two wormkill separate to attack us. A scream tears through me as a strand of poisonous slime burns straight through my sleeve and sears into my arm. It takes every ounce of willpower I have not to cry out.

I force myself to move, darting around the wormkill and grabbing hold of the creature's tail. I dig my nails in, ignoring the bite of the poison as it burrows into my fingers. I fight to keep my grip as the wormkill writhes and bucks in an effort to throw me off. I grit my teeth and hang on.

I glimpse Dayne take a running start and leap into the air. He punches the wormkill's snout with enough force to make the whole beast's head contract. For a second, the wormkill seems stunned. It stops struggling, and I manage to get my feet back on the ground without letting go of the tail.

Taking advantage of the wormkill's momentary distraction, I yank its tail with all of my strength.

I crouch down as the wormkill's body flies over me and sails through the air. I squint through the sweat and tears stinging my eyes to watch as it crumples in a heap in the midst of the darkness tree grove hundreds of paces away.

For several moments, it doesn't move. Then, just as it begins to feel the effects of the black sap, the beast lets out a screech that's loud enough to make me temporarily deaf.

The wormkill twists and writhes, trying to rid itself of the black sap that—luckily for us—burns it the same way it burns humans.

My friends cry out a warning, and I turn to see the second wormkill lunging at me.

Dayne tries to stop it, but with a flick of its mighty tail, the beast tosses Dayne into the air. He crumples in an unmoving heap on the ground.

My shout is lost as the wormkill opens its mouth and bellows. I fall back as a blast of hot, fetid air washes over me.

I can sense the wormkill's hungry anticipation. It darts its head forward in a motion almost too fast to perceive. I throw myself onto my side, hearing rocks shatter as the wormkill's head plows into the ground where I had just been.

Scrabbling for purchase, I manage to get to my feet and face the beast. It stretches its jaws, and I get a full view of its glistening, poison-covered fangs. Each one is the length of my forearm. For a moment, I'm paralyzed with fear.

Move, Hemera!

I fight my instinct to back away. Instead, I lunge forward before I have a chance to think twice about what I'm doing.

I wrap my right hand around one of the wormkill's top fangs and my left hand around one of the bottom. Pain burrows into my hands, but I don't let go. I tighten my hold.

The wormkill tries to snap its teeth shut, but I hold on, keeping its jaw locked in place. The wormkill stops fighting me, and I can sense its uncertainty. It's never encountered prey like me before.

I'm not quite sure what to do, either. My grip is sliding, and as soon as I lose my hold, the wormkill's jaws will shut…on me. Out of the corner of my eye, I see Dayne come up beside me. He mimics my stance as he braces the beast's mouth open.

"Hold him," I gasp out to Dayne as a desperate idea comes to me.

When I can sense that Dayne's hold is as firm as it's going to get, I yank on the top tooth, the longest and sharpest-looking one.

The wormkill writhes and shrieks, but Dayne holds it in place as the tooth snaps away. Green, stinking ichor flows from the hole in the creature's mouth.

"Now!" I shout, trusting in our blood bond and knowing Dayne will understand what I need.

Dayne lets go of the wormkill. We both dive out of the way of its snapping jaws. Before it can recover, I drive the tooth into the wormkill's head.

Dayne throws me out of the path of a jet of poison that shoots from the wound and burns a hole into the ground. The wormkill screeches. It tosses its head in an attempt to free itself from the tooth, but I drove it in far enough that it's never coming out. The wormkill shrieks a final time, and then it falls to the ground with a sickening thud.

Gasping and wheezing, and too afraid to look down at my hands for fear that they've been completely burned away, I watch the wormkill to see if it will get up. It doesn't.

The beast's body wavers in and out of my vision.

"Hemera!" Wade runs over to me.

I can see the lines of worry carved into his face.

"I thought—" He curses. "What in the sun were you thinking, going after them like that?"

"Wasn't thinking," I mumble, letting his familiar warmth encircle me as he wraps his arms around me.

Even though my face is probably covered with wormkill slime, Wade leans down and brushes his lips over mine. It's enough to banish the numbness from my limbs and bring a smile to my chapped lips.

Wade settles me more firmly against him. I'm so comfortable it's a struggle to stay awake.

"Are you hurt?" I ask Dayne, raising my head from Wade's chest.

"Go now," Dayne says, the slits of his nose vibrating as he scents the air. "More coming."

My wounds are already healing, although I'm afraid I'll never be able to rid myself of the stink of wormkill slime. I try not to think about how it's coating my hair and drying on my skin.

"Why can't the wormkill at least have the decency to be delicious?" Ry complains.

The first time a wormkill came close enough to the fortress to be a threat, we had gone out to battle the giant beast. After a terrible fight that cost us the lives of two Solguards, we managed to take the wormkill down.

We had never lived in a world where we could afford to waste anything, but after Darkness, we became more desperate than ever before. Still, the thought of eating wormkill had been almost too unappetizing to consider. *Almost.*

Tut had sliced off a chunk of the rubbery carcass and tried boiling it. After we carefully stripped away the outer layer of poisonous slime, Ry had been brave enough to take the first bite. She'd spent the next twenty-four hours throwing up what she deemed to be the "most disgusting, unpalatable rot this side of Darkness Peak." No one had been desperate enough to try repeating the experience.

After we've gotten our breath back and my wounds have mostly healed, we backtrack to get the supply carts. They're heavy and we could use five more people to help push them, but this burden is one none of us will ever complain about. I lock my arms around the handles of two carts and begin trudging back in the direction of the fortress.

CHAPTER 14

By the time we make it back to the fortress, I'm a bundle of nerves. *What if everyone discovered we're out of food? What if the Halves and humans killed each other while we were gone?*

The Solguards on watch let us into the building. Instead of the dull groans of pain and rattling coughs that usually greet us, I hear…laughter.

Wade and I exchange a look full of suspicion. Laughter isn't a sound we hear much around here anymore…unless it's an Easterner who's gotten too deep into his liquid sun. But even that has become a rare event now that the barley Valior uses to make the liquor no longer grows.

We leave our laden carts with a group of Solguards. Wade gives them orders to evenly distribute the supplies between humans and Halves, and then we go to investigate the laughter that seems to be rising in intensity.

The source of everyone's entertainment soon becomes apparent.

"What have we here?" Ry murmurs.

Bathed in the light of the rose-gold tree, Brogut and Everlyn are…dancing. He's hunched over so far he's practically on his knees to get himself to the right height. Everlyn is barking out orders that the Halve can't possibly understand.

Brogut is still too thin, but there's a gleam in his black eyes that wasn't there when I carried him to the fortress.

Banished and Halve onlookers are laughing in good-humored amusement as Wokee tries to translate Everlyn's commands into Halve-speak. He's getting some of the words right, and the ones he gets wrong are sending the Halves surrounding them into uproarious guffaws.

A few Solguards are playing on their reed instruments. It's a song I recognize from the banquets at Solis, and it makes me feel nostalgic and heartsick all at the same time. I look at Dayne, wondering if the man playing a lute has attracted his attention. But Dayne's gaze is turned down at the floor. I don't feel any change in his emotions through the bond. All I can sense is his ever-present restlessness.

I can't wallow in my sadness over Dayne for long. Everlyn is trying to show Brogut how to do a complicated turn that some human men can't even master, and it isn't going well. Wokee is only confusing the matter by mixing up the Halve words for "left" and "right," and with all of the laughter coming from the onlookers, Brogut seems to be unable to focus on anything more than not stepping on Everlyn's toes.

"How did all of this start?" Wade asks one of the Solguards.

The Solguard's lip twitches in amusement. "Young Wokee and Everlyn thought it would be a good idea for the Halves to learn some of our dances before Jarosh and Camike's wedding," he explains.

"Jarosh and Camike are getting married?" I ask.

"Apparently, Halves go through a mating ceremony," the Solguard replies. "Jarosh and Camike have already done it, so I don't see why they'd have a wedding, too. But when Jarosh told the kids, Everlyn threw a fit that she hadn't been invited to the ceremony. So, she and Wokee decided there would have to be a proper wedding."

I can't help but laugh as I picture what that conversation must have sounded like.

"Well, if you can't beat 'em," Ry says, holding out a hand to Dellin.

"Are you serious?" Dellin asks. Her pale, dirt-streaked cheeks turn pink as she glances around at all the onlookers.

"Why not? It's just a dance." Ry shrugs. "But if you're too embarrassed to dance with me, I'm sure I can find someone else who won't be scared away by my charm."

Dellin narrows her gaze, and then she takes the hand Ry holds out to her.

They join Brogut and Everlyn on the makeshift dance floor. Brogut snarls in frustration when he catches sight of the effortless way Ry spins Dellin.

I feel a smile crack across my wormkill slime-covered face.

There was a time when I resented the affection between Ry and Dellin, but that time is long gone. Over the last six months, I've watched their relationship grow. I saw that they had something Ry and I never would, despite the kiss we'd once shared.

Instead of begrudging their affections, I'd come to realize I didn't want Ry that way.

Watching the two of them has me looking for Wade before I'm even conscious of what I'm doing. I had thought he was still beside me, but when I catch sight of him, he's skirting the crowd around to where Wokee is watching Brogut and Everlyn with an unreadable expression on his face. Wokee tilts his head as Wade whispers something in his ear. Wokee screws up his face in disgust at whatever Wade has told him, but I can tell he's considering Wade's words more than he wants to let on. Wade steps away, and Wokee goes back to studying Brogut and Everlyn with a fierce concentration.

He looks back at Wade, who gives him an encouraging nod. I see Wokee blow out a breath, push back his shoulders, and stride up to Brogut.

In a voice loud enough to carry, Wokee says, "I'd like to cut in."

The Solguards do their best to hide their snickers.

Brogut gives Wokee a confused look. Wokee makes a shooing gesture with his hand. Brogut, seeming more than a little relieved, drops Everlyn's hands and steps aside so Wokee can take his place.

Still chuckling, I slip through the crowd and head for the stairs. It isn't my turn for a bath, but with the dried wormkill slime caked on my skin, no one will begrudge me taking more than my share of the precious bathwater.

I'm shivering and trying to dry my hair over the fire without actually setting it aflame, when the sounds of shouting reach me from the bottom level of the building.

The cold slices right through my clothes to my skin as I run down the steps. I push my way through the throngs of Banished and Halves who are watching the spectacle unfold.

The happy scene from a few hours earlier has vanished. Now, the onlookers are tensed in expectation of trouble.

Wokee and Everlyn are standing on either side of the tree, blocking a crowd of angry Northerners holding axes. Vlaz stands next to Everlyn, growling and snapping at anyone who gets too close. Brogut stands beside Wokee, his tree trunk spear gripped in his fist.

"We're freezing to death," a Northerner with rotting teeth grumbles. "Let us at least have the branches."

"No," Wokee says. "The wood from the abandoned building is already dead. Use that."

"That would involve going outside, which I ain't gonna do in the middle of Dark when there are wormkill about." The Northerner takes another step toward the tree.

I push my way through the crowd until I'm standing in front of Wokee. Dayne stays within my line of sight, his muscles taut and his black eyes narrowed on the Northerners. I know that if any of them make so much as the slightest move toward me, Dayne will break their necks without a second's hesitation.

"Tut told you to stay away from the tree," I tell the man who had spoken.

"We're all doing our part to keep everyone alive, and you're just pouring good water into a tree that doesn't give us shit," the man retorts. "Cut it down and let it do its part, I say."

The Northerners have always been the loudest complainers of all the Banished, and our new hardships haven't changed that.

"There isn't room for anything in this building that doesn't carry its own weight," a different Northerner says with a pointed look in the Halves' direction.

"No one's chopping it down," Everlyn replies stubbornly. "Anyone who tries is going to get a nasty surprise from my burning powders."

I feel a little smug on Everlyn's behalf at the way several of the men step back in the face of the little girl's fury.

"Yeah, or Vlaz will bite you," Wokee adds.

"Speaking of the hyenair," one of the Northerners begins, and I know what's coming next. "We can't keep feeding that creature."

"That creature should be feeding *us*," another Northerner pipes up. "Not the other way around."

"We don't eat hyenair," Wokee says in a tone that is far more reasonable than I feel the other man deserves.

Brogut rumbles out a growl and jabs his tree trunk spear close enough to the Northerner to make his threat clear.

"Get outta my face," the Northerner snarls at Brogut.

"Stupid human brutes," Brogut replies in the Halve language.

"Dumbass monsters!" the Northerner yells.

If their expressions weren't so threatening, it would be funny the way the Halves and humans are using nearly the same words to describe each other, even though neither can understand what the other is saying.

But their fierce looks and grip on their weapons make it clear this isn't idle complaining. More Halves now flank Brogut, and they're all brandishing stone clubs.

"So, is that how you're gonna play it?" the Northerner with rotting teeth asks, lifting his axe.

"Stop," I say, getting in front of him.

The man's eyes are glazed over with his hatred of the Halves, and I don't think he's even heard me. He raises his axe, and I realize his intended target is...me.

Before his stroke can fall, a gnarled hand wraps around the Northerner's wrist and squeezes until he drops the axe.

It's only after he's shoved the man away from me that I get a clear view of the Halve. It's Ekil.

The Northerner spits at Ekil as two Easterners drag him back.

"We'll have our revenge for all the Banished you've killed," he shouts.

Camike and Jarosh have appeared, and between them, they manage to convince the Halves to lower their weapons as the rest of the crowd breaks up.

"Thank you," I tell Ekil.

He gives me the briefest of nods, and then he follows the rest of the Halves back to the part of the building we segmented off for them.

I'm still trying to make sense of the fact that Ekil defended me, even after what I did to the Halves, when a distraught-looking Solguard comes racing toward me.

"Hemera, Wade says to come quickly."

CHAPTER 15

I try to ignore the bite of the cold through my wet hair as I follow the Solguard. With each step, my trepidation grows. The last time Wade needed me, it was because the Easterners had taken down a support beam from the other building for firewood, and the whole thing was about to collapse on top of our building.

I'd rectified the problem with a carefully-positioned boulder. After that, the job of gathering firewood had been given to the Northerners, whose familiarity with architecture would prevent them from making a similar mistake.

The Solguard leads me outside into the Gloom. At the sight of three Solguard archers standing around a Dusker, I hurry forward.

The Dusker is on his knees, and the hood of his cloak thrown back. The man's face is covered with old, ugly scars left behind from his initiation ritual.

Ry and Dellin come running with their bows held at the ready. They both come to stand beside me when they see there's no imminent threat.

"They didn't used to do that, you know," Dellin says to no one in particular, gesturing to the Dusker's scarred face. "That's a new practice the more ruthless Supremes adopted to test their disciples' loyalty."

Her voice trembles with barely-concealed anger. My trust in Dellin is absolute after what she did for Dayne and Wokee, but when she makes these kinds of comments, it's impossible not to remember that she was born as one of the Duskers.

From the little Dellin has told us about herself, I know that Crowe killed her father, and Dellin and her mother were forced to flee to the Banished territory to escape a similar fate.

I still don't know what it was about Dellin that made the Duskers listen to her in Malarusk when Crowe was commanding them to do the exact opposite. I tried asking Dellin about it weeks later, but she made it clear she didn't want to talk about anything having to do with her past.

My attention shifts to Wade and the piece of script tree bark clutched in his hand. He passes it to me without a word.

Even this scrap of bark is evidence of all the Duskers have that we don't. All of the script trees are dead now, but the fact that the Duskers still have enough bark to use for messages is just another reminder of how Crowe knew what was going to happen to our world. It reminds me that whatever we steal from the Duskers is a negligible fraction of all they've hoarded for their own use.

I unroll the bark and read, recoiling at the sight of my name written at the top of the page.

Hemera- my army is coming for you.

My heart pounds against my ribcage as I continue to read.

Your people will turn to ashes just as Hendrix did. I hope you're the last to die, so you can see the destruction and death with your own eyes before you join them.

There's no signature, but even without one, I know who the message is from. *Crowe.*

I don't give myself the luxury of taking all the blame for whatever the Dusker Supreme is planning. Her vendetta against me might be making this attack come sooner than it would have otherwise, but I'm not self-absorbed enough to think I'm the only reason the Duskers are coming for us. Crowe has wanted an excuse to destroy the Solguards since she became the Supreme.

At the Battle of the Iron Gate, Crowe told me she didn't care about killing Solguards anymore. Even then, I knew better than to trust those words. Crowe would never allow us to continue on like we've been, especially now that our survival is partially dependent on the goods we've stolen from her.

We've all been expecting the Duskers to come after us at some point.

Part of me is relieved by this message. Now, at least, we can stop wondering when the reckoning between us and the Duskers will come.

"This is probably happening now because of our raid," Ry says, reading over my shoulder.

Dellin gives a short nod of agreement.

"Maybe, but it was bound to happen eventually," Wade says, echoing my thoughts.

The Dusker Supreme tried to take everything from me once before, and I'm itching to meet her in battle and end this lethal dance between us. I doubt Crowe would lead her own army into battle, though. If the reports are to be trusted, Crowe never comes down from Darkness Peak anymore.

As the supposed Dark God incarnate, Crowe doesn't need to concern herself with the goings-on down below, when she has thousands to carry out her every whim.

I wonder if Crowe will send Jadem with the army that's meant to finish us off. A flash of bitterness goes through me at the thought.

Jadem's probably sitting atop Darkness Peak, reveling in the chaos she's caused.

"He says there's an army coming across the mountains to make good on this message as we speak," Wade says, snapping me out of my reverie.

The Dusker bares his teeth in a menacing smile. "You have angered the Dark God by trying to destroy His trees. Soon, you will be punished."

"Do you have anything else of use to tell us?" Wade asks, his voice dripping with disgust.

"Gather your people. Prepare to fight. It will make no difference." The Dusker gives us a look full of loathing.

Wade nods his head at the Solguard standing behind the Dusker. The other man doesn't hesitate before pulling his dagger from his hip and slicing it across the Dusker's throat.

The Dusker slumps onto the ground, twitching and choking on his own blood. After a few seconds, he goes still.

"Get rid of the body," Wade tells the Solguards, and then he turns around and heads back for the building.

I'm stunned by the empty expression in Wade's eyes as he gave the order. I'm reminded of that recruit's head rolling across the ground, and Wade's face stained crimson from the weaponless man's blood.

Killing a battered, weaponless recruit is not the same as killing a fully-armed Dusker who threatened us on our own land. And yet, Wade treated both like their lives were nothing more than a nuisance. It's so unlike the Wade of the past, that I wonder if I know him at all anymore.

Shaking myself out of my stupor, I hurry after him.

"Wade—"

"I need you to find out if that Dusker was telling the truth," Wade says without looking back at me.

"But, Wade—"

"Now, Hemera."

Wade keeps walking toward the building even though I've stopped. I am a Solguard, but I don't take orders from Wade. As the former leader of old Tanguro and the Zero army, I'm afforded the same privileges as any other leader in the fortress. But the way Wade just spoke to me made me feel like I was little better than a servant.

After the sting of his disregard has passed, I realize there's no point in arguing. We do need to know whether the Dusker's threat is real, and I can make it to the mountain pass and back in half the time it would take anyone else.

"We'll start fortifying the building as best we can in the meantime," Wade calls over his shoulder.

I swallow my hurt at being treated no better than one of his scouts. I twist back my hair and ready myself for the long run.

"Hemera," Wade says, almost as an afterthought.

I turn to look at him, but his back is to me. "Yes?"

"Be careful."

CHAPTER 16

It takes me fewer than twenty minutes of solid running to find the Dusker army. My heart stops beating for several seconds, and then it starts back up double-time. More than a small part of me had hoped the Dusker had been exaggerating. He wasn't.

Even in the thick gray soup of Gloom, I can see the Duskers moving steadily through the mountain path in a long, snaking column.

Their pace is unhurried, but even so, they'll be at the fortress by midday. From just a glance, I can tell that even if every Banished and Halve fights alongside us, we'll be outnumbered.

What's worse is that this army represents only a bare fraction of the Duskers' ranks. Even if, by some unexpected miracle, we can defeat this group, more will come.

Before the familiar stranglehold of panic can take over, I turn and head back to the fortress. After less than a minute of running, I come to a skidding stop as a thought occurs to me.

All I need is a couple of sacks of Everlyn's exploding powders to take out this entire army, and I can stop them before they even reach Tanguro. It's so simple, I can't believe I hadn't thought about it before.

With that realization warming my insides, I sprint back to the fortress as fast as my legs will carry me.

"Hemera," Wade says as soon as I step inside the building.

"Everlyn," I gasp. "Tell her to get all of the explosives she has and bring them to me."

While a Solguard races off to find the girl, I fill Wade in on what I've seen. His jaw tightens, but as I explain my plan, I see him relax. This battle is not one our people could win, so our best option is to make sure it never comes down to a fight at all.

Everlyn, her little face twisted in concern, comes running up to us. "What's happening?"

"Where are your explosives?" Wade demands.

Everlyn shakes her head. There's a frightened look in her round eyes.

"The Duskers are coming," I tell her, thinking that Wade's curt tone has made her nervous. "I need your explosives to kill them before they come within reach of the fortress." I keep my voice low enough that none of the other Solguards and Banished milling around will hear me. The last thing we need now is for everyone to start panicking.

Everlyn's scared look doesn't disappear, nor does she move. Swallowing, she says, "I'm so sorry. I was going to tell you earlier, but I couldn't find you, and—"

"What happened?" Wade asks, cutting her off. He holds up a hand to some Solguards who are trying to get his attention and pins Everlyn with his gaze.

"The flowers I use for the igniting fluid don't grow anymore, and the Westerners haven't been able to find any more on this side of the mountains."

"Meaning?" Wade crosses his arms.

Everlyn twirls her hair around her hand in a nervous gesture. "There are two reasons why you need the igniting fluid. The first is so there's a lag with the explosion. The fluid delays the reaction, which gives you enough time to get away. The second reason is because you would need a really strong flame…a candle or flaming arrow wouldn't be enough to start the reaction."

"And if you were to light the powders with regular fire instead of that fluid?" Wade asks.

"Assuming it was a big enough fire to make the powders work, you'd have two, maybe three seconds before they exploded," she says. "Not even Hemera could escape the blast in that amount of time."

"Why don't we have Ry and Dellin drop it from the air and then shoot a bunch of flaming arrows at it?" I suggest.

Everlyn shakes her head. "The wind would spread the powder around, and you'd have as good a chance of blowing up this building as you would the Duskers. The only possible way would be to go right up to them and dump the powders at their feet."

Wade nods as he digests this information.

"You can't be thinking about it," Everlyn says, looking from him to me, her expression becoming more terrified by the second. "Hemera, you'll get killed right along with the Duskers you're trying to blow up."

I swallow. Before I even have a chance to think about what I'm saying, I tell Wade, "It's my fault Crowe is after us. Let me—"

"Absolutely not." Wade's jaw is set. "I'm not losing one more Solguard to the Duskers." He looks at me, and I see a desperate kind of resolve on his face. "And I won't lose you."

The raw emotion in his voice tugs at my heart.

"Don't give Hemera any of your explosives," Wade tells Everlyn. "That's an order. Where are you keeping the powders now?"

"On the third floor with the other weapons," she replies in a breathless voice.

Wade gives me a look that says he knows exactly what I'm thinking. "I'm going to have some of my people move them elsewhere so you won't be tempted to use them." He glares at me. "Do I need to have you tied up so you don't go trying to sacrifice yourself?"

I feel my cheeks flush with anger. "You're welcome to try," I shoot back.

"Hemera," he growls, his voice low and threatening. "I'm serious."

I can tell from the relative quiet that has fallen that we've attracted the attention of the Solguards hovering nearby, but neither Wade nor I spare them a glance.

I step toward Wade, getting in his face in a way none of the other Solguards would ever dare. I can sense our audience's amusement turn to concern as the tension between us visibly heats up. It's the Solguards' sworn duty to protect their leader, but they also know it would be a waste of their limited energy and strength to try to fight me.

Wade takes my shoulders in a hard grip and pushes me back against the wall.

"Last I checked, you were still a Solguard," Wade says in his most commanding voice. "And that means you are compelled to act as one of us."

He leans closer and presses his lips against my ear. I'm so startled by the contact that I don't immediately react. He speaks against my ear in a low voice. "I'll do whatever is necessary to make sure you don't go after the Duskers yourself. Do you understand me?"

My momentary shock at his nearness is replaced with anger as my temper flares to life. I lean into him, preparing to remind him exactly what I'm capable of. It's then that I see the emotion I hadn't noticed before in my anger. There's fear in Wade's eyes.

The sight of it cools my temper.

Lowering my voice so only he can hear, I say, "I don't have a death wish, but Wade, think of all the lives that will be saved if I do this."

"No." Wade grips my hands hard enough to hurt, but the anger is gone from his eyes. All that's left is a helpless kind of desperation I know all too well. "Please, love. I can't lose you."

I suck in a breath. Wade hasn't spoken to me this way in…as long as I can remember. For as much time as we've spent together since Darkness, this is the first time I've felt like our closeness is more than just physical proximity.

The honesty and emotion in those words are more than I've gotten from him in months. Part of me is surprised he still cares enough to fight me so hard. I find I have no defenses against him like this.

"Besides," Wade continues. "We both know that even if you were to blow up these Duskers, Crowe would just send more."

"It would give us a fighting chance, though," I argue. "And the Duskers' numbers aren't limitless. At least I'd be giving our people time to prepare for whatever else Crowe sends our way."

A muscle flexes in Wade's jaw, and I can tell he sees the truth of my argument, even if he's too stubborn to admit it.

"Do you really want to have this battle when I could end it all?" I press, keeping my voice low enough that others won't be able to eavesdrop.

"Yes." His voice cracks as he pulls me against him.

I hold him back. I had forgotten how right this feels. Wade's warm hands press against my lower back, and his heart thuds against my chest.

"Then we fight?" I ask, leaning my head against him. "Together?"

I can feel his nod. "Together."

When we separate, Wade takes my right hand and kisses the place where the Solguard sun is tattooed onto my skin.

Someone clears his throat. We both turn to see the small group of Solguards who are appraising us with some combination of amusement and wariness. I've always gotten the feeling that some of the Solguards were happier when Wade kept his distance from me…especially since I haven't done much to change the more recent perception that I have a volatile temper. Everyone remembers what I was like when the Zeroes were under my command. The Zeroes' impulses bled into my personality, and the memory of the person I became as a result is still raw for many who live in the fortress.

"What in the nonexistent sun are you all standing around for?" Ry, hands on hips, stomps toward us. The group of Solguards parts for her, knowing not to rouse her temper the same way they avoid mine. "The Duskers are coming. We need to fortify the building. Prepare the front and rear defenses." She claps her hands in mine and Wade's faces. "Chop, chop."

Wade shakes himself, and I feel his leader mask slide back into place. "You're right," he tells Ry. "Get the archers up on the wall. I'll go alert the other Banished leaders."

And just like that, Wade is gone, swallowed up into the crowd of people all vying for a piece of his attention.

CHAPTER 17

Is it true?" a Solguard asks Ry. "Are the Duskers attacking?"

"Yes," Ry replies without any attempt to soften the blow. "So get your armor and prepare yourselves for battle."

A ripple of fear goes through the growing crowd of Solguards and Banished who have joined us.

"I thought the Supreme didn't want anything to do with us," someone else says.

Many had hoped that Crowe, sitting on Darkness Peak and being worshipped as a god, had forgotten about us.

I knew better. I remember the way she looked at me after Dellin thwarted her plans to kill my family in retribution for the death of her daughter. I remember the way she screamed my name moments after Hendrix burned to death.

I know that Crowe won't rest until I, and everyone I care about, is dead.

Still, I can't fathom this being the end. After everything we've been through…everything we've done to survive…. I can't stand the thought of us all becoming corpses in yet another battle for which we're grossly outmatched and underprepared.

If I had my army of Zeroes, we'd stand a chance.

That thought stops me in my tracks. A wave of shame passes through me.

No, I tell myself. The Zeroes are the reason I turned my back on my best friends. All I cared about was the Zeroes, and I was so drunk on the power they leant me that I almost lost myself.

I'll never make that mistake again. We'll just have to defeat the Duskers the same way we won every battle before the Zeroes existed, relying on the strength of our alliance with the Banished and Halves.

"We're not going to die today," Ry snaps at the men and women surrounding us. She sets her mouth in a hard line of determination. "We've all got too much unfinished business. Now, stop moping and help fortify the building."

Wade, joined by Ekil and the other Banished leaders, comes down the stairs. The crowd makes room for them as they head toward Ry and me.

"Hemera," Wade says. "I think Ekil is trying to tell us something."

"If we survive all of this, I'm going to teach you their language," I tell Wade before turning my attention on Ekil.

I listen while the Halve explains.

"Secure building and let them in front door," Ekil says in his gravelly voice. "Kill a few at a time instead of meeting on open ground."

It's a good idea, and I quickly translate it for the other leaders.

When I've finished, Tut smiles, displaying his gold teeth. "The creature isn't as dumb as it looks."

Brogut, who must have picked up enough of the human language from Jarosh to grasp Tut's meaning, snarls.

Before I can interject, Tut continues, "We've got the advantage of a fortress that's been double-reinforced by the best architects in the territory." He waves a hand at his people gathered around him. "The Duskers would need explosives of their own to break down the layers of wood that are reinforcing this building. With only their crossbows, they'll have a difficult time getting into the building unless we let them."

"And we coated the whole lower part of the building with one of young Everlyn's flame retardant substances," Valior points out. "They won't be able to burn it down."

Wade nods. "Get everyone back inside the building," he says. "And I mean everyone. Scouts, archers, Halves…."

While the Banished leaders bark out orders to their people, I go out again to see how much progress the Duskers have made.

A small bit of hope creeps inside me. Now that they're gathered in a group instead of marching in a single-file line, there aren't quite as many Duskers as I'd originally thought. It's still more than I'd want our starving, suffering army to have to face, but at least it's possible we'll stand a chance against them.

When I get back inside, I go in search of Wokee and Everlyn. I find Everlyn first, hovering by the enormous tree and looking lost without one of her chemistry experiments clutched in her hand.

I cut off her worried questions and say, "I need you to get Wokee. Then, the two of you take Vlaz and head north. Bring enough supplies for a few days. Do you understand me?"

"But—"

"Hurry," I tell her, giving her a quick hug. "I'm counting on you to keep Wokee safe. Okay?"

She nods, her eyes brimming with tears.

Wokee and Everlyn are the youngest ones in the entire fortress. Sending them away isn't just about my special love for them. They're the only children we have left, and no one would begrudge my choice to protect them over everyone else.

I head back into the crowd in search of Valior and Tut, trusting that Everlyn will do as I've asked. My mind is occupied by battle strategy and the best ways to configure our soldiers. We'll also need to move our stockpile of goods to the upper levels of the building, just in case the Duskers get through our defenses. It won't do us any good to win this battle if all of our food is destroyed during the fight.

"Hemera, what in the sun is going on?" Jarosh demands.

"Dusker attack," I tell him.

"Camike," Jarosh says, his voice tinged with desperation. "I have to get her out of here."

"There's nowhere to go." I spare him as much sympathy as I can manage with my mind flying in a thousand different directions.

"Vlaz. Where's that hyenair?"

I set my jaw. "I told Everlyn and Wokee to take him and ride north. They're probably already gone."

"No. You don't understand." He grabs my arm, his fingers digging into my skin.

"I understand," I tell him as gently as I can as I slide out of his grip. "We all have people here we love and care about, but—"

Jarosh lets out a low curse, and then he's winding back through the crowd without waiting for me to finish.

Shaking my head, I turn my attention inward, feeling for Dayne through the bond that connects us. I follow the invisible tug until I find him. He's standing against the wall, appearing as still and calm as everyone else is frantic.

"Will you fight by my side?" I ask my brother.

"No other choice." His voice is a deep, inflectionless rumble. "Bound to you."

I nod, swallowing the hurt that gathers inside me.

"I don't know if you can understand this now," I tell him, needing to raise my voice to be heard over the bedlam of the humans and Halves preparing for battle, "but I'm sorry for what I did to you. If there was any other way I could have saved you, believe me, I would have done it."

Dayne doesn't say anything. His black eyes are fixed on mine, but I can't tell what he's thinking…if he's thinking anything at all.

I bite my lip, and then I just say the words because there's no point in holding them back anymore.

"As selfish as it is, I can't be sorry for what I did. I know you aren't like you were before, but you're still here. I've lost so many people who matter to me, but of all of them, you matter the most. I couldn't lose you, too." I take a breath, feeling drained. "I just thought you should know."

Dayne still doesn't speak. I guess I didn't really expect him to, but it doesn't stop the feeling of disappointment from squeezing against my insides.

"Hemera," Dayne says before I can walk away.

"Yes?" That persistent sense of hope returns in full force.

"You should have killed me."

CHAPTER 18

uskers are approaching," a loud voice calls from one of the upper floors of the building.

There's more frantic movement and shouting as everyone gathers their weapons. The one benefit of Darkness is that it's not too hot to wear armor the way it used to be. The Northerners have used their spare moments to craft helmets and shields, but there aren't enough for everyone.

"Hemera, have you seen Wade?" a Solguard asks me. She looks as frazzled as I feel.

I shake my head. "He was here a little while ago, but—"

"A scout just reported there's another group of Duskers approaching from the far north. They must have gone miles out of the way for us not to detect them, but they've made camp a short distance away."

My brow furrows in confusion. "Why would they do that?"

"No idea," the Solguard replies. "They've brought sacks of what we assume are supplies to wait out a siege, although the scouts couldn't get close enough to confirm." She frowns. "But if I were them, I'd attack quickly before my enemy could get their defenses in place, especially since they've got us pegged in on both sides now."

I agree with her. Besides, we have shelter for the hours of Dark. If the Duskers stay where they are, they'll be vulnerable to the wormkill and terrible cold. *What are they thinking?*

"Okay." I nod, trying to get a handle on everything. "We need scouts to keep an eye on those other Duskers and report back if they start making moves."

The Solguard nods and runs off.

"Hemera!"

I turn to see Everlyn, her face pale with terror.

"Why are you still here?" I demand, my own panic rising.

"My explosives." She waves her hands in a frantic gesture. "I went to get some of the powder so Wokee and I would be able to start a small fire, but it's all gone."

Before I can respond, my attention is drawn to a commotion at the door.

"Mer?" Ry waves at me to get my attention. Her mop of red hair is askew, and I can tell from the look on her face that something's wrong.

"Forget the powders," I tell Everlyn. "Just get Wokee and get the hell out of here. Fly high enough that you'll be out of range of the Duskers' crossbows. Now, get going!"

"What's happening?" I ask Ry when she's in hearing distance.

Ry blows a wayward red curl off her face. "Wade said something that freaked me out, and I thought you should know."

"What did he say?" I ask, not quite understanding the fear slithering down my spine.

"He told me that if anything happens to him, I'm in charge of the Solguards. And he said he needed two archers to cover him so he could go check things out."

"*Check things out?*" I demand as the pieces begin fitting together.

"Yeah. I figured he was doing some recon or something to see what kind of numbers we were dealing with, but I don't know, it didn't feel right."

Oh no.

"Was he carrying anything with him?" I ask.

"Um, he had a really big torch, and a couple of big bags. I didn't see what was inside—"

"Ry." I grab her shoulders as my fear turns to full-blown panic. "When did he leave? Which direction was he heading?"

I follow her out the door, my mind screaming in rejection of what I'm becoming increasingly certain he's done.

I blink into the gray mist, scanning the land for some sign of Wade's blue cloak.

"Over there."

I turn at the sound of Dayne's voice. I was so consumed with my terror that I hadn't even realized he was standing right next to me. I follow the direction he's pointing.

Wade is too far away for me to see details, but I know it's him from the way he moves. Even from this distance, I can see the blazing torch in his hand.

"Wade!" I scream.

He's heading straight for the mass of Duskers.

"Stay here," I tell Ry.

And then, I run. I run like I've never run before.

The Dusker archers are ready for Wade. Their grip on their crossbows is lazy, and I think I hear a few of them laugh as Wade approaches.

The two Solguards who were flanking Wade split off at the same time, like he's just ordered them to turn around and come back to the building. Except, they've stopped moving a short distance away. Their bows are pulled taut, and their arrows are pointed at me.

"Stop," one of the archers calls out to me. "Don't come any closer."

About a thousand sarcastic responses are on the tip of my tongue, but I'm too focused on Wade to bother with any of them. I don't have time for this nonsense.

A few more steps bring me close enough for Wade to hear me.

"Wade, stop!" I yell.

He must have heard me this time, but instead of paying me the slightest bit of attention, he takes one of the two sacks slung over his shoulders and fumbles with its opening. That much powder is enough to destroy the whole Dusker army…and Wade along with them.

I take two more steps toward him before pain rips through my knee.

I look down to see an arrow lodged in my kneecap. Beside me, Dayne roars as a hole appears through his pantleg and brown blood spills out. I have to wrestle Dayne back before he tears our own archers limb from limb.

By the time I get Dayne under control and pull the arrow out of my leg, precious seconds have slipped away. I look up to see Wade toss the first sack at the Duskers. One of the Duskers shoots at it, and the material bursts apart. A wave of purple powder arcs across the sky. It falls harmlessly over the Duskers, and they laugh.

Wade overturns the second bag. A light dusting of purple powder covers the ground between Wade and the Duskers.

No, no, no.

The Solguard archers release two more arrows. One hits my left ankle and the other impales the fresh wound on my right knee. I collapse. Dayne's bloodcurdling shriek of pain and rage echoes in my ears.

"Wade, please," I beg him.

He turns to face me. The torch's flame illuminates the determined look in his eyes.

"I'm sorry, Hemera," he calls.

And then he lowers the torch to the ground.

CHAPTER 19

N o!" I scream.

We each make it two steps—Wade toward me, and me toward him—before an explosion rocks the earth.

My body is weightless as it's pitched through the air. Before I can even begin to make sense of what's happening, my body hits the ground with so much force the air is knocked from my lungs. I hear the crack of bone.

I retch from the pain even as I struggle to my feet. I shield my head as bits of debris covered in the sticky black sap of the darkness logs rain down around me.

I hadn't even known the Duskers had the darkness logs.

In the distance, I see the splintered remains of the carts that were used to haul the darkness logs.

Even amid all of the pain, foul-smelling chunks of darkness wood, and patches of small black flames dotting the ground, my thoughts narrow to a single point of focus: Wade.

My eyes sweep the wreckage as I search for him. I take a hobbling step and cry out as my broken leg comes into contact with the ground. I stand, sweat pouring down my face as I grit my teeth against the pain. My vision blurs, and it takes all of my energy to keep from passing out.

The two archers run toward me from the direction of the building. I can see their mouths moving, but I don't hear a word they say. They both look as dazed as I feel.

I look around, forcing myself to stay conscious.

Wade, I think, using that one syllable to ground my foggy brain.

It takes me several moments to find him amid the wreckage of the carts and Dusker bodies. Most of his cloak is covered in black sap, but there's enough blue left that I know it's him.

My vision goes dark as I straighten my broken leg. A strangled, pitiful sound tears through me as I force the bones back into place. I lay on the ground, gasping, while my leg knits back together.

I shove aside one of the archers who tries to help me.

Wade. I need to get to Wade.

I don't wait for the healing to finish. I crawl to Wade. And then, once my leg is whole again, I force myself to my feet and limp to him.

"Wade!" I fall to the ground by his side.

He's lying face down, and my heart lurches into my throat as I turn him over.

I don't recognize the scream that comes from my throat. It doesn't even sound human.

His bare hand is covered with darkness tree sap. It's all over his Solguard tattoo, replacing the beautiful sun with a black, sticky mess.

Even with such a small amount, the beautiful copper skin of Wade's hand is shriveled and blackened from where it is already decaying. As I watch, the black rot travels up to his wrist. I'd cut off his hand to stop the poison from spreading, but it's too late. The fact that the it's spreading means that the sap has already gotten into his veins.

Wade lets out a low, suffering breath. I rip off his cloak, which is covered with the black sap.

"Need to go."

I recognize the rough, emotionless tone of Dayne's voice, even though I can't see him through my tears.

Dayne bends down, picks up Wade, and starts back toward the building. I feel Dayne's rage and all-consuming need to protect me through the bond. All I feel for myself is a crushing weight against my chest. It's what I imagine it would feel like to drown.

By the time we get back to the building, my tears have stopped falling. Numbness has taken hold, making it impossible for me to feel much of anything. I've seen enough people consumed by the black sap to know Wade won't survive.

There's no hope.

Wade is unconscious, and as desperate as I am for him to wake up, I know it's a mercy he can't feel what's happening to him. None of the healing herbs Camike has tried have ever been enough to dull the pain or stop the poison from killing whoever it touches. Banished, Halves, Duskers…it's the single great equalizer. I doubt even my body would be able to recover if the stuff got on me.

I know I should be feeling more than this terrible numbness, but it's almost like my mind can't accept the loss. So many of the people who mattered to me are gone. All I can think is *not you, too.*

As Solguards hover around us, my numbness transforms into fury. I'm angrier than I've ever felt, and all of it's directed at Wade.

He did this to himself…he sacrificed himself.

It was what I tried to do…what he stopped me from doing. It never occurred to me that, the whole time, he was planning to do exactly what he was begging me not to do.

Wade single-handedly destroyed half of the Dusker army. But it cost him his life.

He should have fought by my side. After everything we've been through together, we should have faced this challenge together. And if we died on the battlefield, then at least we would have been together and surrounded by our people.

Instead, Wade was surrounded by the Duskers. My last words to him should have been *I love you*, not *Wade, no.*

"How could you do this to me?" I demand in a hoarse whisper.

Wade doesn't react or give any indication he can hear me. His face has taken on a grayish color.

Tears are coursing down my cheeks, and still, all I want to do is scream at him. I want his golden eyes to open and for him to yell back. His ragged breathing is still audible, but I'm not foolish enough to think he can last like this much longer. The poison is probably already in his heart and lungs.

A howl of agony and rage rips free from me. People stop what they're doing to stare. Some are whispering, while others are trying to offer me comfort. I ignore all of them as I huddle over Wade's motionless body and sob.

How am I supposed to watch him die? How am I supposed to watch Wade disintegrate before my eyes?

The last man I loved died right in front of me, too. I remember the blade that was meant for me slicing through Brice's chest. I remember begging him to stay with me, even as he gasped his last breath.

Now, I'm reliving that nightmare all over again. Except it isn't Brice, it's Wade.

Solguards surround us. Many of them are crying and screaming out Wade's name.

Ry stalks toward us. I don't bother to look up, but I know the sound of her footsteps, even amid the din of grief and despair. I glance at her when she's standing right over me. She takes one look at Wade, lying limp on the ground, and a shudder goes through her. She doesn't break down like everyone else, though. She stiffens her spine and lifts her chin.

"Everyone shut up." Ry's voice trembles, but it's loud and strong enough to get everyone's attention. "I'm acting as Solguard leader while Wade is out of commission, and I'm ordering all of you to pull yourselves together."

She pushes her hair back from her forehead.

"Wade bought us time, and now it's up to us to do what we can to save ourselves."

I stay motionless, devoid of every emotion besides anger, as Ry points and calls out orders. Ekil and the Banished leaders are doing the same. Oaths are shouted about defending the fortress to our dying breath.

In spite of the sadness hovering over the Solguards, I can also sense a newfound glimmer of hope. Now that half of the Dusker army has been demolished in one fell swoop, we have a chance. The thought gives me no comfort.

The Solguards pace around, darting furtive glances in Wade's direction. They clench their tattooed hands into fists and mutter curses and prayers under their breath.

Through it all, I kneel beside Wade's still form, speechless and motionless.

Because Ry is standing near me, I hear when the scouts deliver their report that the other half of the Dusker army hasn't broken camp. Tut and Valior actually shake hands, congratulating themselves on being formidable enough to make the Duskers hesitate.

I don't have the will to tell them the truth: the Duskers aren't afraid of us.

"Wade has given us a chance," Ry tells me, even though her bottom lip trembles with the emotion she's trying to hold back. "We'll win this battle, and then we'll march straight up to Darkness Peak and end Crowe once and for all."

The thought offers me no comfort.

I watch numbly as the crowd parts for Camike, who is shadowed by Jarosh.

"Put him over there," Camike says, motioning to an empty pallet beneath one of the tree's branches. The rose-gold color of its bark makes Wade's copper skin look more lifelike than it is, like the tree is trying to infuse me with false hope.

It's like the tree is mocking me.

Camike kneels beside me, inspects Wade's face, and then lets out a sigh.

"I am so sorry," she tells me.

The sadness in her voice confirms what I already knew, but still, it opens the floodgates.

I lay my head on Wade's chest, heedless of everyone's warnings not to get too close to the sap.

"Mer, we need you and Dayne," Ry says, her words slightly muffled from the metal helmet now covering her red curls and half of her face.

I ignore her and wrap my arms around Wade's body. He's too warm and strong to be dying. My eyes know the truth of what's happening to him, but still, I can't accept it.

Wade feels feverish, even through the layers of clothes separating us. I look up to see his mouth is twisted in pain. Then, I don't see anything, because I'm crying too hard.

I cry until there are no tears left. Then, I just lie there on the ground, huddled next to Wade with my mind in a haze of pain, anger, and regret.

"The Duskers built a bonfire and erected tents," a Solguard reports to Ry. "I don't think they're going to attack today."

"What are they thinking?" Ry asks, puzzled. "Either retreat or attack, but staying on the Outside when Dark is coming makes no sense."

"Maybe there are more Duskers coming," the scout replies.

The scout is probably right, but I don't have the energy to worry about what that will mean for us. I don't even care enough to wonder if Crowe and Jadem will be with the new group of Duskers.

"Perhaps we should gather our forces and attack them first," Valior tells Ry.

I listen with disinterest as the Banished leaders debate whether to attack first or wait until the Duskers come for us. After a heated discussion, they finally agree we should stay put.

I don't know how much time has passed when Ry kneels down on the ground next to me.

"Mer, come on." She tugs at my arm. "He wouldn't want you to see him like this."

"Do you think I care what he would want?" My voice is savage. "He's dying because he made a sacrifice he didn't need to make. It didn't have to be like this."

Some part of me is aware I'm shouting, and that everyone milling around is staring at me. The other part of me doesn't care. I'm shaking with fury. And there's nothing I can do with my rage, because the person it's directed at is dying.

Wade is dying.

A horrible, gut-wrenching sob cuts through the silence in the room. I register that it's my own seconds before I'm being crushed into Ry's embrace.

She holds me and rocks me in her arms while I cry. She murmurs soft words that are drowned out by the force of my sobs. I cling to her so hard it must be painful, but she doesn't try to loosen my grip.

I have no idea how long we stay like that, with Ry holding me as I cry out my fury and grief. I don't stop until my head is pounding and an exhaustion greater than any I've ever known is weighing me down. I don't even have the energy to keep myself upright, and I know I'd be lying on the ground if it wasn't for Ry's embrace.

When we finally separate, I can't bring myself to look at Wade. I know from too much experience with the black sap that his arm will be mostly gone, replaced by a congealed mass of charred flesh.

The last person I saw die from the darkness tree sap screamed for two hours before he was nothing more than a gelatinous puddle on the ground.

In spite of Ry's warning that Wade wouldn't want to be seen this way, I refuse to run away from him and hide in some corner. No matter how painful it is for me, no matter how many years the sight of his decomposing flesh will haunt my dreams, I won't leave him. I feel like I owe him that much, after he made the ultimate sacrifice so the rest of us could live.

When I brace myself and force my gaze on Wade, I have to blink several times. Even though I'm sure at least an hour has passed, he's unchanged from the last time I glanced at him. Dark is replacing Gloom outside the window, so I know I haven't imagined the passage of time. Still, the horrible decay hasn't moved farther than his forearm.

I call out to Camike, who is hovering over another patient nearby.

She gives me a small smile that doesn't reach her black eyes and comes over to rest a comforting hand on my shoulder.

"I do not know why it hasn't killed him yet," she tells me in a soft voice, "but you should not have hope."

I already know that. I've seen too much horror and tragedy to entertain false hopes any longer. I know that whatever the reason Wade is still alive, it's likely only prolonging his suffering.

Dark comes, and still, Wade lies motionless and unconscious, neither better nor worse.

The Duskers still haven't made their move. Scouts have come and gone a number of times, reporting to Ry as she keeps vigil beside me, but nothing has changed. There are no new Dusker troops headed this way, and the Duskers who are here haven't broken camp.

"What are they waiting for?" Tut growls as he paces back and forth.

The only explanation that makes sense is that they're waiting for reinforcements, but no matter how many scouts Ry sends out, none of them find any evidence of more Duskers on the move. I can't make sense of what the Duskers are planning, but I can't bring myself to care.

As the hours slip by, Wade's condition stays the same. I listen to his labored breathing. My heart shrinks a little more with his every gasp of pain. Different people come and go as they stare down at Wade or offer me some meaningless words of sympathy. Dayne's presence is constant, but it doesn't give me any comfort. He doesn't understand my grief.

Hours later, a downpour of gloomy rain forces all of the scouts and Banished keeping watch over the Duskers to come sprinting back to the building. I feel some small sense of satisfaction at the thought of the Duskers outside and unprotected from the rain. With any luck, it'll kill them, and then this battle will be over before it's begun.

And Wade will have died for nothing.

A muttered curse comes from the window. It's echoed by others, and pretty soon, the whole building is abuzz with terror.

I glance up as a scout comes tearing in through the building's entrance. Her face is speckled with burn marks from the gloomy rain and she's wheezing with pain, but her words are still audible as she delivers her report.

"The Duskers' cloaks don't absorb the rain. They've broken camp, and they're coming for us."

CHAPTER 20

The Duskers were waiting for the gloomy rain. They knew we'd have to retreat inside the building, and that we'd be powerless to stop whatever they're planning to do now.

Even the archers posted at each window are of little use. The rain has extinguished all the torches outside, and it's impossible for our archers to see through the dark.

If I had any room left for anger, I'd resent that the Duskers have cloaks that protect them from the gloomy rain.

Even now, I can hear the groans of several of our scouts who are writhing in agony from the poisonous rain, while the Duskers are out there without a single drop harming them. The senseless injustice of it all is enough to drive me insane.

"Mer, we need you," Ry tells me. She takes my arm in a firm grip and hauls me to my feet.

I stand motionless as a Solguard straps armor over my chest and legs, too tired to bother telling her that I'm the last person who needs armor.

I take the sword Tut holds out to me with one hand and accept my sling from Ry with the other. I stand at my post in front of the rear entrance to the building, which is harder to defend than the front. Dayne stands at my side. Solguards and Banished are behind us, their weapons gripped in their hands, as they wait for the inevitable attack. I stand, stoic and emotionless as Dayne, as I listen for the sound of a battering rod against the building's exterior.

The Duskers' camp was close enough that they should already be breaking their way into the building, but it's still quiet. I tense as a muffled thud comes from the opposite side of the wall in front of me. It's not loud enough to be a battering rod or wood splintering against an axe. It's the gentle thud of something coming to rest against the building's outer wall.

Because of the combination of wind and gloomy rain, we covered all of the windows with the specere leave awnings. The leaves keep the rain from coming inside the building, but they also prevent us from being able to see what the Duskers are up to. There's nothing for any of us to do except wait for the Duskers to make their move.

I'm still waiting for the sound of something heavy to come crashing through the wooden boards, when my eyes start to sting. The stinging becomes a burn at the back of my throat. The soldiers standing closest to the window start to cough and wheeze. Finally, understanding begins to dawn.

Oh no.

Smoke begins to filter in through the gaps in the window a few moments later. Hoarse cries and shouts confirm that others have figured out what the Duskers are doing.

The rhythmic thuds I heard were the darkness logs being stacked against the building.

The inky black smoke is filtering in through the gaps in the building's wooden planks. My eyes and nose feel like they're on fire.

"I thought our building was fire proof," Tut roars.

"It is," Valior replies. "We'll be safe for a little while, but the darkness flames burn hotter than a normal fire. They'll get through eventually."

All at once, it occurs to me why the Duskers waited to burn the logs. If we stay inside, we'll all be killed from the black flames—if the smoke doesn't kill us first. If we go outside, the combination of gloomy rain and Duskers will kill us.

We're trapped with no means of defending ourselves.

Too late, I understand Crowe's note.

Your people will turn to ashes just as Hendrix did....

At the time, it hadn't occurred to me that the note might be literal...that my people would die in the same way Hendrix had...consumed by black flames. Now that I know the truth, it's too late for me to do anything about it.

I hear the choked cries from the others in the building as the smoke spreads. There are horrible hacking sounds as people cough up blood. Families wail as they hold their loved ones.

My anger and sense of helplessness transforms to terror when I see Vlaz huddled over two small forms on the other side of the building. The kids didn't leave like I'd ordered them to, and now they're going to die with the rest of us.

I stare around, more desperate than ever for some way to end this…to protect them. Crowe tried to take Wokee from me once. She won't do it again.

Black flames begin to lick around the edges of the window covering.

I know from experience the black flames aren't deterred by the gloomy rain the way normal fire is. If anything, the chemicals in the rain seem to make the darkness fire burn more intensely.

It won't take more than an hour for this entire building, and everyone inside, to become ashes.

"I'm going out," I tell Ry, stifling a cough as I grab my sling and head for the back of the building. "Dayne and I will kill as many of them as we can. Wait until the smoke is unbearable, and then get everyone out."

"The rain will kill us," Ry says, despair in her voice.

I turn to look at her and see that she and Dellin are clinging to each other. They're both holding the sleeves of their cloaks over their noses and mouths in an effort to block out the poisonous stench, but I know it won't do them any good once the flames are inside the building.

"Maybe the rain will stop," I say over my shoulder as I gesture for Dayne to follow me. "Just have everyone ready to get out of here."

I put my hand on the door's handle and wrench it back with a gasp. The wood is burning hot from the fire that must be licking against the exterior of the wood. It won't be long before the flames eat their way through the wall completely.

I'm looking down at my hand, watching as new skin forms over the burn, when a blinding flash of light fills the entire building with a rosy glow.

It's so bright I cry out and shield my eyes. I haven't seen this much color in six months, and my eyes can hardly comprehend what they're seeing.

Surprised shouts echo all around me.

I look around for the source of the explosion of light. And that's when I understand. The pulsing light is coming from the tree.

CHAPTER 21

The giant tree in the center of the building—the one Wokee grew from the golden seed Jadem said would be the Solguards' salvation—looks like it's been lit from within. The tree was big before, but as I blink through the illumination, the branches unfurl and extend. The trunk lengthens. I hear the creak and groan of wood as the tree pushes up and out. It's growing so fast it'll soon tear through the walls and roof.

Glowing pink flowers unfurl and sprout clusters of round, golden seeds. Heat radiates from the branches until it feels like I'm standing next to a bonfire.

My attention is so wholly consumed by the tree that it takes me several moments to realize I'm no longer coughing, and the horrible stinging in my eyes and nose is gone. I glance around, and I see that it's not just some effect of my rapid healing. Everyone around me is taking deep gulps of clean air.

And then I notice something else. Even with all of the shouting and voices surrounding me, I had been aware of Wade's labored breathing. But as I listen for it now, I don't hear it.

I glance down and gasp.

Wade is illuminated in a pool of rosy light. His bare arm is covered in red, angry burns. I look closer, but I don't see any sign of the black sap. I don't think it's some trick of the tree's light. Somehow, some way, the black sap is gone.

That's not all. The harsh, contorted lines of his face have smoothed out. He looks like he's sleeping peacefully instead of succumbing to an agonizing death.

I know my jaw is probably hanging on the floor, but there's nothing I can do to reel it back in place.

Wade's alive. And from the looks of it, that isn't going to change. I kneel down beside him, silent so I won't wake him from this impossible sleep he's in. I reach out for him. My hand is trembling so violently I jerk it back, afraid I'll hurt him.

"The gloomy rain stopped and the Duskers are running away," Ekil reports. He's glancing out the nearest window, which has scorch marks all along the wood beams as evidence of the black fire that was licking at the frame.

From months of experience with the damned black flames, I know there is no way to extinguish them until everything and everyone in its path has been burned down into nothingness. And yet, the flames that were in the process of consuming the building were somehow extinguished.

"Ekil says the Duskers are retreating," I translate for Ry, my voice hoarse.

I'm still in too much of a daze to really process any of what's going on. Part of me is sure this is all just some hallucination from the smoke we're breathing in. The other part of me is trying to find some rational explanation for all the irrational things that are happening.

Finally mastering my own limbs enough to trust them not to flail, I reach out and press the back of my hand to Wade's forehead. His face is warm but no longer feverish. When I look closer, I realize his complexion has lost its grayish hue. His copper skin is gleaming with health.

I can feel the tears running down my cheeks even as my brain tries to find some logical explanation for what I'm seeing.

"What in the sun—look!" Ry yells, almost blowing out my eardrums in the process.

Tearing my eyes away from Wade, I follow the direction of Ry's finger. She's pointing at a new hole in the side of the building, where one of the tree's branches has cracked through the wooden exterior.

I squint, blink several times, and then look again.

"I'll be back," I tell Wade, even though he's given no indication he can hear me. Then, I rush out with the mass of people and Halves emptying out of the building.

The first thing I notice is that the biting cold I was prepared for, the cold that should already be sinking into my bones, isn't here. The air isn't warm, but it isn't painfully cold, either.

I look up to where others are pointing, and my small cry mixes with all the other exclamations and surprised shouts surrounding me. The dark mass that has blocked out the sun for the last six months hasn't disappeared, but there's a patch that's thinner than it is everywhere else. It's more of a light gray, and beams of sunlight—something I thought I might never see again—are filtering through the gray fog. The patch hovers directly over the building and the golden tree, which is still snaking its branches through the newly-formed holes in the ceiling. As I watch, the tree continues to grow up and out. As it does so, the lightened section of sky continues to push back the Darkness.

In the distance, the Duskers are racing away on foot. I can see their panic in the haphazard way they're retreating. I look around, trying to make sense of all the inexplicable sights unfolding around me. That's when I glance down at the ground and see something I never expected to see again.

They're so small I might have missed them. Buried amid the tangled, brown vines of long-dead plants, I see three tiny blue flowers. Each one is smaller than the pad of my fingertip, but they're the first flowers I've seen in the six months since Darkness. Their tiny heads are turned in the direction of the tree, like they recognize it as some kind of life-giving sun.

I kneel down to the ground and, with the utmost care, clear away the dead plant debris to give the flowers more room. I pile the dead weeds around the flowers, making a little barrier to protect them from being trod on.

"Look at this." A Solguard comes up to Ry with a log cradled in the folds of her cloak.

It has the shape and consistency of the darkness logs I've grown so familiar with, but not their color. The log isn't white, exactly. It's more like it's been drained of color rather than possessing a hue of its own. It looks sucked dry, like a fruit that's withered in the sun.

I reach out a hand, and after only a brief pause, run my fingers along the rough wooden exterior.

I catch a whiff of the awful stink of the darkness tree, but I feel none of the burning poison.

Ry, whose arm is still wound around Dellin's waist, looks at me with a mixture of shock and confusion.

"I don't get it," Ry says, her eyes wide.

"Mer!"

I whip around at the sound of Wokee's voice.

"Wokee, why didn't you and Everlyn leave like I told you to?" I ask, all of my fear returning at the sight of him, even though logic tells me the danger has passed.

"Did you really think we were going to just abandon you? Seriously, Mer." Wokee rolls his eyes. "Besides, if we were gone, you'd all still be wandering around with your jaws hanging open with no idea of what's happening."

I just gape at Wokee while I try to summon the rebuke he deserves.

"Do you know what's going on?" Ry demands.

"'Course," Wokee says, a mixture of pride and impatience plain in his voice. "I've been trying to tell you."

We all wait, and I get the sense Wokee is trying to build anticipation. I'm about to tell him that now is most definitely not the time for dramatic suspense, when Wokee finally speaks.

"I knew there was something special about the tree as soon as it started to grow. It just *felt* like one of Jadem's plants. I don't know how else to describe it, but I could sense her as I tended it, just like I could tell it was Jadem's work with those darkness trees." He wrinkles his nose at the thought of those foul trees. "But what I couldn't understand was why the tree didn't do anything. I mean, it had that golden-pink light and was warm to the touch, but something that could grow that fast should do something more impressive. I just didn't put it together until it bloomed."

"Put what together?" I ask.

"It's the darkness trees' opposite. This tree feeds off them."

Ry and I exchange a puzzled look.

"Huh?" Ry asks.

Wokee huffs out a frustrated breath. "I couldn't figure it out at first…why the tree kept growing upward, even though there wasn't sunlight for it to be reaching toward."

"So?" Ry fists her hands on her hips.

"It wasn't reaching for the sun. I think it was reaching for the darkness particles in the air."

"What makes you think that?" I ask.

"Because, it was only when the Duskers started the darkness fire right against the building that the tree really came alive. It let out a burst of heat and light at the exact same time when the darkness smoke started coming into the building. Everlyn was the one to figure it out." It seems to grate on Wokee to make this admission, and he scowls.

We turn our attention on the younger girl, who is racing toward us, her cheeks flushed with excitement.

"It's just chemistry," she says, waving her hands in animation. "Opposites attract, and they work together to help each other. And Jadem's tree is the exact opposite of the darkness trees."

I stare uncomprehending at the kids.

"*Mer.* Our tree *eats* the Dark!" Wokee flails his hands in the air, indicating the small patch of sky that is less gray than the rest.

"So, are you saying…."

"I'm saying that we found the cure to Darkness!"

CHAPTER 22

It hurts my eyes to stare at the hazy beams of sunlight that almost—but don't quite—reach through the gray mist, but I continue to stare until other changes draw my attention away.

A few rodents have scurried out from holes in the ground to see what all the fuss is about. I can't remember the last time I saw a single live animal that wasn't Vlaz or a wormkill. Neither can the Halves, apparently, who are shouting as they try to catch the little creatures.

"Praise the sun!" Valior cries, shaking Tut's hand as he looks down at the tiny blue flowers at our feet. "We can begin growing crops again."

Dellin and Ry are jumping up and down and kissing each other at the same time. Ekil and Brogut are grunting and motioning with their large hands in their own version of excitement.

Some of the Solguards are on their knees, their right hands fisted over their hearts, as they stare up in wonder at the weak beams of sunlight. It's a sight none of us ever expected to see again.

I leave the group of Banished leaders, who are listening while Wokee talks in animated tones about fruit trees and edible roots. My steps feel lighter as I head back toward the building. Its exterior is stained black from the remnants of the darkness fire that would have consumed it and us, if it hadn't been for Jadem's tree.

I'm too overwhelmed by our miraculous survival to give more than a passing thought to the fact that my aunt—the person responsible for Darkness and all the deaths that have come since—somehow saved all of us. Right now, I'm more concerned about convincing myself that all of this isn't just some horrible trick of our imaginations or, more likely, a temporary state that will fade and leave us in the same position we were in before.

I push my way through the throngs of people congregating in the courtyard and let myself back into the building. My heart is in my throat, and more than a small part of me is terrified the tree's light only made Wade appear healed. I'm almost too scared to look at him for fear I'll find him covered in the black sap once again.

Camike is kneeling beside Wade.

"Camike?" I ask, my voice coming out in a scared little croak.

She looks at me, and her eyes are wide with wonder. "It's a miracle." She gestures down at Wade.

I kneel beside him. The burns on Wade's arm are bloody, but the wounds aren't mortal. There's no trace of the black sap.

"Wade?" I whisper.

His eyes crack open.

"Hemera." He tries to sit up and then winces, raising a hand to his chest.

"Three broken ribs," Camike reports. "Do not move."

"I'm alive." Wade looks at me in wonder. "We're alive."

"I must be dreaming." I reach out my hand to entwine our fingers.

Wade gives me a tired smile. "Then can you dream away my broken bones? They hurt like hell."

I let out a choked laugh, still terrified that the moment I let myself believe what I'm seeing, it will disappear.

"It was the tree," I tell him, watching as his gaze goes to the brilliant rose-gold color emanating from the bark. "Wokee says it feeds off something in the darkness logs. It must have somehow absorbed the poison in the black sap."

"Lucky for me." Wade shakes his head in amazement.

Those words turn my blood cold as I remember what brought Wade to the point of near-death. My overwhelming relief at seeing him really and truly alive transforms into anger. I can't stop the tears that are falling down my cheeks and dotting the material of Wade's shirt.

"Shh, it's alright, love," he murmurs, wincing at the slight movement of his chest.

"No, it isn't," I tell him through my muffled cries. "You almost died."

"But I didn't—"

"You left me!" I practically scream the words.

I'm furious, but I can't stop the hot, ugly tears pouring down my cheeks. I cover my face with my hands.

"Do you have any idea what it did to me when I realized what you were about to do?" I demand, my harsh words choked by the tears I can't keep at bay. "Do you have any idea what it did to me when I saw you light those powders, and I knew I wasn't going to be able to stop you?"

My raised voice has drawn the attention of others in the room, but I'm too angry to care.

"Love, please."

"And after that whole speech you gave me about not wanting me to sacrifice myself?! You looked me in the eye and said we'd fight together, and then you turned around and left me. You left me!"

"Hemera, I had to. I'm the Solguard leader—"

"That doesn't mean you get to sacrifice yourself!" I wrench away as he reaches for me.

I take in deep gulps of air as I try to collect myself.

When I think I can speak without my voice breaking, I say, "If you think so little of yourself, then I'm not going to hang around and watch you throw your life away."

"Hemera—"

"Don't ask for my help. Don't try to talk to me. We're done."

Wade ignores Camike's protests as he gets to his feet. His face drains of color, and I have to stop myself from wrapping my arms around him. When he steadies himself against the wall, he holds out a hand toward me. I don't take it. When he takes a step closer, Dayne lets out a warning growl that is more animal than human.

I don't wait for Wade to reach me. I turn around, ignoring the small crowd that's gathered to watch our little spectacle. I push past a shocked Jarosh, who is hovering behind Camike. I don't stop until I'm back outside.

* * *

If I wasn't so angry and hurt, the sight that meets me would be funny. Wokee is standing on top of a boulder, shouting out orders to eager Banished and Halves about which seeds he wants planted where. He's doing an admirable job of using some combination of Halve words and hand gestures to tell the Halves that he needs darkness tree wood.

The sight is enough to thaw the cold layer around my heart just a little.

"What are you doing?" I ask Wokee.

Wokee opens his cupped hands, displaying a dozen of the tree's round, golden seeds.

"The Halves and I are going to plant the golden seeds our Jadem tree sprouted," Wokee explains.

"Jadem tree?" I ask, raising an eyebrow.

"Well, yeah. Like it or not, Jadem is the one who gave us the seed, so I figured it was only fair to name the new species of tree after her."

His words stir new emotions in me, but I push them away before I have to try and make sense of them.

"So, you're going to plant these…Jadem trees…all over the Wild Lands?" I ask.

Wokee nods. "The more we have, the more the Dark will go away. But to make the trees grow, we need to bring the darkness wood to us."

"We need more darkness to make light?" I give Wokee a little smile.

"Pretty much, yeah," he replies with a grin. "Isn't it cool?"

"I guess it is."

I should be as energetic and enthusiastic as everyone else. Instead, I just feel drained.

"We're going to have food again," Wokee says, bouncing on the balls of his feet. "We won't be so cold anymore, and things will go back to the way they were." His grin widens. "Everlyn knows how to make berry tarts, and she said she'll make me one as soon as the rupyberries grow back." He licks his lips in anticipation.

"That's great," I tell him, but Wokee's too much in his own world to be listening to me.

117

"Jadem was right. These trees are gonna save us!"

I haven't forgotten about my aunt's note, and her promise that the little gold seed would be our salvation. Still, it's not enough to erase the sense of betrayal I feel whenever I think about her. She might have given us the key to our survival, but we would have had no need of it if she hadn't created the darkness trees in the first place.

Jadem is the reason so many of our people have died. It's because of her that we've barely managed to survive all this time. Whatever good she did by giving us the golden seed, it doesn't erase everything else she's done.

An uproarious shout goes up from the people standing nearest to the stone wall. Ry is standing on top of the wall, holding up one of her arrows. A small animal that looks like it might be a hare is speared on the arrow's tip. The poor creature is bone-thin, and in times past, its meat wouldn't have been enough to satisfy even a single grown man. Now, it'll be a veritable feast. But more than that, the animal is a symbol of what Crowe has taken away from us. Now, thanks to Jadem's tree, we have a way to fight back.

Vlaz is capering around, his yellow eyes brighter than I've seen them in months. The Westerners are already working to clear the dead plant debris from the courtyard. Everyone is smiling.

Valior hobbles up to me as he leans on his cane. "It looks like we'll live to fight another day after all." He gestures with the hand that isn't holding his cane. "The Westerners are organizing a hunt, the Halves are scampering off to collect more darkness logs to feed our savior tree, and I'm going to volunteer my people to plant more of those delightful golden seeds." He sighs in contentment.

We both stare up at the tree, which is still growing. The topmost branches have broken through the roof of the building and look like fingers grasping for the Gloom.

"I've known your aunt a long time, young lady," Valior says, still craning his neck to study the tree.

That gets my attention. By silent agreement, none of the leaders have so much as mentioned Aunt Jadem since we discovered her betrayal.

"I don't know her reasons for all that she's done," Valior continues, "but I do know one thing. She's given us a chance, and I'll take that over death any day."

"I can't begin to understand her," I say, more to myself than Valior. "Why, after she betrayed us and created the darkness trees for Crowe, would she have given us the key to unmaking all that she's done?"

What in the sun was the point?

"A valid question," Valior says. "Although if all the years I've known your aunt are any indication, she had her reasons."

Wokee races past, and I have to put out a hand to steady Valior before the old man topples over.

"Sorry!" Wokee calls over his shoulder as he continues on his way.

Wokee's cheeks are flushed and there's a vitality in his expression that I haven't seen since before the Battle of the Iron Gate. He's shouting orders to the Westerners about not planting seeds too close together, and babbling in no discernible language to Brogut and the two other Halves trailing behind him.

At that moment, Ry, her hand linked in Dellin's, joins us. "Sorry for interrupting," she says, breathless, "but Dellin has a crazy idea." She blows a spiraling red curl off her face. "And I mean *crazy*."

"Thank you." Dellin gives her a wry smile before turning her attention on me.

"As soon as Crowe finds out about what happened here, she's going to empty out Malarusk and send every last one of her soldiers here to end us once and for all."

"We have got to work on your tact," Ry says, slinging an arm around Dellin's shoulders and kissing her cheek.

Dellin's cheeks redden in between the streaks of dirt smeared over her face, but she continues, "So, my idea is to take Crowe out before she can give the order."

"Have you forgotten we already tried that?" I ask, giving Dellin a pointed stare. "It didn't go so well."

Dellin shakes her head. "I'm not saying we should attack Malarusk again."

"Then, what—"

"I think we should organize a small party…just a few of us we can easily disguise with the Dusker cloaks we stole…and assassinate Crowe."

Dellin's gray eyes gleam at the mention of killing Crowe. It makes me like the other girl more.

"Dayne and I are coming with you," I say without a moment's hesitation. My gaze slides to Valior. "I have some questions for Jadem."

CHAPTER 23

I don't ask Dellin why she's suddenly so eager to face down Crowe when, in the past, she's balked at the bare mention of going into the Dusker territory.

Dellin still keeps her face covered in dirt, but that doesn't seem to be so much because she's trying to hide from the Duskers anymore. It seems like she's more worried about trying to blend in with the Banished and Solguards. When it's clean, her skin is pale enough that no one could misinterpret her Dusker lineage. No one needs to tell me about the way others pass judgment on appearance alone.

Once we've decided to limit our group to Ry, Dellin, Dayne, and me, it takes us hardly any time to gather everything we need. Dayne presents the greatest challenge when it comes to a believable disguise because he's now so much larger than any human. A few of the Halves help us rectify the problem by combining two Dusker cloaks so they cover him. When he hunches down and keeps his hood drawn up, the disguise works well enough that we should be able to pass him off as a Dusker...if we arrive during Dark.

While we finish our preparations, I avoid the part of the building where Camike tends the sick and injured. I'm still furious with Wade, and I can't stand the thought of hearing any more of his self-sacrificing excuses. I know Camike will take good care of him, and outside of that, I want nothing more to do with him. The pain of almost losing him—of watching him do something I knew he wouldn't survive and being unable to stop him—is still too raw. Even knowing he's on the mend, I can't get the sight of him, covered in the black sap and lying unmoving on the ground, out of my mind.

"Do you remember who Crowe is?" I ask Dayne as I hand him a full waterskin.

Dayne's jerky nod is his only response.

"We're going to pay her back for everything she's done, and especially for what she tried to do to you," I tell him.

And for what you've become.

There was a time when I pitied Crowe. My Zeroes killed her daughter before I realized there was a child in the group of Duskers. I tried to stop the Zeroes, but it had been too late. I hadn't known who the little girl was at the time, and when I found out, a part of me understood exactly why Crowe wanted to make me suffer.

But after what she tried to do to Dayne and Wokee, any sympathy I might have felt for her fled.

Now that all of my focus isn't preoccupied with other matters, like our food stores running out, my anger and resentment are returning full force. I want to make Crowe pay for everything she's taken…from me and everyone else.

I want to look my aunt in the eye and tell her what she's done. I want her to see Dayne and know that what he's become is because of her betrayal.

It takes only about ten minutes of walking before the effects of the weak beams of sunlight disappear completely. The cloud of ash covering the sun becomes thick and impenetrable again, and the bone-deep cold returns.

"The Duskers originally formed out of the need for someone to step up and bring all the separate groups in the Subterrane territory together," Dellin says as we walk. "The first Supreme set up a system of rules to protect Dwellers and make sure everyone got what they needed. The Duskers were strong, and they were supposed to use that strength to protect and help people who were less powerful." A dark look crosses Dellin's face. "That was their original purpose, anyway. It wasn't until the later Supremes got drunk on their own power that the Duskers' true purpose was defiled."

"Benevolent Duskers," Ry says in a mock-dreamy voice. "What would that be like, I wonder?"

"Crowe's a tyrant, as full of corruption as any Supreme I've ever laid eyes on." Dellin fidgets with the sleeve of her cloak. "Leaders like her made the Duskers into something to fear."

"I don't fear them," Ry says. "I loathe them."

* * *

We reach the edge of the Dusker territory two days later. Darkness Peak rises before us. It looks like a black, towering mass against a slightly less dark background.

It's easy to find the beginning of the path that will lead us up the mountain. Large torches are anchored in the ground beside the biggest Dark God shrine I've ever seen.

"Look at this rot," Ry mutters.

Messages have been scratched into the sheer rock face of the mountain. *Go in darkness* is the most prominent message. But there are others, as well. Prayers to the Dark God, pleas for food and shelter and the health of relatives…. The whole wall is covered with the evidence of desperate people's pilgrimages to this place.

I avert my gaze from the sight of what are obviously human skeletons that have been kicked to the side of the path.

The husks of flowers long-since dried out, and the brittle remains of food offerings, litter the mountain's base. Bits of scrap metal and other gifts surround messages weighted down with stones. There are charcoal and slate idols of the Dark God, some of them looking downright disturbing in the light of our lanterns.

"What are you doing?" I ask Ry, incredulous.

"Wha'?" She takes another bite from what looks to be a strip of dried capy pig. "It's fresh enough, and the Dark God doesn't seem to be eating it."

"You're unbelievable." Dellin shakes her head.

We watch in amused silence as Ry stuffs her pockets with more of the offerings.

"Why aren't there any guards here?" I ask, feeling unease prickle at my skin.

"Because no one except for us is dumb enough to dare coming here uninvited," Ry replies.

We all draw our Dusker cloaks more tightly around us. I motion for Dayne to hunch down so his height isn't so obvious, and then we start up the path.

Aside from the movement of gravel beneath our feet, and an occasional whispered curse when one of us stubs our toe on a protruding rock, we don't speak. Dayne is a constant presence beside me, but his proximity isn't calming. I can feel his anger radiating within me, and it fans the flame of my own impatience.

The higher we climb, the thicker the ash cloud becomes. I keep my breathing as shallow as I can manage, but even so, I can almost feel the darkness particles scraping against my eyes and throat, like invisible shards of steel. With the extent of the pollution, I doubt they even have Gloom up here. I wouldn't be surprised if the mountain existed in a constant state of Dark.

We're about two-thirds of the way up the mountain when we begin passing small fires alongside the path. Banished slaves in threadbare cloaks silently tend the flames, adding logs when they're needed and stoking the fire to keep it alive.

The fact that the Duskers have enough fuel to keep these fires burning all the time is just one more indication of their prosperity compared to the rest of us. I think of the way Wokee and Everlyn shiver in the crook of Vlaz's paw each Dark, and my anger stirs again.

I'm concentrating on the barely-visible path in front of me and keeping my head down so no Duskers we pass will look at me and glimpse my black eyes. So, I don't notice the Dusker on the path is speaking to me until he grabs the sleeve of my cloak, forcing me to a stop.

I tamp down my instinct to throw off his grip.

"You just passed a captain." He indicates his black armband, which is pretty much invisible in the darkness surrounding us. "Where's your sense of respect?"

I go still. From my time in Subterrane Harkibel, I know it's a lash-worthy crime to pass a captain without bowing your head and murmuring *Go in darkness* in an appropriately meek voice.

While I'm trying to think of some excuse, the Dusker grabs my chin and jerks my face up. I try to keep my gaze downturned, but I see the moment the Dusker recognizes my black eyes.

"Dark God protect me!" the Dusker exclaims.

I hear the sound of his dagger coming free from its sheath. I hesitate, trying to decide what to do. If I kill him, his corpse will alarm the next person down the path that there's an intruder. On the other hand, if I let him live, he's going to report me to Crowe anyway.

The man gives a startled little cry and then falls forward, his weight almost pushing both of us off the narrow path. I wrestle his dead weight off me, only to see Dellin standing behind him. There's a bloody dagger in her hand and a determined look on her dirty face.

"What'd you do that for?" Ry demands, coming up behind Dellin. "Now they're going to know we're here."

"I could throw the body over the cliff," I suggest. "But that won't help us as soon as they realize one of their captains has gone missing."

"No." Dellin wipes her blade on the dead Dusker's cloak. "We're not going to hide the body. I want them to find it."

Ry and I exchange an incredulous look.

"I thought our plan was stealth." Ry raises an eyebrow.

"That was only to get us within Crowe's reach," Dellin replies.

Ry stares at Dellin, her mouth slightly ajar. "Are you feeling alright?" She puts the back of her hand to Dellin's forehead.

"I'm fine." Dellin swats away Ry's hand.

I would have expected Dellin's voice to waver, but there's no hint of fear or indecision.

Of all of us, Dellin is the last one I'd expect to be calm and taking charge this close to her father's killer. And yet, the timid, cowardly Banished girl I first met is nowhere in sight.

Dellin takes a few purposeful steps over to a stone basin on the side of the path.

"Make sure that water isn't contaminated," I warn as Dellin bends down to the basin.

I assume she's going to take a drink, but instead, she dips the sleeve of her cloak into the water. Ry and I watch in silent fascination as Dellin methodically wipes the dirt from her face. When she's finished, her skin gleams Dusker pale.

"What are you doing?" Ry asks.

Dellin smiles at her. "I think it's time I remember."

CHAPTER 24

What do you mean it's time you remember? Time you remember what?" Ry prompts.

Dellin bites her lip in thought. Her pale face, no longer covered in dirt, is luminescent in the dark. It makes her look not-quite human.

"Those were the last words my father said to me before Crowe murdered him," Dellin says in a quiet voice, more like she's talking to herself than us. "My mother is the one who wanted me to forget. She wanted me to stay safe. For a long time, that's all I wanted, too."

"Would you care to explain what's gotten into you?" Ry fists her hands on her hips.

"Ry, there are still some things about me that you don't know," Dellin begins, her confidence faltering, "but—"

"Oh goodie, you're 'ere."

We all turn at the sound of the unfamiliar male voice. A skeleton-thin man with leathery skin and a bent spine grins at us. His missing teeth are like black holes in his mouth.

My adrenaline spikes, but there's something familiar about this man that makes me hold out a hand to Dellin before she kills him, too.

"I know you," I say, trying to remember where I've seen him before.

"Malarusk dungeon," Dayne says in his emotionless voice.

"Shh, not so loud," Morey hisses, looking around to make sure we haven't been overheard.

Of course.

It all comes back to me in a rush. When Jadem delivered Dayne and me to the dungeon—as an excuse so she could supposedly get into the citadel to kidnap Hendrix—Dayne and I were surrounded by a group of the dungeon's prisoners who had thus far survived the daily wormkill feedings. The leader of that motley group of prisoners tried to kill us before Dayne and I made it abundantly clear we wouldn't be easy prey.

Later, when Jadem came down into the dungeon with Fake Hendrix and a horde of Duskers chasing her, it was this man who told us to go while he and the other prisoners held the Duskers off.

I assumed he was killed with the rest of the prisoners when they tried to slow down the Duskers and give us time to escape.

"Morey, right?" I ask, feeling a strange surge of joy at seeing the man.

Maybe it's because I assumed he was killed for helping Jadem, Dayne, and me. Maybe it's because, when I met Morey, my brother was still my brother, and I hadn't known my aunt would betray us.

The man's grin widens. "You 'membered. Flattered, I'm sure."

"What are you doing here?" I ask.

His gaze darts around again to make sure no one else is nearby.

"I'm just a regular ole Banished slave, here to serve at the pleasure of my Supreme." He gives me a twisted, missing-toothed smile.

Morey isn't a Banished slave. He was a prisoner in Malarusk. Still, he saved my life once, and I'm not about to repay him by drawing attention to what he's really doing here…whatever he's really doing here.

"Kill the creep and let's go," Ry murmurs in my ear.

"No, I have a better idea." Dellin turns an imperious gaze on Morey. "Take us to your master."

Morey chuckles and gives her a sardonic bow of his head.

✳ ✳ ✳

Morey refuses to answer any of my questions, and so we trudge up the rest of the way to the summit in silence.

Morey saved my life in the Malarusk dungeon, but that was a long time ago…before Darkness. Everything and everyone has changed since, and I don't know if I can trust him. I keep one hand on my dagger as my eyes scan the path ahead. Ry keeps an arrow nocked in her bow. Dellin is alert, but she doesn't seem worried.

Even though it gets darker the higher we climb, at least it's warm here. There's a new, well-tended fire every ten steps. Slaves are constantly passing us on the path as they bring fresh kindling or come to stoke the flames.

"You do know all of this is going to end eventually, right?" I ask Morey.

"How d'ya mean?" he replies without looking back at me.

I wave a hand at the slaves carrying bundles of sticks on their backs. "Without sunlight, nothing new is going to grow."

"And you can't eat the Darkness," Ry adds, patting her pockets, which are bulging with the sacrifices she stole from the base of the mountain.

"What are you all going to do when your supplies run out?" I clarify.

Morey points above us to a Dark God statue carved into the face of the rock.

"The Dark God will provide for us," he replies, smirking.

I shake my head. Crowe has to know she's condemning everyone to death…eventually. Unless Jadem gave her some of the golden seeds so they could grow more food, I can't imagine what Crowe's long-term plan is.

In a rare moment when we're the only ones on the path, Morey grabs my cloak and pulls me closer to him.

"She wouldn't want you to be 'ere," he whispers in my ear.

"Crowe?"

Morey rolls his eyes. "*Jadem.*"

"Yeah, well, I'm not too concerned with what Jadem wants," I retort.

Morey opens his mouth, but another group of Duskers appears on the path., He hunches down in his cloak and scuttles ahead of us again.

Morey hurries up the last, steep incline.

"Oh good, you brought them," calls a familiar voice that raises the hair on the back of my neck. "You can go now, slave."

Crowe.

"Yes, Supreme." Morey bows and scampers back down the path before I can make up my mind about whether or not I should stab him.

I notice Morey sneaking away, but I stop paying attention to him as soon as I catch sight of the tall seat carved into the mountainside.

Ry snorts in derision, but all I feel is bone-chilling fear.

Crowe knew we were coming. She wants us here now. And that can't be good.

Crowe is sitting in the stone seat. She wears a long gray cloak that trails down to the base of her chair. There's a gray crown on her head, and the two torches burning on either side of her chair make her look almost inhuman with her ghostly pale skin.

Three Duskers, with crossbows in their hands and swords at their hips, stand guard on both sides of her. There are more Duskers standing in the shadows of the Dark God statues ringing the summit.

All my other thoughts evaporate when I see the figure chained to the foot of Crowe's stone seat. In spite of myself, I can't contain the gasp that comes from my lips. Crouched in a defeated heap on the ground, her wrists bound in chains and a gag in her mouth, is Aunt Jadem.

CHAPTER 25

I don't speak. Crowe's eyes glitter with anticipation as she watches what must be evident horror playing out on my face.

"You keep coming back for more, don't you?" Crowe asks. Her gaze moves back and forth between Dellin and me; she ignores Ry and Dayne.

"Your efforts to kill us at Tanguro backfired," Dellin says in a calm voice.

"So I heard." Crowe gives us a little shrug. "But I have no shortage of soldiers at my disposal."

As much as I've tried not to look at her, I can't help but notice how terrible Jadem looks. She's like a shell of the person I remember—all skin and bones. And there's a deadened look in her one good eye. It makes sympathy fill me even though it's the last emotion I want to feel toward my aunt.

She's the one who betrayed us, I remind myself.

"Why is your second-in-command in chains?" Dellin asks.

Crowe gives Jadem a disinterested look.

"I knew, at some point, Hemera would be back to claim her. And now, she has." Crowe smirks. "Besides, I didn't want Jadem getting any ideas about trying to leave without my permission."

I try to catch my aunt's eye, but she's just staring at the ground. Her shoulders are hunched in dejection. I think I see dried blood around her wrists and through the gaps in her torn cloak.

I can't help but ache at the sight of her. Traitor or not, Jadem is still my aunt.

I start when I realize Morey is sneaking behind the fires and Dusker guards ringing the summit. And he's heading for Jadem.

What in the sun is he up to?

"We're not here for Jadem," I say, angling my body so Crowe's attention won't be drawn to Morey. I have no idea what he's up to, but whatever it is, I owe him my help in any way I can give it. "We're here for you."

Crowe's Dusker-gray eyes, the ones she shared with her daughter, gleam in the light of the bonfire. "Then, come and get me," she hisses.

I draw my sword—the one Tut made for me before the Battle of the Iron Gate, and which I hadn't used because I had been relying on my Zeroes.

Instead of drawing her own weapon, Crowe looks at me and laughs.

"You really are a fool, aren't you?" Her gaze narrows. "Just like your dear old aunt."

I hear the simultaneous clicks of many arrows being fitted into crossbows. I hear Ry's sharp intake of breath.

"Guards!" Crowe calls.

Duskers step out from the shadows and all of the paths leading to the summit. We're surrounded. At least two dozen Duskers have their crossbows aimed at us.

"Stop," Dellin says in a commanding voice. "Hold your fire."

Unlike the last time Dellin gave orders to the Duskers, these soldiers don't lower their weapons.

Crowe laughs, her eyes full of amusement as she stares down her nose at Dellin. "Haven't you heard? I'm the Dark God incarnate. No one can take away my authority now."

I expect Dellin to shrink away in fear. Instead, she seems to grow taller. She stalks up to the nearest Dusker, ignoring Ry's hushed protests and the Duskers' crossbows.

"I am Dellin Methuin, daughter of Xander Methuin." She takes the Dusker's chin in her hand and jerks his head down so that they're eye-to-eye. "Do you know what that means?"

To my utter shock and amazement, the Dusker doesn't throw her off, even though he's far bigger than she is. Instead, his crossbow goes slack in his hands. He swallows, his gaze flicking to Crowe.

"Don't answer her," Crowe snarls, clutching the stone armrests of her chair with bone-white hands.

"Answer me," Dellin orders.

"You're the daughter of the former Dusker Supreme," he says.

A muffled shriek of rage comes from Crowe, but she doesn't get down from her stone chair.

"And what does that make me?" Dellin asks, her voice quiet and commanding.

"You're our rightful Dusker Supreme."

My jaw has gone slack. I knew Dellin was a Dusker, and that her family must have been important for the Duskers in Malarusk to obey her, but I'd assumed her father was a captain. I never guessed she was the daughter of the last Dusker Supreme...the one Crowe murdered in order to steal his position. I look at Ry, who is staring at Dellin with a shocked expression on her face. It's clear Ry is as blindsided by this news as I am.

"*I* am your rightful Supreme!" Crowe shouts at the Duskers.

The soldiers' eyes shift from Crowe to Dellin, and I can read the uncertainty in their gazes.

"Dellin," Ry begins, but she doesn't say anything more.

Dellin gives her an apologetic look before turning her attention back on the Duskers.

"Crowe is a usurper," Dellin says in that strong, almost regal tone I first heard her use when she commanded the Duskers to let me, Dayne, and Wokee go. "She stole the office of Supreme from my father and is holding the position that by all rights belongs to me. It is your obligation as Duskers to give your loyalty and strength to your true leader. Me."

"You look like him," a Dusker wearing an armband that designates him as a captain says. "But Crowe is the one who brought the Darkness."

"Jadem is the one who brought the Darkness," I say, unable to help myself.

Dellin spares me a cool glance before returning her attention to the Duskers.

"Crowe murdered my father and installed herself as the illegitimate leader of the Duskers. She would have killed me, too, but my mother took me away and hid me in the Banished lands. I knew that if I ever came near Malarusk, Crowe would kill me the same way she killed my father. So, I hid my heritage and my name, even from the people I love most." She glances at Ry.

Ry's expression has shifted from astonishment to anger. The light of the fire shows how her face has turned almost as red as her hair.

"She's a liar!" Crowe shrieks, on her feet now. "An imposter. I command you to kill her at once!"

None of the Duskers move.

"Crowe has led all of you astray from what you were meant to be— providers and protectors," Dellin continues. "That mission has been polluted by corrupt, power-hungry leaders like Crowe. As the rightful Dusker Supreme, I will help the Duskers become what they were meant to be."

I wouldn't have believed the dirty-faced girl who balked any time we got near Malarusk could possibly be the rightful Dusker Supreme, but I saw Dellin challenge Crowe once before. I heard her give the Duskers an order that directly contradicted what Crowe was telling them, and I saw them obey Dellin. I remember thinking she looked like a leader then.

I never guessed at her true identity, but now that I know, I can't say I'm surprised. All those times I thought there was something proud and imperious about her, even when she was dressed in rags and her face was covered in dirt, make sense now.

Dellin continues, her gaze and voice unwavering. "I am the rightful Dusker Supreme, and I am here to take up the position that is my birthright."

I see the flicker of movement out of the corner of my vision. Crowe, who was standing by her chair only a few seconds before, has been moving silently around the edge of the summit. Now, she is almost behind Dellin, and her sword is poised for the killing blow.

"Watch out!" I yell.

Dellin turns. Moving faster than I would have thought her capable of, she draws her dagger and blocks Crowe's blade.

I've never seen Dellin fight with anything other than her bow and arrows, but she parries Crowe's strike and even manages to drive the Supreme back a step.

But a dagger is no match for a sword.

I pull out my sling, preparing to use it the first chance I have at a clean shot. Ry's bow and arrow are at the ready as she waits for the same opportunity, but Crowe and Dellin are too close. We both risk hitting Dellin instead of Crowe.

The Duskers surrounding all of us still have their weapons raised, but they're looking around like they don't know where to aim them.

I decide to take advantage of their indecision. I feel for the bond with Dayne, silently communicating with him. At the same instant, we spring.

I rush the Dusker captain. I catch him by surprise before he can fire his crossbow and knock him into the two Duskers on either side of him. I release my sling, and a Dusker across the way goes down. Two more fall to Ry's arrows.

By the time I've knocked a third unconscious with a single punch, I look up to see that Dayne has put down six of the Duskers.

"Dayne!"

I don't wait for him to react. I throw myself at the Dusker who is aiming his crossbow at my brother. We both go down in a tangle of limbs and weapons. I knock the hilt of my dagger over the Dusker's head and scramble to my feet. Ry and Dayne are standing back-to-back, each of them parrying three opponents.

I wind my sling and release, taking down one of the Duskers aiming his weapon at Ry before he can pull the trigger.

Crowe and Dellin are locked in combat on the other side of the summit. Dayne, Ry, and I are making short work of the rest of the Duskers as they continue to hesitate over who to obey—their rightful Supreme, or the one they've been worshipping as the Dark God incarnate.

Jadem, who is bound and gagged, violently twists her head as she tries to loosen her gag. Behind her, almost invisible in the shadow of Crowe's stone chair, Morey is bent over Jadem's shackles. It looks like he's trying to free the chains around her ankles, but I can't be sure.

I don't spare them another glance. Right now, Crowe is my priority.

Leaving Dayne and Ry to deal with what's left of the Duskers, I sneak around behind Crowe, trusting that she's sufficiently preoccupied by Dellin that she won't notice me. I'm not worried about honor or the injustice of killing someone from behind. All I know is that Crowe needs to die, and now, for the first time, I have a chance to see it done.

I raise my dagger and let out a steadying breath as I wait for the pair to move close enough for me to strike.

Dellin's gaze flicks away from Crowe at the sight of me.

"No!" she tells me. "I have to be the one—"

She stumbles back as Crowe's sword crashes down against her smaller weapon. Dellin cries out in pain, and her dagger goes skittering across the ground.

At the same moment, I feel the point of a sword digging into the back of my neck. From the emotions surging through our bond, I know Dayne is being similarly restrained. I look over and see two Duskers with their weapons held against his sinewy neck. Another Dusker is restraining Ry.

There is no hint of uncertainty in these Duskers' eyes. It's obvious they have made their choice about whom they serve, and they have no interest in switching their allegiance.

Ry tries to grab a Dusker's sword. He strikes her on the back of the head, and she crumples to the ground. I call her name and try to go to her, but the Dusker behind me digs his blade in far enough to break the skin. I stop moving.

Crowe advances on Dellin. In the light of the fire, I can see the tear in the arm of Dellin's cloak. The fabric is stained dark from her blood.

Still, Dellin doesn't cower in fear even in the face of her enemy.

"Tell these people the truth," Dellin says. Even though Crowe is the one holding the sword, it seems like Dellin is the more powerful one. "Tell your followers the Darkness won't be their salvation, but rather their doom. Tell them that once all the supplies you hoarded in Malarusk are gone, there won't be anyone to provide for them." She takes a step toward Crowe, heedless of the blade held inches from her. "Tell them that no matter how many darkness trees they burn or how many prayers they say, they'll die just like everyone else."

When Crowe speaks, her voice is quiet enough that only Dellin and I, who are nearest to her, can hear her words.

"Do you think I care about the Duskers' longevity when the only two people who have ever mattered to me are dead?" She keeps a steady hold on her weapon as she glances at me.

"So, you're going to let everyone else die because you want to join Hendrix and Laurel?" Dellin demands.

Crowe gives her a twisted smile, but for just a moment, I can see the pain of her loss reflected on her face. There's something so haunted about her expression that, for a second, I forget she's my enemy. For a second, I forget all the suffering and destruction she's brought on all of us.

Then, the moment passes, and I remember what she's done.

There are more Duskers on the summit, now. They form a ring that encloses us so we couldn't escape even if there weren't swords held at our throats. We're trapped.

Crowe raises her sword for the killing blow.

"No!" Ry yells.

Before Crowe's weapon can descend, a blur of motion draws my attention. Jadem, now free of chains, throws the full weight of her body at the Duskers restraining her.

"Jadem, no!" Morey screams, just before the hilt of a Dusker's sword connects with his head. He collapses.

My aunt lunges. She knocks Dellin to the side, out of the path of Crowe's sword.

Jadem glances to the side, searching for someone in all the madness. Whoever she was looking for, she doesn't have time to find them before Crowe's sword—the strike that was meant for Dellin—drives straight into my aunt's heart.

CHAPTER 26

Screams fill the air, and I'm only dimly aware that some of them are coming from my own lips. I move to the side, too fast for the blade at the back of my neck to do anything more than slice through a few strands of my hair. I elbow my captor in the face and throw my dagger at the Dusker who is standing over Ry's unconscious form.

Dayne has taken care of the two who were holding him. I race forward, all of my attention on Jadem.

I sink to my knees beside my aunt and cradle her head in my lap.

I glance up in time to see Dellin grab the sword that lies abandoned on the ground—the one Crowe used to stab my aunt—and hold it against Crowe's neck.

The Dusker Supreme goes down on her knees before Dellin. A trickle of blood slides down the white skin of Crowe's throat.

"I am the Dusker Supreme," Dellin says in a clear voice. "And I am reclaiming my birthright."

With a single, clean sword stroke, Dellin separates Crowe's head from her body.

There's a dull thud as Crowe's head hits the hard ground, and a whisper of fabric as her long cloak pools around her lifeless body.

For a moment, no one moves.

Dellin drops the sword to the ground. She's breathing hard, but she straightens her spine and meets the shocked gazes of everyone around her.

"I am your Dusker Supreme," she tells them. "You answer to me. Now and until your death."

I'm aware of the Duskers falling to their knees and murmuring the prayers I remember from my time as a Dweller in Subterrane Harkibel. And then I turn all of my attention back on my aunt.

I stare at the wound on Jadem's chest. I don't have to be a healer to know it's mortal. Aunt Jadem coughs, and bloody spittle slips between her lips.

"Mer." Jadem says the word on a gasp that ends in a rattling cough.

That one word is enough to undo me. Even with her voice thick with blood, the harsh edge to her tone is gone. With that single word, the Dusker she's been for all of these months is gone. All that's left is my aunt.

"Aunt Jadem." I wrap my arms around her as my vision blurs. "We're going to get you out of here and get you some help. Camike can—"

"No, dear niece."

The last few times I saw her, Jadem looked and sounded like the rest of the Duskers. Now, she sounds like the aunt I remember. It makes all of this so much harder.

"This is a sacrifice that was worth making." My aunt coughs again. "This is my redemption."

"No." I'm shaking my head back and forth. "I'm going to get you help. We're going to save you."

"You already have." Aunt Jadem's good eye fixes on me. "I always knew you would be the savior of us all, my darling Mer."

A sob is pulled from my throat.

I haven't done anything, I want to tell her. But her head is lolling to the side, and whatever words I might have spoken stick in my throat.

"Aunt Jadem!" I command, willing her eye to turn back to me instead of staring up into the dark nothingness above.

"She's dead," Dayne says without emotion.

I don't know whether it's right for me to grieve for her, but I can't stop the tears from coming. I can't stop myself from clinging to my aunt as I beg her to come back to us…to come back to me.

Even though the evidence of her betrayal is all around us, I can't stop myself from remembering the woman I met when I first set foot in Solis. I remember the woman who fought by my side at Tanguro, and who told me stories about my mother I never would have known otherwise. I remember the woman who helped me to embrace my identity as a Bisecter instead of trying to run away from it.

That's the woman I'm mourning now.

Ry, looking dazed but otherwise unharmed, kneels on the ground beside me. She doesn't say anything. She reaches over and closes my aunt's vacant, unblinking eye. And then she wraps her arms around me.

A cry of pure devastation cuts through the silence and rips the air from my lungs.

"Jadem!" Morey cries.

He falls to his hands and knees beside us. He lowers his forehead to Jadem's unmoving chest as his body convulses with sobs. He's repeating something over and over, but his words are muffled.

At the slight ripple along the bond that connects Dayne and me, I look up at him. He's standing beside me, his posture rigid. A single tear, illuminated in the firelight, leaks out of his black eye. If I wasn't so overcome with heartsick grief, the sight of such a reaction from Dayne would fill me to overflowing with emotions.

Morey lifts his tear-stained face from Jadem's chest. It's then that I hear the words he's been repeating over and over.

"My Jadem. My Jadem. My Jadem."

Confusion replaces some of the raw pain filling me from top to bottom. I had no idea Aunt Jadem and Morey even knew each other, but from the way Morey is reacting now, it's obvious they were more than mere acquaintances.

This revelation, along with the one that Dayne has experienced an emotion besides rage, barely registers in my consciousness. I'm being crushed beneath a weight of grief. It's a familiar one, and yet it's one I'll never get used to. With each tally added to the list of loved ones I've lost, the pain gets harder to bear.

And I love Aunt Jadem.

After her betrayal, I had cursed her name and sworn I would kill her if ever given the chance. Now, as her body is cooling in my arms, I know the truth. Regardless of what she did and why, this woman is my aunt. My family.

I turn into Ry's embrace and do the one thing I swore I'd never do for my aunt's sake. I cry.

I cry until my throat is raw and there are no tears left in my body. Morey, who hasn't moved from his own place beside Jadem, takes one of my aunt's lifeless hands in his. He raises it to his lips as fresh tears stream down his cheeks. His voice is soft and choked with sobs as he kisses her hand, but I still make out the words.

"Until the nex' life, my love."

CHAPTER 27

We're roused from our vigil by the sound of the Duskers shouting, "All hail the rightful Dusker Supreme!"

Someone has disposed of Crowe's head and body, but her blood still stains the ground. Dellin is seated on the stone chair that used to be Crowe's. The still-bloody sword rests across her lap. She looks as much the part of the Dusker Supreme as Crowe ever had, and I wonder what Ry thinks about this new development. There's a smear of blood across Dellin's Dusker-pale cheek, which makes her look somehow even fiercer.

All these observations are just background. Only a single thought exists in the forefront of my mind.

Aunt Jadem and Crowe are dead.

Crowe tried to take everything from me, and now, she's no longer a threat. Still, I don't have the heart to feel the sense of victory I know I should. All I feel is a mountain of regret and the weight of so many questions whose answers died along with my aunt.

"How did you know Jadem?" Ry asks Morey, who has stopped crying and is now staring straight ahead with a vacant expression in his eyes.

"What does it look like I was to her, eh?" Morey asks without turning around.

"It seems like you were…um…involved." Ry tugs on one of her curls with uncharacteristic awkwardness.

"Met her when she came back to Malarusk and made you lot think she was dead."

I stiffen at the memory. It was right after we'd kidnapped Fake Hendrix. I believed Jadem had gotten trapped on the wrong side of the Malarusk gate, and that Crowe had killed her.

I had grieved for her then. Later, I'd felt a very different kind of pain when I realized my aunt was still alive and had betrayed us. Now, I've lost her again.

"Crowe made her sleep in the dungeon during high day," Morey continues. "Tha's where she met ole Morey and we got 'quainted." A sad smile touches his lips as he stares out into the nothingness beyond the mountain. "Fell in love. Ya believe tha'?"

He doesn't look back at either of us, and it doesn't seem like he expects a response.

"After Crowe decided to come 'ere to Darkness Peak, Jadem had to go with her." He raises a trembling hand to wipe away the fresh tears that have started to fall. "Jadem convinced the Supreme that she needed all us prisoners to bring supplies. Jadem knew it was the closest I'd ever come to freedom."

He says these last words quietly, and he looks at Jadem when he says them.

I'm too stunned to come up with a response. *Aunt Jadem…in love? With Morey?*

It seems impossible, and yet, there is no mistaking the expression on Morey's face as he stares down at my aunt.

"I been 'ere on this mountain for three months now, just waitin' on my opportunity to get Jadem away from these wretches. I almost had her." His voice wavers, and then it grows so quiet I know he isn't talking to us anymore. "I almost had her."

He sniffles as his tears begin to flow again.

Ry puts a hand on his arm. "I'm sorry for your loss, Morey," she says in a husky voice.

"I talked to her a few times. Crowe kept her in a cage when she wasn' parading her around on the summit, and I got to see her. I promised her I'd get her out. I promised."

"It's not your fault," I say, my voice thick.

Morey blows out a breath and turns around to face us. His tear-swollen eyes fix on me. "Reckon you oughta know why she done what she done, now that she's gone." His voice cracks. "She'd want ya to know."

"You know why my aunt betrayed the Solguards?" I ask, letting Ry's hand drop from mine so I can turn all of my attention on Morey.

He nods. "She told ole Morey everything."

I wait, my breaths coming in shallow little gasps, as Morey twines his fingers with Jadem's.

"It all started with your mother. When you was born, your mother knew you'd have a tough time of things, on account of you being a—" He waves his hand in my general direction, as though it's a sufficient explanation. "She made Jadem promise that if anything ever happened to her, Jadem would protect ya."

"I didn't even know my aunt existed for most of my life," I say.

"Tha's why she felt like she failed ya," Morey replies. "Back when you was a little kid, Jadem was in the Malarusk dungeon. That was before I got 'rested. And during that time, your mama was getting murdered and you was left to fend for yourself. Jadem felt like she'd betrayed your mama by not being there for ya, seeing as how she'd promised to protect ya."

We both look at my aunt. The blood on her cloak has already darkened and congealed. Ry takes off her own cloak and drapes it over my aunt like a blanket, covering up the wound on her chest.

Even with the bloody gash covered, there's no sense of peaceful restfulness to my aunt…no mistaking her death for sleep. The firelight brings my aunt's gray skin into stark relief. She looks almost like a stranger.

"When the Duskers first found out about ya, Crowe was determined to kill ya along with the rest of the Halves," Morey continues. "Jadem knew Crowe had enough soldiers to do it, so she made a deal with the Supreme. Yer aunt said she'd do whatever Crowe wanted as long as she spared you."

A sick feeling pools in the bottom of my stomach. The last time I saw my aunt, she admitted that she'd betrayed the Solguards…betrayed me…in order to save my life. I hadn't wanted to hear it then, and I don't want to hear it now. I never needed my aunt's protection. I needed my aunt….

"She made the darkness trees because it was the only way to keep Crowe from hurting ya." Morey wipes away more tears. "She didn't know it'd all go so wrong. She thought what she was doin' would stop a war."

"She's the reason why thousands of people are dead," I choke out.

"She knew she'd done wrong." Morey nods. "She tried to make amends for it. That's why every minute she wasn't being watched, she was working on a way to save all of ya."

"I don't understand," I whisper.

"She told the Supreme she needed special soil from the crystal caves to make the darkness trees. That's when she made that golden seed that would save all of you's." Morey gives me a hard look. "Crowe sent Duskers to watch Jadem at the Crystal Caves. I helped distract 'em as much as I could, but Jadem risked her life every time she slipped away to her secret orchard."

There's pride in Morey's voice when he says, "I'm the one who hid that golden seed in the crystal caves for ya." He lets out a whistling breath between his missing teeth. "Jadem knew Crowe would eventually find out, but she did it anyway. She was tryin' to make amends."

"It doesn't make up for all the terrible things she's done," I argue, feeling my fury war with my grief. "What about Dayne and Wokee? My aunt told Crowe about them. It's her fault Dayne is the way he is now. If it hadn't been for Dellin, both Dayne and Wokee would be dead."

A bottomless pit of grief takes hold of me at the memory of what my aunt did…what almost happened because of her. What did happen.

I look at Dayne. He's standing beside me, and his pitiless black eyes are fixed on Jadem. There's no sign of the tear I'd seen before, and I wonder if I imagined it.

Morey says, "Jadem didn't mean for that part to happen. Crowe tricked her into talking about the two of them. Jadem never knew Crowe was gonna use them against ya until she already had." Morey dabs at his eyes with his sleeve. "Your aunt was terrible broken up about that."

"Maybe that's true," I say, "but if she was only helping Crowe to save me, then why didn't she try to kill Crowe? That would have been far more useful to me than what she actually did." Another thought occurs to me, and I interrupt Morey before he can answer my first question. "Crowe almost died at the Battle of the Iron Gate, but my aunt pulled her back from the fire. Why would Jadem do that if she was on my side?"

"Because." Morey stretches out the word, like the answer is obvious and he can't fathom how daft I'm being. "Her agreement for your safety was with Crowe. If the Supreme died, the rest of the Duskers would attack the Solguards. Yerself included. You wouldda been killed. It was only yer aunt's agreement with Crowe that kept ya alive."

"But—"

"Look," Morey says. "Yer aunt was trying to keep her last promise to her sister. They both thought you'd save the Solguards, and Jadem jus' figured no price was too high to pay to keep ya safe.

"But after, when she saw the death the darkness trees brought, she realized she—and the rest of us—had paid too high a price for her promise. More 'portantly, she knew Crowe wouldn't have any reason to keep ya safe no more." He jabs an accusing finger in my direction.

Words stick in my throat. Morey has told me so much, and yet the only thought I can hold onto is that my aunt died thinking I hated her.

Finally, I know the truth. It doesn't do me an ounce of good, though. Aunt Jadem is dead. I'll never be able to tell her that I forgive her. I'll never be able to tell her I love her.

"Come here, Mer." Ry wraps her arms around me, pulling me into a tight hug.

Now that I know the truth, there's so much I want to say to my aunt.

"She died an honorable death," Morey says, his eyes filling with tears again. "She deserves credit for tha', no matter what else she's done."

"So what am I supposed to do? Forgive her?"

I know it's stupid to be angry now. Aunt Jadem sacrificed her own life to save Dellin's. But I can't help it. I'm angry with Aunt Jadem for betraying us and not telling me why. I'm even angrier at her for leaving me again.

Morey looks down at where his hand is still clasped with Jadem's. "I ain't gonna tell ya what to do. But don't try to tell me you've never done somethin' outta love, only to come to find it was the wrong choice." His intelligent gaze swivels on Dayne, like he knows exactly what I did to my brother and the way it's haunted me ever since.

I feel my cheeks flush with shame.

That's different, I want to argue. I don't say anything, though, because I know Morey is right.

Still, how am I supposed to forgive my aunt?

"Jadem's greatest crime migh' have been tha' she cared too much. That woman loved ya to a fault. She wouldda watched the whole world burn for yer sake." Morey shrugs his bony shoulders. "But I think, after she seen what she done with those darkness trees, she realized how much had been sacrificed for her choice."

Those words startle me. In her letter, my mother said something similar…about some sacrifices being too great. It was part of her apology for making me into a Bisecter. My mother had been searching for a way to make the Solguards stronger, and she'd believed she found her answer in experimenting on her own unborn child. Only afterward, when she saw the way the Dwellers treated me, did she realize I was the one paying for a choice she had made.

"She done a good deed here," Morey tells me. "She deserves yer forgiveness."

I look at Dayne. His eyes lock on mine, but I don't sense any emotion from him or any indication of what I should do now.

"He's right," Ry whispers beside me. "Jadem died to save Dellin so we could fight another day. Whatever else she's done, that has to count for something. Besides, if it hadn't been for her tree, we'd all have burned to death inside the fortress."

I know Ry is right, even if I don't yet feel the emotions I know I should. I give her a nod as I let out a shaky breath.

"Thank you," I tell Morey. "Knowing the truth…helps."

Morey gives me a nod as his lip trembles.

"What are you going to do now?" Ry asks him.

"Comin' with you, ain't I?" The ghost of a smile crosses his lips. "Seems the least you can do for ole Morey. Besides, the Duskers never seemed to quite take to me."

CHAPTER 28

I want to bring Jadem back and bury her at Tanguro," I tell Ry, who nods at me in understanding.

We all look up at the sound of Dellin's voice. She's addressing the crowd of Duskers and slaves who have gathered around her.

"The Darkness is an artificial one wrought by a greedy woman bent on wielding more authority than is due to the Dusker Supreme." Dellin's voice is clear, strong, and unapologetic. "I am your Dusker Supreme now, and I pledge to you that life will be different under my rule."

She takes a breath. Her gaze flicks to Ry before returning to the Duskers. "And that begins with an end to the Darkness. From this moment forward, it is my decree that no more darkness trees will be burned. Instead, the wood will be used to help grow more of the trees that will reverse Darkness."

The Duskers mutter to themselves. It's obvious that no matter how much they want to accept Dellin as their new Supreme, her words go against everything they've ever believed.

I wonder if Dellin is pushing for too much change too quickly, and whether she'll be able to maintain her hold over the Duskers after the initial shock of Crowe's death wears off.

After Dellin dismisses the crowd of Duskers, she gets off the stone seat and approaches us. Her uncertain gaze is fixed on Ry. All of her confidence seems to have slipped away, and at the way Ry is glaring at her, I can't say I blame her. Morey busies himself with laying his own cloak over Jadem, muttering about how he wouldn't want her to get cold on the trip back to the Wild Lands. The sight of it makes my raw heart ache all the more.

"Dusker Supreme?" Ry asks, her voice and eyes hard as stone as she regards Dellin.

"Ry, I'm so sorry," Dellin says. Her voice trembles a little, sounding nothing like the self-assured leader she projected to the Duskers. "I should have told you."

"You think?" Ry laughs, but there's no humor in it. "It's not bad enough that you're the Dusker Supreme, but I had to find out along with everyone else? Is that what I deserve after everything? I thought I mattered more to you than that." Her voice breaks, and I can see the gleam of her tears in her eyes.

"You do matter more," Dellin says. She tries to take Ry's hand, but Ry twists away from her.

I know this conversation is meant to be private. I try to make some excuse and slip away, but Ry grabs my arm and hangs on, refusing to let me leave.

"I just didn't know how to tell you," Dellin says, her voice pleading. "You have to understand that I've been hiding who I am for my entire life. My father was as bad as Crowe, and I didn't want anything to do with him, even after he was dead."

"Don't think I'm going to fall for your pity routine," Ry snaps.

Dellin reaches out a hand to Ry. In this moment, she's no longer the Dusker Supreme. She's just a girl with her heart on her sleeve.

Ry keeps her stubborn gaze fixed on the ground.

Dellin's voice is barely above a whisper when she says, "It was more than I ever could have hoped for when you accepted I was a Dusker by birth. I was afraid you would see me differently if you knew the truth." She takes Ry's hand—the one that isn't still holding my wrist in a death grip. "I was afraid that if you knew the truth, you wouldn't love me." Dellin brushes a tear off her cheek.

I try to leave again, but Ry won't let me go. I turn my back on the two of them, attempting to give them as much privacy as I can.

"I do love you," Ry says, her voice choked with tears. "Damnit, Dellin. I would have loved you no matter who you were. But you lied to me."

My heart aches at the pain I can feel radiating off both of them. Even with the strange chemistry I'd had with Ry months ago, it hadn't taken long before we realized that aside from a passing attraction, there was nothing romantic between us. But I had seen those deeper feelings between her and Dellin. The same way I'd felt them between Wade and me.

The thought of him sends a sharp jab of pain through my chest.

Ry clings to my arm with both hands like she's drowning, and I'm all that's keeping her afloat. I keep my eyes turned down to the ground as I try to be invisible.

There was a time when I was convinced Dellin was our enemy and couldn't be trusted. Now, even knowing who she really is, I trust her. She's had my back countless times over the last six months, and I've had hers. She saved the two people who matter most to me in this world, and she did that for me when we hadn't even been friends. I know there's nothing Dellin wouldn't do for Ry's sake, and knowing that makes me ache for both of them.

Whatever reservations I might have had in the past, I've come to respect Dellin. Amazingly, those feelings haven't changed now that I know she's the Dusker Supreme.

"I didn't think the truth would ever come out," Dellin pleads with Ry. "My mother was terrified of anyone ever discovering me. It was my father who wanted me to remember who I was. After my mom died, I became even more paranoid about staying hidden. I never intended to claim my birthright."

"So why did you?" Ry asks. "What changed your mind?"

I look up in time to see Dellin's face soften. "You did, Ry."

Ry makes a small, incredulous sound.

"Do you remember when you told me I had to choose a side?" Dellin asks Ry.

I'd been there when they had that fight. It was right after Wade had asked for Dellin's help in getting into Malarusk, and Dellin had refused out of fear of the Duskers discovering her. Ry had called her a coward.

Knowing what I know now, I think Dellin might be one of the bravest people I've ever met. She went into Malarusk again and again to help the

Solguards, all the while knowing that if Crowe caught sight of her, she would be tortured and killed. Still, she'd fought alongside us for Ry's sake.

"I saw how fearless you were, and how you were always there when your people needed you," Dellin continues. "You made me realize I could be strong enough to be the person I'm meant to be."

Dellin goes quiet, and I find myself holding my breath in anticipation of what Ry will say.

"Dellin." Ry lets go of my arm and gets to her feet.

They each take two steps toward each other, and then Ry envelopes Dellin in her arms. Dellin holds Ry back. For several long moments, they cling to each other.

"I love you so much," Dellin says, her voice muffled because her face is pressed against Ry's neck. "I'm sorry I lied."

"I understand why you did." Ry pulls back and brushes her fingertips along Dellin's cheek. "And I'm proud of you."

Dellin chokes out a laugh. "Really?"

Ry nods. "If there's anyone who can exorcise the evil from the Duskers, it's you."

Dellin's happiness retracts back into her, and she seems to wilt. "I'm not sure I can do it," she admits in a quiet voice. "There have been too many Supremes with a more selfish agenda—my father included. The Duskers might…they might not accept me."

I can read the subtext of that statement as easily as if she had said *The Duskers might decide to kill me.*

A jolt of fear goes through me, even though Dellin's words shouldn't come as a surprise. After all, I've seen the Duskers' cruelty firsthand. It would be insane of me to expect that all the Duskers would have a complete shift in personality just because a new Supreme is in charge.

"You can't stay here with them," I say, unable to keep silent any longer. "Come back to the fortress. We can send you back with Solguards to protect you while you establish yourself with the Duskers."

Dellin shakes her head. "Either they will submit to my rule or they won't, but bringing in soldiers they view as enemies will only get all of us killed faster."

Dellin lifts her chin, even as she's acknowledging that she likely won't survive long enough to enact the changes she talked about.

"There has to be something we can do," I say, more desperate now. I can't just leave one of my friends to be devoured by a pack of ravenous wolves.

Ry laces her fingers through Dellin's. The look on my friend's face is so pained that it stabs a hole through my already-bruised heart.

"I don't want to leave you," Ry says, choking on tears she won't allow to fall. "But I'm the Solguard leader until Wade is strong enough to command them again."

"I understand." Dellin raises Ry's hand—the one with the Solguard sun tattoo—and kisses it. "You're needed in Tanguro."

"And you're needed here." Ry's voice sounds broken.

Dellin gives Ry a shaky nod. "I'll count the days until we can be together."

As Ry and Dellin kiss and whisper soft words to each other, I hope with every inch of my breaking heart that they'll see each other again.

CHAPTER 29

Ry is dry-eyed when we leave Dellin on the summit, but when she brushes against me on the path, I can feel how her entire body is trembling. I'm sure her shaking has nothing to do with the cold, but I still take off my own cloak and slide it around Ry's shoulders. Ry doesn't even seem to notice.

Dellin got a few of the Duskers to make a stretcher to transport Aunt Jadem's body down the mountain more easily, which Morey and Dayne are carrying between them.

Even though we're no longer disguised as Duskers, and we're carrying the corpse of the previous Supreme's prisoner, no one tries to stop us as we snake our way down the mountain. We get more than a few threatening looks, but not even a single Dusker raises a weapon against us.

Maybe Dellin will be able to change them, after all.

I try not to get my hopes up. There's a vast difference between letting us go free, and changing generations' worth of malice and tyranny.

Aside from Morey's sniffling and the crunching of our boots on the gravel path, we're all quiet, lost in our own thoughts. My mind is filled with everything Morey told me. While it isn't enough for me to forgive my aunt for what she did—for all the pain and death she's caused—I can't deny she did what she could to make things right. She gave us the tree that will enable us to provide for ourselves again, and she is the reason why Crowe is dead and Dellin is the new Dusker Supreme. If it weren't for my aunt, the rest of us would be dead twice over.

There's another part of my mind that can't stop thinking about how Jadem betrayed the Solguards and made the darkness trees for the sake of protecting me. I realize it isn't so different from my choice to turn Dayne into a Zero, or even my decision to make the original one-hundred Zeroes.

If I hadn't made the one hundred, we would have lost our entire army at the Battle of the Iron Gate. If I hadn't turned Dayne into a Zero, I would have lost him altogether. But I know better than anyone that those choices came with costs.

"You okay?" I ask Ry, wincing at the stupid question.

None of us are okay.

Ry lets out a shuddering sigh. "I'm afraid I'll never see her again. I keep wondering what in the sun I'm doing, leaving her here. The Duskers are going to chew her up and spit her out."

Ry turns away from me, so I can't read the expression on her face.

"Dellin never told you that she saved Dayne and Wokee's lives in Malarusk, did she?" I ask.

Ry shakes her head.

Now that Dellin's secret is out in the open, I doubt she'll mind if Ry knows what happened. So, I swallow my own unwillingness to relive this memory and tell Ry what happened in the depths of Malarusk.

As I talk, I keep seeing Dayne and Wokee at opposite ends of that cave, and Crowe telling me to choose between them. I keep reliving those moments after the Dusker ran my brother through with his sword. I hear Wokee's screams. I hear Crowe give the order to kill Wokee, too.

I force out the words now, because I want to give Dellin the credit she deserves, and I want Ry to know that Dellin is made of stronger stuff than she seems.

By the time I've finished, silent tears are sliding down Ry's cheeks.

"Thank you for telling me," Ry says, taking my hand in hers and squeezing.

"You really love her, don't you?" I ask.

I'm surprised by the shock of emotions that go through me at saying those words. Not because I feel that way about Ry—whatever brief attraction we shared never went deeper than that. I don't feel an ounce of jealousy or resentment toward Dellin for capturing Ry's heart. But those words conjure another face…one I don't want to think about.

"Yeah, I love her." Ry wipes her eyes with her sleeve. "I never thought I'd feel that way about anyone, but I feel it for her."

I return Ry's wobbly smile. "Everything will be okay," I tell her with a confidence I don't feel.

"I'm not so sure about that. But even if it is," she gives me a little laugh, "I still don't know if we would work."

"What do you mean? You're perfect for each other."

Ry keeps her gaze fixed on the ground, hiding her expression in shadow.

"I think I'm…jealous."

"Jealous?" I ask, startled.

Ry nods, still refusing to meet my gaze.

"I've always been the one to take orders. I'm Wade's second, and I'm okay with that, but there's always been a part of me that wanted to be the one in charge. After Wade was…injured…and I became the Solguard leader, it felt *good*." She gives me a guilty look. "I know Wade will take back over as soon as he's better, but I don't want to give it up. And now, my girlfriend is the most powerful woman alive. I don't want to feel resentful, but I do."

I'm too surprised by this revelation to immediately respond. I had always thought Ry was content with being the best archer of all the Solguards. I never knew about her desire to be the one giving the orders.

"I'm sick of talking about me," Ry announces while I'm still wrestling over an appropriate response. She turns a mischievous look on me.

"What about you?" She raises her eyebrows in challenge.

"What about me?"

Now it's my turn to look away and fidget in discomfort.

"This stupid dance you and Wade are doing. You're in love, and yet you both insist on letting your dumb fights get in the way. You pretend like you don't belong together when everyone else in the fortress—and I mean *everyone*—knows you do."

I reach for the Solguard pendant hanging around my neck. It feels like a lifetime ago that Wade gave it to me.

I should have given it back when I told him we were finished.

"It's—"

"Complicated?" Ry asks, her mouth quirking.

"I watched him almost get himself killed." My voice cracks. "And he's never going to stop. He thinks he somehow deserves to die more than the rest of us. He's trying to meet an impossible standard, and I can't stand by and watch him throw his life away."

"Mhm." Ry gives me a too-keen look.

"Whatever is or isn't between Wade and me is irrelevant right now," I say, falling back on practical arguments and pushing aside my growing discomfort. "He has the Solguards to think about, and I need to kill my father before he can create more Zeroes. After all of that is done…if there ever is an end to all of it…we can see if there's anything left for us."

"Don't you think you can find a way to do all of that *and* be together?" she asks.

I laugh before realizing Ry is serious.

My humor fades as I think about the ever-widening divide between Wade and me.

"I don't know if I can fix what's broken between us," I whisper.

"Do you want to?"

The answer is obvious, and I don't need to say it.

"Well, then." Ry shrugs. "I think you owe it to both of you to try."

CHAPTER 30

We get back to Tanguro at the time of day when it should be Dark, and yet, the sky is still as light as if it was Gloom. The beams of sunlight are mostly hidden behind the ash cloud, but the visibility is the best it's been in months. And that isn't the only change.

When we'd left, the three blue flowers were the only signs of plant life in an otherwise barren courtyard. That's no longer the case.

I can't stop the feeling of awe and hope that spreads through me at the sight of dozens of tiny golden saplings that have been planted all over the courtyard. Even though it's only been four days, their thin branches are already sprouting and reaching toward the darkness logs that have been stacked around them.

The darkness logs don't give off the rancid, burning scent I'm used to, and their poisonous sap isn't oozing onto the ground. In fact, they're looking shriveled and harmless. As I watch, I could swear I see the little gold saplings grow taller as the darkness logs dry out.

Solguards, Halves, and Banished are working on the saplings under Wokee's watchful gaze. I almost laugh at the sight of all these adults and Halves following Wokee's bossy instructions, but then I remember that these little trees are our salvation. Jadem might have created the seed from which they've all sprung, but without Wokee, that golden seed would still be in its box, forgotten in some corner while we continued fighting an impossible battle to get through each day.

The Westerners are hard at work clearing away the dead foliage and planting the seeds they've kept since the beginning of Darkness. At the time, it had seemed foolish to hope that we'd be able to plant them one day. Now, I'm grateful for the Westerners' optimism.

Some of the older fruit trees, which we long ago gave up any hope of reviving, are coming back to life. Their branches are covered with tiny leaves and buds that will eventually become fruit. My mouth waters in anticipation of a taste that is almost gone from my memory.

All around us, I see the promise of life. After months of death and suffering, and the sadness weighing me down from Aunt Jadem's death, it's enough to warm me to my core.

For the first time in as long as I can remember, we won't be consumed with the question of whether we'll survive until the week's end.

Even with all of the activity in the courtyard, my eyes are drawn to a solitary figure standing against the wall of the building. Wade is leaning on a crutch and observing all of the activity in the courtyard. My knees go weak with relief at the sight of him on his feet, since he'd barely been conscious when we left. As relieved as I am, though, I don't try to catch his eye or go to him.

"You're back!" Wokee calls, waving to us. "Did you kill Crowe?"

Ry and I move to stand in front of the stretcher Dayne and Morey have lowered to the ground.

"Dellin killed Crowe," I say, before we're joined by Wade and the other Banished leaders.

It takes enormous effort not to look at Wade. Even though I keep my gaze fixed on Ekil, Valior, and Tut, I can feel the heat from Wade's golden eyes boring into me.

"Did you just say Crowe is dead?" Tut asks, his jaw going slack.

Ry and I nod.

Tut raises his hands up in victory.

"Crowe is dead!" Valior shouts, waving his cane around.

Everyone in the courtyard stops what they're doing. They look at us, then at each other.

Cheers erupt.

I watch as people cry and hug each other. Some of the Easterners have produced dusty bottles of liquid sun they must have stashed somewhere.

The bottles clink together in toasts as they're passed around for everyone to take a sip of the fiery liquid.

After I translate the news for the Halves, they nod their heads and grunt their own approval.

"This means we can start planting the golden seeds in all the other territories and not just Tanguro," Wokee says, jumping up and down in excitement.

"Halves will plant golden trees in all the territories and no Duskers can stop us?" Ekil asks.

I'm not sure if Ekil understood Wokee's words, or if he was just sharing Wokee's thoughts.

"It means we don't have to worry about another attack from the Duskers," Tut adds. "My people can put their efforts into fixing up the inside of the building instead of using all our time to fortify the outside."

"It means we're no longer the Banished," Valior says. "We belong only to ourselves, and we no longer need to fear retribution from the Duskers. I never thought we would live to see a day when the Duskers didn't threaten our way of life."

Tut claps Valior on the back, and then reaches out to steady him as the older man wavers on his feet.

"I only wish Liglette was here to witness our triumph," Valior says.

Tut's expression sobers. "She would have been damn proud of us."

Tut and Valior exchange a knowing look, and then they both smile in a shared recollection of the kind, gentle leader of the Westerners.

Echoes of *Crowe is dead* and *the Dusker Supreme has fallen* fill the air. It's almost enough to make me want to join the celebration. It's almost enough for me to forget about the terrible burden we carried back from Darkness Peak. *Almost.*

"What's that, Mer?" Wokee asks, peeking around me to get a glimpse of the stretcher Ry and I have been blocking from view.

I try to stop him, but my movements are sluggish with exhaustion and grief, and Wokee pulls down the cloak draped over Aunt Jadem before I've managed a word.

For a long moment, everyone just stares down at my aunt. Before we left Darkness Peak, Dellin commanded the Dusker healers to use an embalming cream that would preserve Jadem's body for the amount of time it would take to travel back to the fortress. Her skin has retained its grayish color, but with the wound on her chest covered, and with the weak sunlight brightening everything, it's possible to believe she's only sleeping. Especially compared to so many others I've seen these past months—people whose skin was burned off from the gloomy rain, or whose bodies disintegrated from contact with darkness tree sap—her death seems almost peaceful. The lines on her brow and around her mouth are smooth, and the frown she wore every time I glimpsed her as a Dusker has disappeared.

Together, Ry, Morey, and I manage to tell everyone what happened.

Wade kneels beside the stretcher and puts his right hand, the one with his Solguard tattoo, over his heart. The rest of the Solguards surround him. They all bow their heads as they fist their tattooed hands over their chests.

My heart swells to the point of bursting at the sight of all these people paying their respects to my aunt.

"She died well," Morey says into the silence. "She wouldn't want you all to grieve her."

"You're right," Valior says. He clears his throat. "Jadem might have done wrong by her own people, but as far as I'm concerned, she's redeemed herself. She has my forgiveness."

"And mine," Wade says in a low voice.

"Mine too," Wokee says.

The others around us murmur their agreement.

"We'll remember her as a fearless Solguard and aunt to Hemera and Dayne," Valior declares.

"And how she was a good bot-i-nist," Wokee adds. "We can't forget that."

Valior chuckles. "No, we can't forget that."

✳ ✳ ✳

I help dig the grave into which we lower Aunt Jadem's body. All of us—Banished, Solguards, and Halves—stand around the grave as people who knew my aunt take turns telling stories about her. Some of the stories are familiar to me because I was a part of them, and others are new.

We laugh and cry as we remember all of the good my aunt did in her life. At the end of it all, Wokee places a golden bough, taken from what he had earlier announced would forever be known as *Jadem trees*, on top of her grave.

After the funeral, I feel strangely lighter. It's like a burden has been lifted from my shoulders. My exhaustion is catching up with me, though. I decide to take advantage of the fact that no one seems to need me right at this moment and sneak away to get some sleep.

I'm heading toward the building when two scouts come racing into the courtyard. Both of their faces are pale with fear. I feel all of my muscles tense in anticipation of whatever bad news they're about to share.

"Wade, Hemera," one of them gasps. "He's coming."

CHAPTER 31

Who's coming?" Wade asks.

I already know the answer to that question. There's only one *he* that could put that look on a Solguard's face.

"Captain Harkibel," the scout says, giving me an uncertain look. "Hemera's father. He has three-hundred Zeroes with him."

Everyone holds back their questions until the scouts have finished delivering their report. When they're finished, the courtyard becomes a flurry of panic. As the anxiety around me grows until it's reached a fever pitch, I feel my own emotions spike for a very different reason.

Anger and anticipation roll through me, and I can tell from the strength of the emotions across our bond that Dayne and I are feeding off each other. The confrontation we've both been waiting for is no longer some hope for an ambiguous time in the future.

My father and his army are coming to Tanguro.

"You said *three*-hundred Zeroes?" Wade asks. "Where did he get so many of them?"

"Rumor has it he turned what was left of the Subterrane Dwellers into them," one of the scouts replies.

"And he had my blood," I say, feeling Dayne's and my anger combine to a force that is almost combustible.

The scouts also report that my father has added a herd of reptors to his army.

Zeidan started breeding the reptors back when he was in control of Tanguro and was conducting his first experiments on the Halves and humans. The Halves, in particular, remember the vicious reptilian creatures.

Brogut and a handful of the others pace around the courtyard with their weapons clenched in their fists.

I have no idea what my father could be using to feed the reptors now that meat is so scarce, but I decide it's better not to dwell on that particular mystery.

I also know better than to think the reptors are the greatest threat. They are fierce predators, but they're nothing compared to my father and the Zeroes.

The others are in the midst of a heated debate about whether to defend Tanguro or abandon it. The fear in the crowd grows by the second as they consider what it would mean to be attacked by an army of reptors and Zeroes. But I'm barely listening. I'm almost jubilant with the knowledge that, instead of having to chase him down, Zeidan is coming to me.

My father has eluded me for too long. His Zeroes have caused more pain and death than I can bring myself to consider, and it's all been possible because of the blood Zeidan stole from me. Now, I'll be able to face him and make him answer for all he's done.

Finally, one way or another, this is going to end.

Once my father is defeated and his Zeroes destroyed, there will be nothing to stop the humans and Halves from living a life free of oppression.

If I can defeat him.

My euphoria seeps away and is replaced by a cold knot of dread.

All the times in the past when I had an opportunity to kill my father, I hesitated. I was swayed by his honeyed words or my own desire to cling to the only parent I still had. None of those hesitations remain. But will I be strong enough to be able to kill him?

Zeidan was a formidable force before. Now, he's a Bisecter. He's my equal.

I think about the sense of weakness that's weighed me down since I lost control of my army. I'm still many times stronger than any human or Halve, but I remember what it felt like to share the strength of a hundred Zeroes. And my father has three-hundred of them tethered to his soul.

Not only will the Zeroes lend him strength, their very existence depends on protecting him. They'll defend him with every bit of their strength.

The only one I have who can help me face this enemy is Dayne.

I exchange a glance with Ry and Wade. We've all seen what my father has become. He's as powerful as I am now, and with his army of Zeroes behind him, I'm not sure I can beat him.

The realization would have filled me with a paralyzing kind of despair if it wasn't for Dayne. His anger is palpable through the bond, and it gives me a strength I wouldn't be able to conjure on my own.

"Should we evacuate?" Wade asks me.

"Where would we go?" Tut interjects before I can respond. "Our people aren't going to leave Tanguro now that it's finally coming back to life. The Northerners would rather take our chances and fight for this place or die trying."

"The Easterners are with you," Valior agrees. "This fortress is our home. We're not leaving."

"The Halves will stay," Ekil says. "We cannot wander anymore."

"What does he want from us?" Tut asks, pulling my attention back. "Does he want to retake Tanguro?"

"No." I force myself to meet the gaze of every member of the group. "He wants me."

"Well, he can't have you," Wade snaps.

In spite of myself, a little flutter goes through my stomach.

"Alright, so what do we do to put this monster down?" Tut asks.

"We need to call everyone back to the fortress," Wade says. "As important as it is to plant the Jadem trees, that can wait until Hemera's father is dead. Right now, we need all the help we can get."

I nod and then translate Wade's response for Ekil. Even as I speak the words, I know that no matter how many Halves and Banished we have on our side, it won't make any difference in a fight against my father's army.

That's when the truth hits me. I need to kill Zeidan before the battle even begins. Once he's dead, the Zeroes won't be any threat, since I will become their master again in the absence of my father's influence.

I will become their master.

I tamp down the automatic thrill that passes through me at the thought of controlling the Zeroes again. The Zeroes need to die just as much as my father. I won't allow them to hurt anyone else, and I won't let their hold on me drive me to become the monster I was before. The only way to make sure that doesn't happen is to kill them before the blood bond between us can re-form.

Once Zeidan is defeated, I'll keep control of the Zeroes just long enough so that the Halves and Solguards can kill all of them. Only then will I truly be rid of my father.

"There's more," another scout says now that he's caught his breath. "We met some Dwellers who escaped before they were turned into Zeroes. They reported that the Captain isn't…right in the head. They say he talks to himself, and that he's been growing madder by the day."

Ry wrinkles her brow. "He didn't seem insane the last time we saw him." She cocks her head. "Well, no more insane than usual, anyway."

"Maybe he's given away too much of himself to create the Zeroes," Wade says.

I feel the heat of Wade's gaze on me, but I don't look at him.

"Is that possible?" Ry asks me.

I hesitate before answering.

"Every Zero connected to him gives him strength, but it's true that he also has to give some of himself to them."

I look inward at my blood bond with Dayne as I search for the right words to explain our connection.

"Dayne belongs to me in every sense of the word. But he exerts control over me in some ways, too. The few emotions he experiences influence mine."

I glance at Ekil and feel my cheeks heat under his scrutiny.

"With a hundred, or three-hundred, of those subtle influences, it could be enough to change someone entirely."

Even though it's the last thing I want to do, I translate what I've just told the humans for Ekil.

"That is why you became bad," Ekil says with all of the bluntness I've come to associate with him.

"Yes," I say, because after what I did to the Halves, they deserve my honesty.

It's more than a little troubling to consider that, if my father hadn't stolen the Zeroes from me, I might have gone insane. Drunk on my own power and with no one to stop me, what else would I have done? Who else would I have hurt?

These thoughts are enough to curdle my insides and any remaining hints of desire I might have had to reclaim the Zeroes.

"So, what do we do now?" Tut asks.

"We gather our forces here and build the best defenses we can manage," I say. "And then, we wait for my father's army to come to us."

CHAPTER 32

As it turns out, we don't have to wait as long as I would have expected. My father's army is moving quickly. They crossed the other territories in record time and have nearly reached the mountains bordering the Wild Lands before Gloom on the next day. It's a pace no human could ever match, and it just serves as a further reminder of all the ways his army outmatches ours.

Since the scouts can't come and go fast enough to keep us informed about his location, Ry takes Vlaz and tracks Zeidan's progress from the air. Every hour, she returns to report that the army has crossed an impossible stretch of land at an impossible speed.

"What's his rush all of a sudden?" Tut grumbles.

I don't bother to explain that everything—from the speed, to the two-hundred new Zeroes added to the army's ranks—is my father making a direct appeal to me.

Look at how strong I've become, Daughter, he's saying. *Look at what* you *could have become.*

When my nerves can't take the waiting around anymore, I tell Ry to give Vlaz a break, and I take over tracking my father's advance.

I keep my distance and hunker down beneath the hood of my gray Dusker cloak so I won't be noticed. Then, I take advantage of the speed my mother gifted me when she made me into a Bisecter. I'm not as fast as I was when I had the strength of one-hundred Zeroes flooding through my veins, but I'm fast enough.

The closer I get to them, the more I sense the barest hint of a connection between us. The bond hasn't been entirely erased like I'd thought. After my father stole the Zero army, I'd searched in vain for my connection to them. Now that I've grown accustomed to being without the Zeroes, I feel that barely-there connection.

It's like they're calling to me across some vast distance. It's a tug on my heart, making me sick with loss and need. It's a cruel reminder of the strength I possessed when the Zeroes belonged to me. I have to remind myself of all the reasons why I have no intention of reclaiming them, and why the bond needs to be destroyed forever.

When I get my first glimpse of my father's bolstered army, the sight sends alternating shocks of fear and anger down my spine. The scout who reported their number in the three-hundreds was right. The Zeroes' metal armor blends in with the gray Gloom, but the sickle blades of their scythes flash in the hazy beams of sunlight. Even at this distance, they're imposing.

In spite of their rapid progress through the territories up to this point, they stop just past the mountains.

The army could be upon Tanguro in a few hours with the pace they've been keeping, but instead, they start building a camp. I watch from afar as bonfires spring to life. The Zeroes make a perfect, unmoving ring around the camp. I can imagine my father standing inside their protective circle. Anger churns in my gut.

I can't figure out why they would stop now, after keeping such a brutal pace for so many hours. I know it can't be because they're worn out from their journey. The Zeroes don't tire.

As my gaze roves over their campsite, I catch sight of movement. My breath hitches as I realize a small fragment of the army—ten reptors and a single Zero—are on the move.

The reptors' mud-brown hides blend into the ground they're running on. Even at this distance, I can see how huge they are.

The creatures are as big as Vlaz. Unlike Vlaz, these beasts don't appear malnourished. One of them opens its mouth, displaying long, dagger-sharp fangs.

The Zero runs behind the reptors, using its scythe to whip the beasts into a frenzy as they race toward us.

It takes me several precious seconds to understand what my father is up to. When I do, I curse out loud. Then, I race back to Tanguro.

* * *

"He's going to make us fight these reptors first," I report to the leaders.

There's a terrible brilliance to my father's plan. He's going to let us take on this insignificant slice of his army first. We'll fight, and many will die. Then, just as we're recovering, he'll launch the full force of his army on us.

"He wants us to see how pointless it will be for us to try to resist," I tell the others.

Tut makes a derisive sound as he pulls his golden sword from its scabbard. "Let the bastards come."

What Tut doesn't understand is that we will defeat the small group heading toward us…eventually. But it will take every ounce of strength we possess. Once it's over and we're all bloody and exhausted, my father will attack with the rest of his army. Then, instead of ten reptors and one Zero, we'll be facing three-hundred Zeroes. We won't stand a chance.

Some of our soldiers will try to flee. The rest will take the only other option Zeidan will give them: surrender. They'll become my father's slaves, and eventually, they'll be added to his army of Zeroes.

Unless I can kill him first.

It was my plan from the beginning, and it's still the only hope we have. I'm determined that for once, I won't let down the people who are depending on me.

Everyone inside the fortress spills out into the courtyard, dressed and ready for battle. Archers line up behind the stone wall and wait for Ry's signal. The Halves and Banished shore up the defenses of the building and set guards around our precious supplies. All the busyness is just that…movement to make everyone feel like we're doing something, even though the truth is that none of our preparations will matter once the army arrives.

"Hemera!"

I turn at the sound of Wokee's voice. He and Everlyn are darting through the crowd of Banished and Halves to reach me.

"Good news," Wokee announces. "The touch-me-not trees I thought were dead just went dormant, and there's been enough sun in the past few days for them to bloom again. We've got a good number of the pods we can use against the reptors."

That is good news. The touch-me-not pods in Tanguro are powerful enough to penetrate a reptor's thick hide and will cause them enough pain to give our fighters a chance.

"Distribute them to the archers," Wade orders. "We'll use them first before we attack on foot."

"What's the bad news?" I ask, reading the expression on Wokee's face.

Everlyn is the one who answers. "The plants I need to make more explosives did die, and Wokee says it'll be weeks before the new ones we planted grow enough to be useful to us." She frowns. "I scraped together enough for one good burst, but that's all."

"Save it," Wade tells her. "We'll use it as a last resort."

I consider making a sarcastic comment about keeping Wade far away from the explosives, but that just seems cruel and unnecessary. Besides, it would require me speaking directly to Wade, which I refuse to do.

"One other thing," Wokee says. He marches over and stands toe-to-toe with me. "Everlyn and I aren't leaving. We're going to stay and fight with the rest of you."

Before I can even open my mouth to protest, Wokee continues, "I'm not a little kid anymore. Everlyn and I have been training with the Solguards, and we've survived this long. We have the right to defend Tanguro along with the rest of you, and you know it."

I stare at Wokee, and it's then that I realize I barely have to look down to meet his gaze anymore. He's almost as tall as I am.

"We won't fight on the front lines," Everlyn adds, giving Wokee a sharp jab in the side when he opens his mouth to disagree. "But we will be fighting." There's a stubborn determination on both of their faces.

Absolutely not! my mind shouts. They need to be kept somewhere safe…somewhere out of harm's reach. If such a place even exists….

I turn to Wade, who is leaning on his crutch, his bronze skin pale.

"I don't know," he begins.

"They're right," Valior says in a quiet voice. "They should have the right to stand alongside our army."

Even as my instincts scream at me to get Wokee as far away from here as possible, part of me knows he's right. If I were in his position, I wouldn't be content to stay behind while everyone I cared about fought for our home without me.

I let out a breath, feeling a heavy weight settle into place against my heart.

"Okay," I hear myself say. "You can fight with us."

The two kids nod their heads, and I can tell how much they're struggling to maintain grown-up facades when all they really want to do is whoop and high-five each other.

"Go see Jarosh, and he'll put you to work," Wade tells the kids. More quietly to me, he says, "Jarosh will make sure they're as far from the fighting as they can possibly get."

I give him a grateful nod.

Ry turns to Wade and puts her hands on her hips. "You, on the other hand, will be sitting this one out."

"Excuse me?" Wade deadpans.

As the second-in-command of the Solguards, Ry has every right to challenge Wade, but she's never done so before. Maybe it was the sight of Dellin stepping up and becoming the Dusker Supreme that has made Ry bold in a way she never has been before.

"You're one of my best friends," Ry tells Wade. "And I've sat back and watched you throw yourself into the line of fire too many times. I get that you want to protect all of us, but I don't get you trying to sacrifice yourself for every one of the Solguards. That's not your role. Your role is to stay alive and keep us all together."

Wade starts to reply, but Ry isn't finished.

"We all know you're not up for walking across the courtyard right now, let alone battling the reptors. You're sitting this one out, and that's the end of it."

It's the same message, more or less, that I've been trying to convey to Wade for months now. But for the first time, it seems like Wade is listening. I hold my breath as I wait for him to tell Ry that she should mind her own business and demand that someone bring him a sword. He doesn't.

"I guess you're right," Wade concedes.

Ry and I exchange a stunned look.

Wade waits until Ry has turned back to him before he asks, "Think you're up for leading this one?"

Ry gives him one of her confident grins. "You know I am."

CHAPTER 33

After a few more words are exchanged between the leaders, we all disperse. Ry gets onto Vlaz's back with another archer. They each carry a bag full of touch-me-nots. We watch them fly out to meet the reptors, which are now only a few miles from the fortress. Valior and Tut take charge of lining up our soldiers, with the strongest Solguards and Halves split between the front lines and rear defenses.

I walk back to the main building with Wade and Dayne. The three of us are quiet as the organized chaos of pre-battle preparations unfold around us. There is so much I want to say to Wade, and yet, I can't seem to manage a single word.

As we reach the door to the building, red sparks explode in the air. We turn to watch as the archers continue to launch the touch-me-nots at the reptors. The enormous beasts snarl and rear up on their hind legs, trying to claw out the sparks embedding in their flesh. Their roars, which are audible even from this distance, make the hairs on my arm stand on end.

All too soon, the touch-me-nots are gone. The reptors thrash as they fight against the fiery sparks burning into them, but it won't be long before the Zero starts chasing them toward us again. We have precious few minutes before the beasts are on us.

"Ry's more cut out for this job than I am," Wade says in a hollow voice.

I turn to look at him. "Everyone respects you and would die for you without a second's hesitation. If that isn't the mark of a great leader, I don't know what is."

Wade nods slowly. "I don't have the head for it, though." His gold eyes meet mine, and for a second, the mask that he so often keeps in place, even with me, starts to slip. "I can't take it, Hemera…all the people who died because of orders I gave. And there's nothing I can do to stop it. No matter how hard I try, more of our people die. I don't know how to live with all of it."

Wade and I stopped being vulnerable with each other sometime after I took control of the Zeroes and he became the Solguard leader. We were both so consumed with our own need to feel powerful that we stopped confiding in each other altogether. Now, I'm more grateful for his honesty than I could put into words.

"You're trying to be perfect, and that isn't possible in the world we live in," I tell him. I laugh a little as a thought occurs to me. "Something I've learned from all the times I've messed up is that no matter what your intentions might be, reality seems to have its own agenda."

He smiles, but it doesn't reach his eyes.

I'm overcome with a desire to touch him. Pulling my hand free from my glove, I reach up and let my hand rest against his cheek.

Part of me expects him to pull away. Instead, he leans into my touch.

"We can't lose you, Wade," I tell him. "*I* can't lose you." The words come out quiet and a little hoarse, but I know he's heard me because I feel his breath hitch.

"Everything's broken," Wade tells me in a harsh whisper. "And I don't know how to fix it."

Something inside me aches at those words. I get the feeling he's talking about more than the Solguards' survival as emotions fill his eyes.

"I feel the same way," I admit. "But the Jadem trees are giving all of us another chance to make things right. Once I take down my father, everything will be alright again."

Wade shakes his head. He looks…sad. "When you get the Zeroes back, I'll lose you forever."

He steps away from my touch…away from me. My hand feels cold without the warmth of his cheek.

His words feel like a slap. I start to feel angry, and then I realize there's no one to blame for his distrust but me. I gave my friends every reason to believe I would choose the Zeroes over them. Wade doesn't know about my change of heart, because I've never bothered to tell him.

I open my mouth to do just that, but I never get the chance. A frantic-looking Jarosh bursts through the door and almost knocks Wade over in his haste.

"Wade, you have to help me get Camike out of here before they come."

"Jarosh," Wade begins.

"I've been watching her work since we were mated. I can heal any human or Halve as well as she can. We don't need her." The look in his eyes is fierce, bordering on violent.

He's always been protective of Camike, but not like this. I can't imagine what's gotten into him. I can't imagine Camike appreciates it.

"Jarosh—"

"I've never asked you for anything, damnit. But I'm asking for this." Jarosh's voice breaks, and it's then that I see true terror in his eyes. "Please, Wade. We all know what's going to happen when the Zeroes get here. My mate has to survive."

Wade puts a firm hand on the other man's shoulder. "We're going to do everything we can to defend the fortress. I'll even—"

"She's pregnant."

Wade and I stare at each other.

"What?" Wade asks.

"Camike's pregnant," Jarosh repeats.

All of a sudden, Jarosh's strange protectiveness and insistence on keeping Camike away from the fighting makes sense. I had thought his obsession with keeping her warm and giving her his food rations was over the top, even for him. Now, I understand.

There hasn't been a single pregnant woman—human or Halve—since Darkness. We assumed it was because of the ash in the air or the darkness tree smoke, but no one knows for sure.

"What?" Wade asks. "How?"

Jarosh's panic eases up just enough for him to raise an eyebrow at Wade. "I'd be happy to give you the details later."

"No, that's not what I meant. I mean—" Wade runs a hand through his hair, looking more than a little out of his element.

After months of seeing him as the ever-calm, collected Solguard leader, I can't hide my smirk.

"Please, Wade," Jarosh says, his humor dissipating as quickly as it had come. "She's weak, and if she keeps straining herself, she'll lose the baby. If anything happens to her, I won't survive."

"I understand," Wade says, although he still looks completely bewildered. Frankly, so am I, but I try not to let it show on my face. After all, just because there's never been a Halve-human union before, it doesn't mean it shouldn't theoretically be possible….

Jarosh continues, "She's refusing to leave, so I need you to make up some excuse that will convince her. Tell her you need her to go heal someone to the north, or whatever it takes. Just put her on that hyenair and get her out of here."

"You'll have to go with her," I say, even though Jarosh has been directing his plea to Wade. "She won't leave without you."

Wade frowns. "Then, we wouldn't have a healer at all."

"Dayne has some experience with that," I say with more confidence than I feel. Dayne's abilities were never as good as Camike's to begin with, and I have serious doubts about how he would fare as a healer now that he's a Zero. Healing requires sympathy as much as the knowledge of how to stitch a wound or set a broken bone, and Dayne doesn't have access to that emotion anymore. Still, he's the best option we have.

I may not share Jarosh's panic for his mate, but I understand what it means that Camike is pregnant. If their baby survives, he or she will be the first our fortress has seen since Darkness.

The birth of a child was sacred before Darkness. Now, it seems like an impossibility. Camike and Jarosh's child would be the proof we all need that there's hope for our future.

"We have to do whatever it takes to keep her and the baby safe," I say.

Jarosh turns to me. After I carried Brogut back to the fortress, Jarosh stopped hating me. But he still didn't trust me. Now, for the first time since

I exiled the Halves, the way he looks at me reminds me of when we were friends.

The memory of how horribly I behaved to the people I care about most fills me with shame.

Never again, I promise myself. I'll never succumb to my blood bond with the Zeroes and trade it for all of the relationships I truly value. I'll never lose myself to them again.

While these thoughts are still occupying my mind, Ekil and Brogut come out of the building. They're clearly looking for Jarosh, and when they see him, they head toward us. When Brogut catches sight of me, he lowers his head in a sign of deference.

Another rush of guilt hits me. I might have done a good deed by helping the Halves when they were mere days away from death, but if it hadn't been for me, they wouldn't have been in such dire straits to begin with.

I almost killed Brogut after he attacked my Zero in the Eastern settlement. If Wade hadn't stopped me, I would have. I would have killed Ekil for trying to protect Brogut from me, too.

The scout's report about my father fills my thoughts.

The Captain isn't…right in the head.… He seems to be growing madder by the day….

"We can send you with a few Solguards to help protect her," I tell Jarosh, raising my voice so it drowns out the doubt and shame echoing in my own head.

"I'll go with you," Wade tells him. "I might not be good for much right now, but I know this land better than most. If anything attacks, I'll do whatever I can to give you time to get her away."

"Brogut go too," Brogut says in the human language, pointing to himself. "Protect Camike and Jarosh."

Ekil nods in approval. Jarosh puts his hand over his heart and bows his head.

"Thank you," Jarosh says, making eye contact with all of us. "I won't forget that you did this for us."

He turns to go.

"Jarosh," I say. "Congratulations, by the way."

He looks back and grins at me. It's the cocky, friendly smile I haven't seen from him in months. The sight of it fills me with warmth, but at the same time, it's a stark reminder of everything I gave up when I chose the Zeroes over my friends.

And that makes me wonder whether I really have any right to judge Wade for putting the Solguards above himself, when I chose the Zeroes over everyone.

CHAPTER 34

rchers," Ry calls out.

The men and women standing in front of our army nock their arrows, preparing for Ry's order to fire.

As I track the reptors' progress, I think about Wade. He and I didn't exchange any goodbyes before his small group left, and now, with the sight of the beasts barreling toward me, I wish we had.

My only consolation is that there's no time for regrets. Each second brings the reptors closer.

Ry paces back and forth on top of the stone wall as she shouts orders to the Solguards. When we're all organized to her satisfaction, she puts her hands on her hips and lets her gaze roam across the lines of soldiers.

"Solguards, Banished, and Halves," she says in a voice loud enough to carry even to the back of our ranks, "today is our chance for vengeance."

The Solguards stamp the ground. I translate her words for the Halves surrounding me.

"We will defeat these beasts just as we've taken down every wormkill that's dared to come within our grasp."

There's more foot-stamping and murmurs of approval. I try not to think about how, as formidable as the wormkill are, they're nothing compared to the reptors. And they're less than nothing compared to the Zeroes. I also don't let myself dwell on the fact that we've never had to battle ten of the wormkill at once. Right now, our army needs hope and motivation more than anything else.

"This is our land," Ry continues. "Are we going to let some insane tyrant take it away from us?"

Choruses of *No!* echo back from every member of our army.

"Are we going to send these foul creatures back to the pits of hell they came from?"

"Yes!" everyone calls back.

I find myself pounding my sword against my armor to add to the ruckus everyone else is making.

"We are the people and Halves of Tanguro, and we don't back down from a fight. We answer to no one but ourselves."

More cheers.

"We'll chase off these creatures and any others that dare cross us. And then, we're going to fight the Darkness the same way—with all of our strength. Because that's who we are."

She holds up the back of her hand, showing off her Solguard tattoo.

The rest of the Solguards fist their right hands over their hearts. The Banished and Halves stamp the ground in approval.

"We won't fear this army. It is they who should fear us!"

I shout myself hoarse along with the rest of our soldiers. Ry takes off her helmet and thrusts it into the air. Her red curls fly in every direction, shining like flames amid the weak beams of sunlight. Looking at her, I can almost believe we're as invincible as she's made us feel.

"Now," she gives us a feral grin, "let's go kick some reptor ass!"

Ry jumps down from the stone wall and picks up her bow just before the reptors come into range.

I release my sling along with the archers' arrows, but our barrage seems to do nothing more than infuriate the beasts. Only the touch-me-not pods seemed to have had any real effect on them, and there are none left.

From my vantage point, I can see two reptor bodies stretched out on the ground in the distance, their hides still smoking from the effects of the touch-me-nots. That still leaves eight reptors and one Zero almost within range. The Zero hangs back, staying just out of reach of my sling and the archers' arrows.

The reptors' six legs move so fast they're a blur. Their legs are barely visible beneath the bulk of their midsections, and it looks like they're slithering across the ground like giant serpents. Their spiky hides are riddled with arrows, which seem to be having no effect on their progress.

Even Vlaz looks unthreatening in comparison.

As weak and thin as he's become, Vlaz still defends us as viciously as ever. He flies down, fangs on full display, and grasps a reptor's tail between his jaws. He tries to lift the entire creature into the air, but he doesn't have the strength to manage it. Instead, he bites down. I wince as the reptor lets out a terrible shriek. It turns its head to snap at Vlaz, but not before the hyenair has bitten its tail clean off.

Even from this distance, I can see the greenish-yellow ichor pouring from the gaping hole. Vlaz lets go of the detached, still-flopping tail and lifts back into the air, missing the reptor's snapping jaws by inches.

The beasts' muddy eyes gleam with the promise of violence. They open their mouths to display jagged, wicked fangs that are easily the length of my forearm.

Before Darkness, the sight of these creatures would have sent the Banished into a state of panic as they raced for the illusion of safety. Now, every member of our army holds their ground. Shields are raised and weapons are drawn. No one whimpers or backs down.

The reptors barrel through the stone wall.

I yell to the others fighting beside me to aim for the beasts' bellies, since it's the only part of them that isn't protected by the plated armor of their hides. But to get near their stomachs, we have to risk their teeth and claws. The air fills with the sound of screams—both human and animal—as our forces collide.

As I fight, I try to keep Wokee and Everlyn in my sight. Wade ordered a group of Solguards to watch out for them before he left, but true to my word, I haven't done anything to try to keep them away. Knowing they're here, not only witnessing but being a part of all of this, is terrifying.

"Pay attention," Dayne snaps at me. He uses his sword to slice off a reptor's claw that was within inches of raking across my chest.

I return my focus to the reptor that is rearing up on its hind legs and swiping at the air. With a ferocious cry, I lunge for the beast.

When it opens its mouth to swallow me whole, I step into the reek of its cavernous maw. I drive my sword up and through the roof of its mouth.

The beast lets out a gurgling shriek as blood pours from the wound. Dayne tosses me a new sword as I dive out of the reptor's mouth. While the beast writhes and digs its snout into the dirt to rid itself of my sword, Dayne and I attack its vulnerable underside.

I know when I've hit the beast's heart. Blood spurts, and the reptor begins to twitch. I yank out my blade and jump to the side, pulling Dayne with me before we're crushed underneath the lifeless creature.

My breathing comes in short, ragged gasps. Too many of our own are already dead, and there are still five reptors to battle. I can see the weariness and fear on our soldiers' faces. I feel a sinking dread in the pit of my stomach.

The single Zero my father sent to face us hasn't even joined the battle yet. I can sense it waiting just on the fringe of the action, where it seems to be watching to make sure none of the reptors lose track of their purpose.

Our army is fighting fiercely, but all it takes is a quick recollection of the sheer number of Zeroes at my father's disposal to realize we don't stand a chance. It's a stark reminder that the only reason any of us are still alive is because he's allowing it…for now.

This bare fraction of the strength he possesses is almost more than we can deal with. I'm beginning to see the growing hopelessness of those around me, just like I can feel my father's growing sense of victory as he listens to our battle from afar.

A cry of rage rips free from my throat. I won't let my father win. Not this time.

With that thought, I raise my sword and charge at the next reptor.

* * *

"One more to go!" I shout, egging on the Solguards and Halves fighting beside me.

We're all exhausted and bloody, but we rally for one final push. Ry and the archers rain down arrows on the reptor from above, while Dayne and I brave its flailing claws to strike at its underbelly.

No single strike is enough to kill the beast, but each one makes it bleed a little more, slows its reactions just a bit.

Dayne gets in a wicked stroke that nearly cleaves one of the reptor's hind legs off. The beast roars, and I see an opportunity. I duck between its thrashing claws and go for the creature's heart with my sword.

At the last second, the reptor jerks back, and my strike goes wide. It swipes a claw at me. I throw myself to the ground and roll, feeling a burst of air as its claws miss me by a hair's breadth. When I manage to get to my feet, I realize I'm directly in front of the beast's snout. The smell of its blood and breath is so rancid I'm momentarily stunned. It's enough time for the reptor to open its mouth and snap at me. I throw my body to the side, but I'm not fast enough. The beast's jaws snap shut on my leg.

I cry out as the fangs sink through flesh. When my bone cracks under the pressure of the beast's grip, my vision goes dark.

I'm aware of Dayne close by. Not because I can see him, but because I can feel his agony and fury inside me. I sense his incredible burst of strength, and then the reptor's teeth are gone from my leg. I fight to blink away the darkness, even as a horrible scream continues to echo all around me.

To stay conscious, I force myself to focus on the sight of Dayne hacking away at the beast's snout. With a snarl, the reptor turns on Dayne. Someone else drags me back, away from the reptor's immediate reach. My leg is on fire, which is a strange comfort because at least I know it's still attached.

The horrible screams filling my ears must be mine, but I can't make myself stop.

The reptor is flailing in the final throes of its fight for life. Even in my barely-aware state, I can tell it's only a few good sword strokes away from death. While the other Solguards finish the beast off, Dayne crouches on the ground beside me. His own leg is bleeding. His face contorts in a grimace as he bends down to lift me in his arms. As he does so, my eyes lock on the source of that terrible scream.

It wasn't me, after all.

The Zero, which is standing just outside the crumbled remains of the stone wall, is doubled over. Its piercing wail cuts through all the other sounds and sends shivers down my spine. As I look closer, I realize the Zero is clutching its leg.

No one has dared to attack the Zero, and the last remaining reptor is lying dead as the rest of its blood drains out of its body. When I look closer, I realize the Zero is holding its leg in the same place where mine is throbbing. A suspicion takes root in my mind.

"Wait," I tell Dayne, who is already limping back to the building.

I motion for him to set me down. When he does, I'm able to get a better look at the Zero's injury. Its calf is bloody and mangled, but not so much that I can't see the puncture wound that is oozing brown blood. Even though the Zero is under my father's control and was standing outside all of the action, there can be no debate about the source of its injury. The Zero's wound is the same shape, same placement…same everything…as the reptor bite on my leg.

CHAPTER 35

I look at Dayne's leg. "Let me see," I demand, pointing to the stains of brown blood seeping through the fabric of his pantleg.

He rolls up the fabric and, sure enough, there is a bite mark on his leg. The injury is identical to mine and the one I saw on that Zero.

Even though I no longer have any control over the one-hundred Zeroes, the whisper of a connection that still exists between us was enough for the Zero to somehow absorb my injury.

Were the other Zeroes harmed the same way as this one, or was it something to do with our proximity? Since my father is connected to the Zeroes—and to me, because it was my blood that turned him into a Zero— was his leg wounded, too?

"There you are!" Ry drops onto the ground beside me, her eyes widening at the dried blood all over my leg. Already, new skin is healing over the bite mark.

"I'm okay," I tell her, trying for a smile and managing more of a grimace.

Ry wipes a smudge of dirt or blood from her brow. "Your father sent those reptors just to play with us, didn't he?"

"A predator with its prey," Dayne says in his flat, rumbling voice.

Ry huffs out a breath. "I'd evacuate everyone, but there's nowhere to evacuate to. If we lose control of Tanguro, we won't be able to survive more than a few weeks. Besides, your father's Zeroes could track us down in a matter of hours."

"We fight until the end," Dayne says.

"The only chance we have is if I can get to him before he gets to me," I tell Ry.

"I agree, but how are you going to do that?" she asks. "It's not like he's going to let you walk right up to him. He isn't arrogant enough to take that chance, especially when he has all the strength and advantage on his side." She frowns. "If I were him, I'd just keep sending in the Zeroes until everyone dropped dead from exhaustion. Then, I'd ride in on one of my reptors and force anyone still standing to surrender."

"In that case, I'm glad you're not him," I grumble.

"Seriously, Mer." Ry throws up her hands. "What are we going to do?"

"He doesn't want to kill me," I remind her. "That gives me an advantage."

"Not enough of one," she replies.

"I just need you to help me get close to him." I stretch out my leg and feel the tight pull of new skin and muscles. "It's time for this to end."

I feel Dayne's surge of emotions in response. Anger, bloodlust, and something that feels like approval.

* * *

As soon as the last reptor died, the Zero limped back in the direction of my father's camp. I knew it was going back to Zeidan to report what had happened.

Solguards, Halves, and Banished all gather in the building under the light and warmth of the Jadem tree. We eat a small meal, although for once, no one has an appetite. Then, we try to come up with a plan to face the rest of my father's Zeroes.

My guess is that Zeidan will give us time to really consider what a fruitless endeavor it would be to go up against his three-hundred Zeroes. Knowing what I know about him, he'll make us wait until the next Gloom before he launches his attack.

Even with everyone's brave words and all the preparations we're making, I wonder if, by the time the Zero army arrives, the Banished and

Halves will all be contemplating surrender the way my father expects them to.

The thought of all of these people and Halves—my friends and brothers and sisters in arms—being turned into Zeroes isn't one I want to even contemplate. But that's exactly what will happen to them if my father gets his way.

At this point, the whole concept of a battle plan is really just an exercise to make everyone feel like they have some measure of control. I have no illusions about what will happen when the Halves and Solguards try to go up against an army of Zeroes. There's no point in discussing it…not when I have a plan for ensuring it never comes to that.

If Ry knew what I was really planning, she'd lose her mind.

A group of Solguards enters the building, and my heart speeds up at the sight of Wade. He's walking without his crutch and doesn't even seem to be limping, but he's covered in scratches and shallow wounds.

"What are you doing back here?" Ry demands.

Wade's gaze cuts straight to me.

"I got Jarosh and Camike to a cave that's as safe as anywhere else. They'll be able to hide there until all of this is over, and Brogut stayed to guard them. But I had to come back."

He pulls his gaze away from me to look at Ry.

"I'm still going to need you to lead the army," he tells her, "but I'm not sitting this one out."

Ry gives him an assessing look. "Did you fall into a nest of briars or something?"

Wade gives her a small grin.

"Apparently, the Tanguro wolves we thought were extinct…aren't. There was a family of them holed up in the first cave I checked out. Suffice it to say, they weren't really looking for roommates."

Wokee gasps. "You didn't kill them, did you?"

Wade gives Wokee an amused look. "For some reason I'm still trying to work out, no, I didn't. They were starving and it would have been a mercy if I had, but I couldn't bring myself to do it."

Wokee lets out a sigh of relief. "They'll find food again soon. With all of the plants we're growing, the smaller animals will come back, and then they'll be able to feed the bigger animals, and then everything will be back to the way it was before. Except *better*."

The one enormous caveat to Wokee's plan hangs unspoken over all of us. If we can't survive against my father's Zeroes, none of us will be doing anything.

CHAPTER 36

I'm still thinking about the Zero and its bloody, identical injury when the lookouts announce my father's army is on the move.

While Ry, Ekil, and the other Banished leaders prepare for the coming fight, I go in search of the one person who will be able to help me bring down the most powerful army ever created. Everlyn.

I find her pressing some sticky moss-looking stuff to the base of the Jadem tree.

"Wokee says this'll help the tree absorb the darkness sap better," Everlyn explains to me.

I nod as she chatters about the Jadem trees and Wokee's plan for bringing life back to all the territories.

"Everlyn, I need you to do something for me," I say, interrupting her partway through some commentary about river-cleaning algae.

She stops spreading the goopy moss around the tree and looks up, curiosity in her eyes.

"You know that last batch of explosives Wade asked you to save?"

She nods.

"There's something I need you to do with it."

Everlyn listens as I explain what I want. Her eyes widen, but when I've finished, she nods in understanding.

"Wade's going to be mad," she says, a little smile curving her lips.

She's right.

"Let me worry about that," I tell her.

If everything goes according to my plan, he won't be able to stay mad. I'll kill my father and reclaim the army of Zeroes before even a single one of our people can raise a sword.

After I'm done with Everlyn, I go to meet with the rest of the Banished leaders. I nod along and pretend to agree as they strategize about the best way to thin out the Zeroes and make use of the pathetic resources we still have at our disposal. Their faces are all grim; everyone knows we don't stand a chance against the Zeroes, and that any plans we make will fall apart as soon as my father commands his army to attack.

I want to tell them not to worry, but if I reveal my plan now, they're all going to try to stop me. I can't take that risk, so I stay quiet. They can talk and plan as much as they want, but I know I'm the only one who can save all of us now. The thought is both comforting and terrifying.

The scouts deliver reports every hour to update us on Zeidan's progress. His army is advancing at a slow, almost leisurely pace. Even though they could be in Tanguro in only a few hours if they wanted, they're moving at the speed of a human army. It's no secret why.

My father is building suspense and anticipation. He's confident we won't be able to pose any kind of meaningful threat. By giving us more time to prepare, he's letting our fear grow along with the knowledge that his army can't be beat.

As I look around at the terror being hidden behind brave faces, my blood boils with rage.

My father is going to pay for all of the pain he's caused. He's going to pay for what he's taken from me. He's about to know what it feels like to be alone and without the Zeroes that are everything to him.

At the speed his army is moving, they'll arrive in the early hours of Gloom, which gives us a full twelve hours of Dark to worry and wait.

The leaders have yet another meeting where we go over numbers and weapons. The whole time, we avoid talking about the fact that the Zeroes are unbeatable. I feel my anxiety rise even more when Valior and Tut start discussing whether a strike to the heart or a slit throat is the most effective way to kill a Zero. The thought of what will happen to everyone in the fortress if it comes down to a real battle has my stomach churning.

It won't come to that, I promise myself.

If my plan works, the only ones in harm's way will be Zeidan and his army. I cling to my plan, because it's all that's keeping me grounded.

"Alright," Ry announces, looking as exhausted as I feel. "Let's all get some rest while we can. Sun knows we're going to need it."

"I'm sure we're all going to sleep wonderfully with the threat of imminent death hanging over our heads," Tut grumbles.

Ry purses her lips, but she doesn't argue. What little morale our company has is slipping away as the hours of Dark creep by. It's precisely what my father intended. By the time he arrives, everyone in Tanguro will be suitably panic-stricken and hopeless.

I'm just about to head upstairs to try and get some sleep, when Ekil stops me. He hasn't sought me out since the Halves came to Tanguro, so I'm more than a little surprised when he calls my name in his harsh, gravelly voice.

"Zeroes will kill everyone," he says. His tone is matter-of-fact, but I know him well enough to see the concern in his black eyes and in the way his huge fists open and close in an anxious gesture.

"I'm going to make sure that doesn't happen," I say. Because I know he won't balk like Ry or Wade, I tell him my plan.

When I'm finished, I expect Ekil's face to slacken in relief. Instead, he frowns.

"That sounds like a bad plan," he tells me.

I inwardly curse the Halves and their inability to understand or implement tact. At the same time, I realize how much I've missed talking with Ekil these past months. That revelation is enough to keep me from saying anything sarcastic.

"It's a great plan, and it's the only one that will work," I say in my defense. "I'm going to convince Zeidan I'm ready to rule alongside him. It's what he's wanted since the beginning. It's why he started experimenting on people and Halves in the first place."

Ekil hisses in fury at the bare mention of those experiments. He, like so many of the other Halves, was tortured by my father in his early attempts to create the Zeroes. None of them have forgotten, least of all Ekil.

"He's going to think I'm agreeing to join him," I say, keeping my voice calm in the hope it will soothe Ekil's temper. "I'll tell him I want to make an agreement with him to let everyone else in the fortress go free. He'll have to let me in close enough to negotiate the terms of our alliance, and then I'll kill him."

"The Zeroes will stop you," Ekil points out, still unenthusiastic about the plan I've begun to think is quite brilliant.

"No, they won't, because they won't know I'm going to kill him until I've already done it," I explain. "And then, once he's dead, their blood bond with my father will be severed. The only bond that will be left will be the one they have with me. Then, they won't be able to hurt anyone because I won't let them."

Ekil still doesn't seem impressed, though, so I say, "I'm going to make sure not a single one of our people dies."

"You'll kill him, and then you'll become like him." Ekil points an accusing finger at me.

I take a step back at the unexpected wave of hurt those words carve into my heart.

"I'm not going to be like my father."

"They will change you." Ekil shakes his head in anger. "Just like they did the last time."

It's a fair point, and Ekil has every reason to think I'll fall prey to the call of the Zeroes' power once again. More than a small part of me is worried that, despite my best intentions, I won't be able to resist their influence. Once Zeidan is dead and his blood bond with the Zeroes is severed, they'll automatically belong to me again.

I can't imagine the rush of power that will come when three-hundred Zeroes fall under my command. Will I be able to fight that connection, or will I be so drunk off their raw strength that I won't remember my original plan?

The scout's words from earlier play over again in my mind.

The Captain isn't…right in the head…. He's been growing madder by the day….

My palms have started to sweat.

This fear and self-doubt is exactly what my father wants. It's why he's waiting to attack us. He wants us all questioning ourselves and our abilities, me most of all.

"I'm not going to end up like him," I promise Ekil, forcing myself to meet his black gaze.

"So much power is no good for one person," Ekil says.

"I know that now." I keep holding Ekil's unblinking stare. "I won't fail you again."

I only hope it's a promise I can keep.

CHAPTER 37

It's hours later when all the people clambering for a piece of my attention have drifted off to sleep. I go upstairs to the second floor, only to find that Wade has just gotten back himself. The sleeping spots we claimed for ourselves are near enough for us to see each other and slightly off to the side of the main part of the room.

Wade is in the midst of pulling off his cloak, and the bandages around his midsection peek out from under his shirt. He hasn't noticed me yet, and he winces as he sits down on top of his bedroll.

He looks up, and that's when I realize I've been staring. My face heats. Before I can make some excuse or try to escape, he motions for me to join him.

I don't move. I'm still furious with him for putting himself in so much danger. And besides, I'm already anxious enough about the battle to come. I don't need to add to that discomfort by having yet another confusing and emotional conversation with Wade.

"Please," he says, his voice quiet.

That single word breaks through my hesitation and the residual anger I'm still carrying. I cross the room and, after only a slight pause, sit down on the edge of Wade's bedroll.

We don't speak. I watch the play of light from the Jadem tree in Wade's gold eyes, and I assume he's doing the same in my black ones. It's been so long since I've been able to tell what he was thinking just by looking at him, and I can't begin to guess what's on his mind now.

Wade is the first one to break our silence. "I owe you an apology," he says.

I start at that. "Apology for what?"

"For being so hard on you about the Zeroes." He blows out a breath, making the soft waves of his hair look windswept. "While I was out there with Camike and Jarosh, all I could think about was all of you back here fighting without me. It occurred to me that if I had the ability to create something like the Zeroes—something that would be strong enough to give our people a chance—I'd take it without question. The fact that you want to fight them instead of just going right back to them is…amazing, really. I'm not sure I would have that kind of strength."

He reaches out like he's going to touch my cheek, but he pulls his hand back at the last second. "I was angry with you before because creating those Zeroes changed you, and I saw the way they stole a piece of you away from the rest of us.

"But I realized I was being selfish. It occurred to me that if I'd been in your position, I'd have made the same choice." He looks away from me, like he's debating whether he wants to say more. Finally, he says, "And I think some part of me was jealous of those creatures, because you had given more of yourself to them than you ever gave to me."

Wade's confession sends an unexpected spike of pain through my chest.

"Wade," I begin, but I cut myself off because I don't know what to say.

Instead of denying his words, I reach out and take his hand. His fingers curl around mine.

"You were right to be angry with me," I admit. "The Zeroes made me different, and I know that everything that went wrong between us was because of my blood bond with the Zeroes."

I've never been good at apologies and admissions, but I force out the words anyway. They're long overdue. Besides, Wade has always been honest with me. It's about time I start returning the favor.

It feels strange to be so close to Wade and talking about something other than battle plans or darkness tree groves. It's a good kind of strange, though. There's a rightness to all of this that neither of us can deny.

I wish I hadn't spent so much of the last six months distancing myself from him.

"My blood bonds replaced my other relationships and made it impossible for me to hold onto them in any real way," I tell him. "I hadn't realized the price I was paying for the sake of my connection to the Zeroes until it was too late."

I'm reminded of something my mother wrote in the letter she left for me. After telling me she turned me into a Bisecter to create a weapon for the Solguards, she said some outcomes aren't worth what is needed to achieve them.

I had the best of intentions when I first created the Zeroes, but at the time, I hadn't realized the price I would be paying for them.

After we left Darkness Peak, I told Ry I didn't know if I could fix what was broken between Wade and me.

You owe it to both of you to try, she said.

Before I can lose my nerve, I say the words I've wanted to say to Wade for more than a year.

"I love you," I tell him.

Wade's golden eyes become impossibly bright.

"I don't know how everything with my father will play out, so I just wanted you to hear it, at least once." I swallow. "I know things have been…difficult…between us. But you're the only one I want to be with."

"Hemera," Wade murmurs.

He pulls me to him. We don't kiss. Instead, we just wrap our arms around each other and stay like that, breathing the same air and feeling our hearts beat against each other's chests.

"I love you too," he whispers against my hair. "And maybe once all this is over, we'll be able to be together."

"Together," I repeat.

The word sounds nice. It also sounds like an idea, or a dream, that's just out of reach.

I don't think either of us really believes all of this can end with us being together, but for these next few hours, there's no harm in pretending.

I nestle closer into his familiar warmth, careful not touch his wounds. Wade wraps his arms around me and pulls me down onto the bedroll beside him. We lie like that for a long time before his steady breathing drives away my doubts, and I fall asleep.

✳ ✳ ✳

We wake to a sound I've become familiar with. There's the clanking of weapons as they're thrust into scabbards, and the loud voices and tramping boots of hundreds of humans and Halves preparing for battle.

Wade leans over, kisses my forehead, and nods to me. We both get up, pull on our cloaks, and head downstairs to meet whatever the day will bring.

I notice the light streaming in through the windows is less gray and more of a pale yellow. When I look outside, I actually have to squint from the brightness. The sun is a barely-visible circle hidden behind the layers of ash, but it's the first time in six months I've seen its shape. It seems like a good omen.

"Mer, hold up!" Wokee calls, stopping me before I reach the stairs.

I give Wade a nod, letting him know I'll catch up with him. Then, I turn my attention on Wokee.

"I didn't know we were exchanging gifts," I say as Wokee hands me a messily-wrapped parcel.

"We're not." Wokee gives me a knowing smile. "I just thought you could use this before the battle."

I tear open the package and let out a little *oh* as the blue cloak spills out of the package.

"The plant that makes the dye grew back," Wokee explains as I slip on the beautiful cloak. It's not as lightweight as the first one he ever made me; there's a lining that gives the cloak a sturdiness I can tell will keep me warm during the hours of Dark.

A Solguard sun is stitched in gold thread right over my heart. When the light streaming in through the window hits the threads, they glisten and shimmer, mimicking the flicker of actual sunlight.

"It's perfect," I tell Wokee. "Thank you."

"I figured you might want it before you go up against your father. For luck, you know?" He grins at me. "Not that you need luck, though. You're a Bisecter. How much luckier can a person get?"

That gets a laugh out of me.

Wokee only grumbles a little when I give him a long hug, and I marvel once again at how he's almost as tall as I am. He even has a few hairs growing on his chin, which Everlyn has been mercilessly teasing him about.

As soon as I pull on the cloak, I feel like myself in a way I haven't in months. It fits perfectly. When I look down, I can see the Solguard sun stitched onto the fabric.

Bisecter or not, I'll take all the luck I can get.

"Ooh, that cloak looks so good on you, Hemera!" Everlyn, who was coming down the stairs, swerves to examine the beautiful fabric.

Part of me feels guilty about wearing something new and beautiful, when everyone in the fortress has been making do with tattered cloaks for months. But if we survive this battle, there will be enough time and resources for everyone to have new clothes. And if we don't survive…. Well, at least I'll get to look good during my last few hours.

"Now, you look like the captain you are," Everlyn says, nodding in approval.

"I don't have an army anymore, so I can't be a captain," I remind her.

"Yes, you can," Wokee and Everlyn say at the same time.

Wokee comes closer, like he's about to tell me a secret. "With this cloak, your father will never be able to deny the truth."

"Oh? And what truth is that?" I ask, playing along.

Wokee gives me a sly grin. "That you're the *real* Captain Harkibel."

CHAPTER 38

Ry, who is dressed for battle, looks like she didn't take her own advice about getting some rest. Bluish-purple bruises hover beneath her eyes, and her hair is even wilder than usual. Still, she doesn't waste time with pleasantries before telling Wade and me that my father's army is an hour out.

The Halves and humans assemble themselves outside with an astonishing degree of professionalism. Everyone moves quickly and without any argument or fanfare.

They're not my soldiers, but I still feel a fierce sense of pride at the way everyone polishes their blades one last time as they prepare for an unwinnable battle. Even Tut, who in months past would have been trying to worm his way out of the fighting, is giving a pep talk to everyone within hearing. It's a good one, too.

I try to hold this moment in my mind so that, once I've defeated my father, I won't forget the real reason behind everything I've done.

I haven't been able to get Ekil's warning out of my mind. I don't want to become the person I was before…the one who was too full of rage and impatience to see reason when it was staring me in the face.

The nature of the blood bond is that the Zeroes are forced to give all of themselves to their master, but that doesn't mean I need to give myself to them in return. I don't want to forget why I'm doing what I'm doing, or who I'm trying to protect.

Just because I succumbed to the power of the bond before, it doesn't mean I have to do it again.

I look down at the Solguard tattoo marking my right hand and run my palm over the smooth material of my blue cloak. Both make me feel more grounded…more sure of myself.

I look to my side where Dayne, a silent and ever-present force, stands awaiting my orders. With a sudden fierceness that steals my breath away, I wish I could talk to him the way I used to. I know he'd say the exact right words to give me the courage I need to face my father. Now, all I feel is his simmering anger.

Outside the fortress, my eyes are immediately drawn to the gleam of weak sunlight off the Zeroes' scythes and armor. As they cross the open stretch of land between the mountains and the fortress, they spread out. It makes their already-formidable numbers even more intimidating. I can feel the other soldiers standing around me tense at the sight of so many Zeroes. I can sense the doubt and fear spreading through our company.

I look to Everlyn, who is waiting off to the side where I asked her to be. She gives me a terse nod, telling me she's ready to do as I've asked.

Good.

After the leaders have finished giving out orders and the last-minute preparations have been made, everyone goes quiet. The silence lets us hear the Zeroes' heavy metal boots stomping the ground in rhythmic, unhurried steps long before they reach us.

I can feel Dayne's impatience and bloodlust, and it's only making me more anxious to get this over with. I force myself to stay still, even though all I want to do is rush forward to face my father here and now. I scan the crowd of Zeroes, looking for him.

I'm not surprised when I find him in their center. He looks even more imposing because he's riding one of the reptors. My father doesn't wear armor. Instead, he wears a cloak that looks far warmer and better made than the threadbare ones covering my people. Everything about him exudes power and confidence.

When I look inside myself, I feel a whisper of his power, and I know it must be because of the blood we share. I remember the way he forced me to drain my blood into a glass jar so he could turn himself into a Bisecter. The thought heightens my need for revenge until it's barely containable.

When the Zeroes out in front are no more than two-hundred paces from the courtyard, I start to move. Dayne's strides are in sync with mine, even though I haven't spoken a word to him.

"Hemera?"

I hear Wade's voice, but I don't turn around.

"Hemera!" he calls again.

I break into a run. Dayne's footsteps pound the ground beside me. I get to the ruined stone wall and raise my arm. For a moment, nothing happens. Then, an explosion rocks the earth.

Right on time.

Earlier, Everlyn set her remaining explosives in the half-collapsed tunnels that run beneath the fortress. They were mostly filled in when the Duskers took apart my father's catacombs, but I knew there were still some openings in the ground beneath us. I told Everlyn to align her explosives so that a mile-long swath of ground between the Zeroes and our army would collapse into a giant chasm, preventing either from easily reaching the other.

Now, I stand in the direct path of my father and the Zeroes. Behind me, the ground begins to crumble.

CHAPTER 39

ust puffs up in great, billowing clouds as the ground trembles and slides down into the chasm that Everlyn's explosives have opened up. The hole is too deep for anyone to scale down, so the only way to come after me is by going around. The network of tunnels running beneath Tanguro is extensive, and Everlyn placed the explosives so that a long stretch of tunnels near the stone wall would collapse. It's far enough from the building that the foundations won't be in any danger.

A mile-wide detour would be virtually meaningless to the Zeroes, but it would take the army standing behind me at least twenty minutes to cover the distance. That will give me just enough time to do what I need to without having to worry about the Zeroes attacking the rest of my army. I'm betting my father won't part with his Zeroes to send them after my people until he and I have struck our bargain. By then, it will be too late for him.

I hear voices shouting my name behind me, but I keep all of my attention forward. Aside from Dayne, I'm alone. I'm cut off from the Banished and Halves. There's no one and nothing to protect me from my father's army.

But at least my friends won't be able to cross the chasm that now divides the two armies.

Thank you, Everlyn.

I curl my hand, reassuring myself the dagger I hid in my sleeve is fixed to my wrist in a place where it won't be seen but will be easily accessible. It's a trick Brice taught me years ago, and it's one that has saved my life more than once. Once I've confirmed the dagger is in place, I raise my hands in the air to show my father I'm holding no weapons. I silently order Dayne to do the same.

"I just want to talk," I call out when I'm close enough for Zeidan to hear.

I feel the whisper of my connection with the Zeroes growing stronger. They call to me, but I do my best to ignore the pull.

I imagine what it will feel like when I plunge the dagger into my father's heart and sever his blood bond with the Zeroes. I think about how it will feel when the Zeroes' power floods inside me once again. And then I imagine rejecting that power. I imagine commanding them to stay still while the Solguards go from one to the next and slit their throats.

Queasiness fills my insides.

The Zeroes all jerk to a halt at precisely the same moment, making it clear my father has uttered some silent command. My blood pounds faster.

"Father," I call.

My eyes catch movement in the sea of Zeroes. They hold their scythes loosely in their hands in a way that doesn't fool me—I know they could slice my head off my body in less than an instant. Still, I don't back away or flinch as they move out of the way so Zeidan can ride forward on his reptor.

I can feel Dayne's emotions tugging on our bond.

Attack. Kill, his silent voice urges.

Not yet, I think back to him.

I want to step back as the reptor comes close enough for me to see its slitted pupils, which hold a ravenous anticipation, but I stand my ground. I keep my hands raised in the air and try to display the appropriate amount of fear and anger on my face. Dayne stands beside me. Even though he's as still as stone, I can feel his hatred radiating off him at the sight of my father.

I remember when Dayne begged me to kill Zeidan, and how I hadn't done it because I'd been persuaded he had changed and really wanted to help us. I was so naïve...so delusional. I won't make that mistake again.

As the reptor continues its slow pacing through the crowd of Zeroes, I study my father.

I only saw him as a Bisecter once before, and it's still a shock to observe him in this new form. The man I knew as my father is gone. In his place is a black-eyed warrior.

He looks strong, healthy, and more powerful than ever. As I continue to study him, though, I realize his black eyes are different from those of his Zeroes and even from Dayne. I see now what the scouts had been talking about. The twisted sneer of his mouth and glint in his black eyes hint at violence and insanity.

My father has always been ruthless, calculating, and full of ambition. Madness was the last emotion I ever expected to sense from him. But I can see it in his expression as much as I can sense his instability through the blood bond that connects us.

Zeidan watches me from the back of his reptor. There's an air of victory surrounding him that makes a shudder go down my spine.

"Do you think a little earthquake will stop my army from swallowing yours whole?" my father asks when the reptor comes to a standstill only a few paces from Dayne and me.

Your army? Not for much longer, Father….

I lift my gaze above the level of the reptor's snout so I can look into my father's cruel eyes.

"I know nothing can stop your army." I pause, pretending to hesitate, like I'm wrestling with a decision. "But I needed time to talk to you before our armies clashed."

"And what is it you wish to say?"

His eyes dart to either side. He doesn't seem to be looking at anything in particular; he just seems impatient. That's something else that's new for my father. In the past, he's been content to bide his time for years while his careful plans were set into motion. Now, though, he seems barely able to suffer through the length of a conversation.

"I know there is no army that can stand up to your Zeroes," I say, emphasizing the point. There's nothing pretend about the bitterness that comes through my voice at this admission, or the acknowledgement that this army belongs to him. "That's why I've decided to take you up on your offer."

"My offer?" he asks, his gaze still darting around.

"You once said you wanted to rule the world by my side," I remind him, distracted by his fidgeting. "Now, I'm agreeing to do just that, so long as you promise to leave the people in this fortress alone and return the original one-hundred Zeroes to me."

I throw in that second part because it's what I would have asked for if I actually intended to negotiate with my father. Even though the only purpose of this fake deal is to get close enough to my father to kill him, it grates on me to have to pretend to pander to him. Every reminder that the Zeroes are his, rather than mine, makes the flame of my hatred burn a little hotter.

At this point in the conversation, I had expected Zeidan to discuss terms. He might insist on turning a portion of the fortress's inhabitants into Zeroes, or he might demand that I be his second-in-command rather than his equal. Those were the conditions I'd been expecting. But what comes out of his mouth next takes me aback.

"Ruling the world with you by my side was my original plan," he agrees. "For years, everything I did was to help you to realize your true strength and ensure that others would appreciate your magnificence. But all that has changed. Now, I find I hunger for…more."

The pale sunlight reflects in his eyes, and I see it again…that glint of madness.

All the words I'd planned to say slip from my mind at the sight of my father's expression. I grasp desperately for some way to regain control over this conversation.

"I thought you wanted to build a world in which I belonged…where I was worshipped rather than feared. Did you forget about that part of your plan, Father?"

"I may be your father, but there's only room in this world for one Captain Harkibel." He gives me a cruel smile.

My father jumps from the reptor's back and lands on his feet. Even in that one movement, his new strength is evident. He reaches his hand into his cloak pocket and produces a roll of script tree bark I instantly recognize.

It's my mother's letter. On the side facing me is her explanation and apology. On the side facing my father is the recipe of the steps she took to make me into a Bisecter. I never bothered to read that part of the letter. I had been too angry, and there'd been no point. Now, I wish I had, if for no other reason than the fact that it would put me on more even footing with my father.

It infuriates me that, in addition to everything else he's stolen from me, he's taken this last piece of my mother, too.

Zeidan dangles the letter between his thumb and forefinger. A breeze catches it, pulling it in my direction. My father gives me a taunting smile, and then he lets go of the letter.

I snatch it out of the air without taking a step. I know Zeidan expects me to tuck the letter into the pocket of my cloak where it will be safe. It's what I long to do.

Instead, I ball up the letter in my fist without taking my eyes off my father. The script tree bark is so old and brittle that pieces of it flake off and flutter to the ground. It's a physical ache to destroy this piece of my mother, but I don't hesitate.

"I think there are enough Bisecters in this world, don't you?" I ask.

"Hemera, what are you—"

I throw the balled-up letter at the reptor's snout. Just as I expected, the reptor's teeth flash, and the creature snaps the letter out of the air.

My father hisses in annoyance, but there is nothing he can do. My mother's letter is gone.

CHAPTER 40

Even though I know it was the right decision to destroy my mother's letter, its absence still leaves me shaken. I'm not exactly sure why I care so much that the letter is gone. Maybe it's because it was a piece of my mother, and no matter what she did to me, anything that was once hers is precious to me. Or maybe it's the fact that, without that letter, my father is the only person alive who knows the secret of creating a Bisecter.

In spite of my reservations, I know I made the right choice. Now, no one else will be able to mutilate human beings in their own quest for power.

My father draws the sword at his hip and steps forward. I'm dimly aware of the sounds of shouting from the other side of the crater Everlyn's explosives created, but I block out the noise. I don't so much as glance back. I keep all of my attention fixed on my father.

The prickling sense of unease that's been steadily growing within me is now more of a roar.

Run away, my instincts warn.

Fight, Dayne silently commands me.

My father looks back at the army of Zeroes awaiting his command. Something like restlessness flashes across his face. I see the emotion again in the way he shifts on his feet. It's the opposite of the way my father used to be.

I remember that feeling of restless energy the Zeroes gave me. I had been almost desperate for a fight or some way to make use of the strength bubbling in my veins. I felt like a pot constantly about to boil over.

There was no end to my ambition…my desire for more…when I had the power of the Zeroes flowing through me.

"Come on, Daughter," my father says, his black eyes watching the emotions play out over my face. "I know what you really want."

He flicks his sword, like he's inviting me to come closer.

"You want to take my Zeroes for yourself, don't you?"

I nod. It's mostly a lie, but not entirely. A part of me does still hunger for that connection…that raw power. Looking at my father, I can see what would happen to me if I succumbed to that desire.

"Come and get them, then." My father smiles. "If you can."

I don't step forward, but it isn't fear of my father's strength that keeps me in place. It's the sight of him, bouncing on his feet and twitching as he waits for me to lunge at me.

Instead of moving closer to their master to defend him, the Zeroes are making a wide ring around us. It seems to be taking all of my father's concentration to control his whole army. Some of the Zeroes wander aimlessly until he gets them back under his control. Once the Zeroes stop moving, I realize what my father is doing. He doesn't just want me dead. He wants to destroy me alone and single-handedly, to prove to everyone watching that he is superior.

It's a risk I know he never would have taken before he became a Bisecter. He would have been more concerned with the results than the means, and he especially wouldn't have cared what others thought about him. It's not like the Zeroes can choose not to follow him if they think he's less strong.

My father's arrogance is unfamiliar. It might make him easier to beat. Instead of having to fight off all the Zeroes, I'll only need to defeat him.

Still, I hesitate. If I kill my father and take back the Zeroes, will I be strong enough to resist the intoxicating feeling of the blood bond?

The power was overwhelming when I was creating one Zero at a time. When three-hundred of them suddenly come under my control, what will happen to me?

Ekil was right. I might not be strong enough to fend off the Zeroes' influence.

But what can I do? My only choices are to either kill my father and reclaim the Zeroes, or let him continue his reign of terror.

The Zeroes seem as antsy as my father, and he needs to keep pacing around the circle to push them back into position.

"Hemera," Dayne says.

I spin around to face him. The way he just said my name, it almost sounded like the way his voice had been before he was changed. It might be my imagination, but I could have sworn there was emotion in the way he spoke my name. As his gaze meets mine, I see that same hint of emotion in his black eyes, which have been devoid of feeling since I first changed him.

Another one of the Zeroes falls out of line. When my father goes to wrangle it back into position, I'm able to turn all of my attention on Dayne.

"I was never meant to be this way," Dayne tells me. "None of us were."

His voice is deeper and harsher than it was when he was a human, but I know now the emotion I'm seeing and hearing isn't a figment of my imagination. I feel it through our bond, and that's how I understand what he's feeling. It's desperation.

"You have to let me go."

It takes me several seconds to process what Dayne is telling me. I look over at where my father is shoving the Zeroes back into place. As Dayne continues to give me that meaningful look, a memory nudges against our bond in such a way that I know he has sent it to me. It was the moment I looked at the Zero clutching its leg, and I realized its injury was identical to mine.

I think about the bond that all of us—Zeroes and Bisecters—share. And I understand what Dayne is asking me to do.

My throat goes dry. I'm shaking my head before I can even process the full extent of the sacrifice Dayne's asking me to make.

Dayne nods his head at me. I feel it again, that pulse of desperation.

"Sacrifice." He whispers the word, and it immediately makes me think of Aunt Jadem.

What had she once told me?

There's nothing more powerful than a willing sacrifice.

But is this a sacrifice I'm willing to make?

I don't even know if it would work. If I died, would that put an end to my father and the Zeroes, too?

I can feel the spider web-thin connection to my father and each of the Zeroes through the blood we share. If what happened to that Zero's leg is any indication, it should be possible. But what if I'm wrong? I'd sacrifice myself for nothing, and then everyone at the fortress would be vulnerable to my father and the Zeroes. There'd be no one with the strength to defend them.

But if I don't do this, I'm condemning myself to becoming just like my father.

There's something else holding me back. It isn't just a matter of my life. That would be one thing, since I'm the reason the Zeroes exist and why my father has become a Bisecter. If the price for reversing that damage was only my life, then it's one I would pay. But my brother...he's already sacrificed so much because of my mistakes.

If I die, so will he.

I meet my brother's eyes. That emotion I saw before is still there. His gaze is softer than it has been every other time we've looked at each other.

It makes hope and despair pulse through me.

As I look at him, trying to decide what to do, Dayne does something else he hasn't done in the six months he's been a Zero. He smiles at me.

It isn't the warm smile he used to give me when he still had our mother's eyes and his own personality, but it isn't cruel and merciless, either. It makes me think he understands my dilemma, even though the emotions churning through my gut aren't ones he should be able to feel anymore.

"Do it," he says in his deep, rasping voice. He glances at my father, whose attention is still on his Zeroes. "Save everyone."

I push down the surge of panic that comes from some deep part of me, the part that hollers for me to live...to survive...no matter what.

"If I do this," I say, my voice barely a whisper, "then you'll die, too."

Dayne holds out to his hand to me—another first. I take it, feeling the unfamiliar strength and size of his rough palm curl around my own.

"Should have died before," he says.

I know he's referencing the Battle of the Iron Gate, after he'd been stabbed. I was begging my father to do something. Everyone else was telling me to let Dayne go. I couldn't then, and I can't now.

"No," I whisper.

"Some fates worse than death." Dayne's black eyes pierce mine.

Tears burn my throat and stream down my cheeks, but I can't make them stop.

Dayne reaches up a finger and touches my tears, and I can sense something in the bond…curiosity, maybe.

"Was meant to die," Dayne says, studying the droplet hovering on his fingertip. "Let me."

I shake my head. He releases my hand from his and steps away from me.

I look up through blurred vision to see my father stalking forward.

"Time to finish this, Hemera," he says. "Time to determine who the one and only Captain Harkibel will be."

CHAPTER 41

My father's black eyes glitter with murder and madness.

Not a good combination, I think, as I let out a shaky breath and pull the dagger from my sleeve. There's no point in hiding my weapon now.

My father creeps forward. His body is hunched, his muscles tensed and ready to spring. I keep my distance, watching him as my mind spins in a desperate whirl of indecision.

"Bringing a knife to a sword fight, Hemera?" he tsks. "I would have thought the daughter of Captain Harkibel would know better."

When I don't say anything, he shrugs and tosses his blade onto the ground. He unsheathes a dagger from his belt.

"No matter." He crouches into a fighting stance. "I will destroy you in front of all of these witnesses and solidify my bond with the Zeroes." He laughs, and even the sound of it is wrong and unfamiliar. "I don't expect your brother, even as a Zero, will pose any more threat to me than he did as a human." My father's black eyes flick to Dayne with disinterest. "He's always been weak."

Dayne snarls in response and he tries to lunge, but my earlier command for him to stay still keeps him in place.

I realize the whisper of the Zeroes inside me has grown louder now that I'm so close to them. I can feel their strength and the way our connection calls to me. My father must also be able to sense that at least a small part of his army is distracted by my presence. I can see the anger written plainly on his face, and I know he's as eager to snuff out my connection with the Zeroes as I am to destroy his.

I can feel the threads of every one of the Zeroes deep inside me, and that's when I know without a shadow of a doubt…. We're all bound together, and the essence tying us together is my blood. I am the anchor for all of their abilities. If I die, my father and the rest of the Zeroes will be lost with me. The fortress and all its inhabitants will be safe.

And I'll be dead.

My palms are cold and sweaty, making it almost impossible for me to grip the dagger in my hand.

If I die, I'll never hear Wokee laugh again. I'll never sit by a fire and trade stories about Aunt Jadem with Ry and the other Solguards. I'll never feel Wade's lips on mine.

My thoughts turn to Camike with her growing belly. I remember when she told me I wouldn't be whole until the Zeroes were gone. I remember her saying that not all people are meant to be leaders.

My father brings the blade of his dagger down with so much speed I barely manage to throw myself out of the way. He laughs. It's a high-pitched, maniacal sound that makes the hairs on my arms stand up.

Fight back, my instincts scream. *Win.*

I think about the hope and despair in the eyes of the Solguards. I think about the betrayal in Ekil's gaze when I banished the Halves. I remember Dayne begging me to kill him as I dripped my brown blood into his veins.

The Zeroes are mine. I could have them back….

The Zeroes are not my people. Dayne, Wokee, Wade, and everyone standing on the other side of the chasm are my people. And with this one act, I'll finally be the leader my people need…the leader they deserve.

I spare Dayne another glance as my father prowls closer, preparing to strike again. At the look I see in my brother's eyes, I know what I'm going to do.

There's nothing more powerful than a willing sacrifice.

I raise my knife and go to meet my father.

"I can feel my power growing as you weaken," my father says, meeting me step-for-step.

"Are you forgetting something?" I ask. My voice trembles, but my hands are steady.

My father's next strike comes fast and hard, but I'm ready. I raise my own dagger to block it.

"What's that?" he asks, already preparing for his next slice of the blade.

He grabs hold of my cloak and yanks me to him. His hand tangles in the delicate chain around my throat—the one that holds my mother's key. I feel the necklace's clasp break under the pressure.

"My blood runs through your veins, and yours runs through mine," I say. "We're connected, just like the Zeroes are connected to both of us."

My father's dagger is already in motion. I see his look of surprise, but he put too much momentum behind his strike to stop it.

Instead of bringing my blade up to defend myself or ducking out of the way, I let the dagger come.

It's like everything has slowed. My gaze drops down, to the tiny silver key that is falling to the ground. I hear the whoosh of the blade. I feel it pierce the cloth of my cloak, and then my shirt. I feel the breath leave my body as the dagger cuts into my flesh.

My father's aim was true. The blade enters my heart.

I hear a scream. It's the scream of someone who is dying, and even as my world fades, I know the sound came from my father.

CHAPTER 42

I'm on the ground with my father's knife in my chest, but I'm not dead...not yet.

My breathing is shallow and every inhalation feels like a thousand needles in my chest. But my eyes still work, and I manage to keep them open long enough to see the Zeroes collapse on the ground. Brown blood leaks from their hearts in an injury identical to my own.

It worked.

Exhaustion and pain threaten to push out every other thought.

My brother, one hand pressed against his own gaping wound, crawls to where my father is doubled over and clutching his chest. I don't have the energy to wonder at how he's still moving.

I feel the slick heat of blood across my chest as I watch Dayne bend and pick up the blade my father discarded. My vision blurs, but I force my eyes to remain open as Dayne raises the dagger.

He slices the blade across my father's throat.

I see the spray of blood. I hear the gurgle of despair. Then, my father crumples. The barely-there tether inside me that linked us through blood wisps away.

Dayne hovers over my father's body for several more seconds, grasping the bloody knife. Then, slowly and painfully, he crawls back to me.

"Hemera," he pants, one hand still hovering over the bloody wound on his chest.

I try to speak, but no words will come. I furiously blink away the darkness, desperate to speak to my brother with my eyes even if I can't make the words come from my mouth.

It's okay, I want to tell him. *You were right about everything. Forgive me.*

All these thoughts flee from my mind when Dayne leans over me, and I look up through blurry vision into his eyes. They're no longer the black I've never quite gotten used to. They're blue.

With that last thought, I succumb to the darkness and know nothing more.

CHAPTER 43

More pressure on the wound," a voice commands. It's soft and feminine and accented, like the language isn't wholly familiar to her.

Camike.

"She should be healing. Why isn't she healing?" This voice is masculine and full of panic, and I'd know it even if I couldn't make sense of anything else.

Wade.

"There are all those others," Camike says.

"I don't give a damn about the others," Wade snarls. "Fix her!"

I crack open my eyes, surprised to discover they still work. Part of me expects to find myself inside a dream. Or encased in a spirit hovering over my abandoned body.

"Mer?" Ry's pale, tear-stained face wavers in and out.

My lids are too heavy, and they fall shut again. I sink back into dark oblivion.

* * *

Something has settled on my chest, making it difficult to breathe. It hurts. It's worse than any pain I've ever known. There were times before when I thought I was close to death. I realize now those were scratches compared to this.

I open my eyes, cringing as the flood of rose-gold light sends pain shooting through my skull. The sunlight streaming in through the building's windows is too bright. It makes everything somehow more agonizing.

"Hemera!" Wade's face is slightly blurred as he hovers over me, but not so much that I don't see the shock on his face.

I must look as bad as I feel, I think without much emotion.

I'm tired and my chest hurts, and I just want to close my eyes and succumb to the insistent pull of quiet nothingness.

But some primal, stubborn part of me knows that if I let the darkness reclaim me, I might never come out of its depths again. I blink a few times, forcing Wade's face to come into focus.

He's staring at me like I'm a ghost. If it wasn't for the pain, I would think I was one.

Wade's eyes are wide and filled with emotions I can't begin to decipher. My mouth forms the shape of his name, even though no sound escapes me.

"Hemera, your eyes—" Wade says, and then he breaks off like he doesn't know how to finish the thought.

It's not my eyes I'm concerned about. Whatever has happened to them, it can't be too horrible if I can still see out of them. It's the wound on my chest Wade should be worrying about. It feels like someone lit a fire inside me and then sat on top of me for good measure.

Wade shakes his head, like he can't believe what he's seeing. When he speaks, the words are so unexpected I don't at first comprehend their meaning.

"Hemera, your eyes are blue."

✳ ✳ ✳

When I open my eyes again, I can tell time has passed. The rose-gold light from the Jadem tree still floods the room, but the sky outside the building's top windows is dark.

The pain in my chest is still there, but it's more bearable than it was before. I try to sit up, but several pairs of hands push me back down.

"What's going on?" I croak, amazed to find my voice works.

I turn my head, ignoring the way it somehow makes the fiery pain in my chest spread, and take in the people surrounding me.

There's Wade, Ry, Wokee, Everlyn, and Ekil. Jarosh and Camike are here, too. Behind them stand Valior and Tut. Even Vlaz is pacing and whining behind them, trying to nose his way into the crowd.

"I'm dying," I say.

It's the only explanation for why everyone has been standing around and watching me sleep.

Someone—Ry, maybe—chokes on a sob.

"You're not dying, little sis."

My eyes find my brother. He looks different, and it takes my sluggish brain a few seconds to realize why. I squint at his face. Sure enough, his blue eyes weren't some trick of my imagination. They're there, just like I remember them…just like I remember our mother's. And it's not just the color that's right. Dayne's eyes are full of emotion in a way they never were when he was a Zero.

His hair is still thinner and grayer than it was before his transformation, but his inhuman height and muscles have shrunken down. He doesn't look weak. Instead, he looks like himself…like the brother I remember.

"You're alive," I manage, feeling those words burst into meaning inside my aching chest.

Dayne chuckles and wipes a tear from his eye. "I am indeed. It seems your stubbornness has won the day once again." He strokes a gentle hand over my hair. "You did good, little sis."

"I don't understand." I struggle into a sitting position, waving away all the hands that try to push me back down.

The hazy darkness lifts a little more, and I'm assaulted by memories of what happened in the minutes before I stopped remembering anything at all.

My father brought his army of Zeroes to Tanguro. He wanted to kill me so he would be the most powerful force in all the lands. I chose to let my father kill me so the threat to my people would be destroyed. I died so my friends could live.

Except…I'm not dead. Neither is Dayne. I remember watching as he cut my father's throat.

What happened to the Zeroes?

When I listen for the whisper of my bond with them, I feel nothing except the roaring pain inside me.

I look down and see that my chest is covered with expertly-wound bandages. *Camike's work, no doubt.*

I look at Wade. "Did you say my eyes are blue?"

Everyone around me nods their heads in unison.

"You also seem to have lost your ability to rapidly heal," Dayne says. "I think—" His words cut off, and he looks troubled.

"You think?" I prompt.

"I think that after what you did…after what you sacrificed for us…you lost the non-human part of yourself."

"What?" My already-wounded heart gives a painful stutter.

"Mer." Dayne covers my hand with his own. "You aren't a Bisecter anymore."

CHAPTER 44

My mind goes fuzzy. I have to focus on breathing through the pain in my chest before I slide back into the darkness.

"I think maybe we should back up a little," Ry suggests. "She might not remember or have seen everything that happened."

"I think that's a good idea." My voice comes out rough and strange to my own ears.

"Well, apparently you and Everlyn arranged for her to blow up the ground between our two armies," Wade says. He glances at Everlyn, who ducks her head. Her long hair hangs around her face and hides her expression.

"We couldn't get to you." Wade's face blanches, and I get a glimpse at how it must have affected him in the moments after he understood what I had done, and he realized that Dayne and I were beyond his help.

"I'm sorry," I say, reaching out for his hand. My grip is pathetically weak.

"It's going to take a lot more than an apology for me to get past what you did, but we can talk about that later." Wade's tone is filled with suppressed anger, but he raises my hand to his lips with infinite tenderness.

Ry clears her throat. "*Anyway*, there you were, facing off against your father. We all thought you were going to try to kill him, but then you just dropped your knife and let him stab you. We all thought you were dead." Her voice breaks on the word.

Everyone goes silent.

"Why didn't you fight the Halve killer?" Ekil asks.

I look into his black eyes. For the first time in months, his gaze isn't filled with disappointment and betrayal.

"Because I realized all of you were right, and that as long as the Zeroes existed, I wouldn't be free." I take a few shallow gasps, fighting against the screaming ache in my chest. "I realized that if I took control over them again, I would become a slave to the bond between us."

I don't know if my words make sense, but Ekil nods his head in understanding.

Camike reaches out and touches my cheek with her fingertips. Then, she bows her head to me in a show of respect and deep thanks.

"I didn't think you'd be able to resist the temptation of getting your Zeroes back," Jarosh says, switching to the human language. "I was wrong about you."

"I almost didn't resist," I tell him honestly.

"What changed your mind?" he asks.

I crack a small smile. "The Halves and Solguards. My mother and Aunt Jadem." I look around at my friends. "All of you."

Camike's eyes water in understanding.

"That was so brave of you, Mer," Wokee says, his big eyes even wider with all of the emotions he's trying to hide. "I can't believe you did that, even though I'm really mad at you. If I'd let someone stab me to save everyone else, you would've been furious!"

There are a few chuckles at that. Brogut puts one of his enormous hands on Wokee's shoulder. Strangely enough, Wokee seems familiar with the gesture and to be comforted by it. Everlyn takes Wokee's hand and squeezes. For once, Wokee doesn't act disgusted or try to pull away.

"The Halves thank you for what you have done," Ekil says. "You have regained my trust."

"And mine," Jarosh says.

"Mine too."

This reply comes from Brogut. His gravelly voice is unusually subdued, and I notice he isn't carrying his tree trunk spear.

"Thank you," I tell them, unable to express how much their renewed faith means to me.

"You did well, young lady," Valior says, giving me his missing-toothed smile. "Your aunt would have been very proud of you."

"She always said you'd save everyone," Morey chimes in, stepping out from behind Valior's shadow. "An' here I was thinkin' she was jus' braggin' about her niece."

I realize all of the anger I felt toward my aunt is gone now.

I understand how she got to the point where she was willing to make any sacrifice to bring about an end she was desperate to achieve. It was the same with my mother, and with me.

All three of us made a choice that we thought would help the ones we loved, and after we realized our error, we tried to undo the damage we'd done. Both my mother and my aunt paid the price with their lives. I had been willing to sacrifice my own life. But I didn't die.

I'm still here.

And yet, for the first time, it occurs to me that I don't feel quite like myself. I had been so focused on the pain in my chest I didn't realize it before, but now that I'm paying attention, I feel…lighter.

That's when I understand.

My bond with the Zeroes, as frail and whisper-thin as it has been these last few months, is gone.

"How am I still alive?" I ask.

Fast healer or not, a blade through my heart should have killed me.

"I believe it was your connection with your brother that brought life back into you," Camike says. "You share blood, both from birth and the nature of his connection with you as a Zero."

I look at Dayne.

"We both lost the part of ourselves that was inhuman." Dayne's blue eyes gleam with unspent emotion.

I shake my head, trying to make sense of what's happened to me—of what I've become.

My eyes are blue. I've lost my connection to the Zeroes. I'm no longer a Bisecter.

The changes are almost too big…too impossible…to process.

My whole life, I've wanted nothing more than to be normal. I hated my black eyes and everything that came with them. I did everything I could to convince myself and everyone else that I wasn't so different. I wanted nothing more than to be just like everyone else.

Now, it seems, my wish has come true.

The terrible irony is that now that I'm ordinary, I want to go back to the way I was.

I can't imagine looking into my reflection and seeing blue eyes instead of black. I can't imagine only being able to run as fast as any other human, or to be unable to lift something that is several times my own weight. Even though high day doesn't exist anymore, I still grieve for those hours when I was on the Outside alone…when I was the only creature strong enough to withstand the power of the sun's rays.

With one slash of my father's dagger, all of that is gone.

My eyes burn, and I have to blink several times to keep the tears at bay.

I remember making the decision to destroy my mother's letter so no one else would be able to use that knowledge again. I remember the way the reptor snapped its jaws and the page—and all it contained—disappeared forever.

"There will never be another Bisecter," I say.

It shouldn't make me so sad to say those words, and yet, the pain of them leaves me gasping for air. All of the things that made me *me* are gone. And they're not just gone from me, either.

How am I supposed to mourn something that has been stricken from this world and will never exist again?

Dayne squeezes one of my hands. Wade holds the other.

No one says anything. I guess there is nothing they could say—nothing that could make the loss I've suffered easier to bear.

"You're the same person you always were," Wade says in a low voice, understanding what I'm thinking even though I haven't spoken a word.

I nod, but I'm not sure I believe him.

His lips quirk, reminding me of the good-humored boy I met so long ago in Solis. "Although I'm going to have to get used to looking into blue eyes instead of black."

"I wouldn't be trying to stare too lovingly into her eyes while he's around," Ry says, inclining her head at Dayne. "He might not be a Zero anymore, but he could probably still kick your ass."

"And don't you forget it," Dayne tells Wade, who gives my brother an innocent grin in response.

It's almost like old times. Except everything's changed.

"What about the Zeroes?" I ask, still trying to wrap my mind around the fact that I'm alive instead of buried under several feet of earth. "What happened to them?"

Dayne's expression hardens, and I prepare myself to hear that they're all dead. But he surprises me.

"They are human once again. When your heart stopped and Zeidan was killed, the bond broke. They were no longer affected by either of your injuries."

That sounds like something Dayne should be happy about, but I can tell from the grim expressions of everyone around me that there's another part to the story I haven't heard yet.

"Unlike me, they also had your father's blood inside them," Dayne continues. "Severing that bond impacted them…deeply."

That didn't sound good.

"What does that mean?" I prompt.

"They haven't come back to themselves the way I did." Dayne sighs. "They're confused and don't remember anything that happened during the time when they were Zeroes. They're also struggling because they crave the severed bond, except they don't understand what it is they've lost."

Guilt at what I did to Dayne…at what I did to all of them…threatens to crush me.

"Don't." Ry gives me a stern look. "Whatever mistakes you might have made, you've more than made up for them. Don't beat yourself up over what's done."

"What's going to happen to them?" I ask, imagining three-hundred people feeling bereft and cut off from their lifeline…a lifeline that also enslaved them.

"Given my unique situation," Dayne frowns, "I believe I'm in a position to help them. I intend to use all of my skills as a healer and our shared experience to bring them back to themselves. I believe those who have the will for it will be able to recover in time."

"This must be a lot to take in," Camike says, giving me a sympathetic look.

"The important thing is that you saved hundreds of lives today," Valior reminds me.

"You sacrificed yourself for all of us," Jarosh says. His arms are around Camike, but he's looking at me with a fierce pride.

"You did it, Mer," Wokee says. "You saved everyone."

"You are the true Captain Harkibel." Valior lifts his empty flask to me in a toast.

"No." I shake my head. "I gave up the right to that title when I gave up the right to reclaiming the Zeroes. Besides," I take a deep breath. "I don't want to be the leader of an army anymore."

"What do you want?" Tut asks, his voice filled with genuine curiosity.

I shrug. "Just to be me, I guess. Just Hemera."

I don't know if I believe my own words, and I'm not sure I know how to be *just Hemera*. But I know that in time, I'll figure it out. I know if I repeat the words enough, I'll start to believe them. More importantly, I know they're the right words.

I didn't die the way I expected to, but I'm not the same person I was, either.

"It never occurred to him that you would sacrifice yourself," Valior says.

I laugh a little at that. "It almost didn't even occur to me."

Valior nods. "And that is the difference between you and your father. He assumed you would fight him for the right to the Zeroes until the bitter end, since his thirst for power overshadowed his ability to see anything else. That was his greatest flaw."

The others murmur in agreement.

"We should let you get some rest," Tut says, his voice uncharacteristically subdued. "You did get stabbed in the chest, after all."

I nod, even though sleep is the last thing I want right now. I'm still weak enough that I'm afraid of letting myself slip back into that dark place. I'm afraid if I close my eyes, I'll never open them again.

As painful as it will be to come to terms with all I've lost, I don't want to die. My life was the price I'd been willing to pay to atone for my mistakes and protect everyone I care about. Even at the end, though, I craved life. Now that I have it back, I'm not giving it up.

"Wade! Ry!" a scout races into the building, shoving Halves and Banished out of the way in his frantic dash for the Solguard leaders.

All I can think is *what now?* before my eyelids start to droop closed against my will.

"What's happened?" Wade asks, letting go of my hand so he can get to his feet.

"The Duskers." The scout sucks in a ragged breath. "They're here."

CHAPTER 45

Ignoring Camike and the other leaders' protests, I get to my feet. The room sways and I barely manage to keep from heaving, but I somehow stay vertical.

Someone wraps a cloak around me, since I'm not wearing anything on my top half except for the bandages. My blue cloak is gone, presumably because it was sliced through and then soaked in blood.

Slowly, painfully, I take a step. And then another. Without a word, Wokee slips his shoulder underneath one of my arms to help support my weight. Everlyn wraps a skinny arm around my waist on my other side, even though she's not quite tall enough to bear my weight the way Wokee is. And that's how I make it outside the building, with Wokee and Everlyn on either side of me, keeping me from falling.

When I see what's going on outside, I force myself to stand without Wokee and Everlyn's help.

"Go back inside," I tell them. "Tell the other Banished leaders to get their people out here. And then barricade yourselves inside the building."

They both stare at the mass of troops crossing the open plain and heading straight for our fortress. Without a word of protest, they do as I say.

I turn all of my attention on the Duskers. It looks like the whole of Malarusk has emptied out and is heading straight for us. I can see the crossbows in their hands and the swords sheathed at their hips. I don't have enough energy to feel angry or scared. I'm just tired…tired of all of the fighting and pain and death. All I want to do is curl up and wait for all of it to be over, come what may.

I take one hobbling step after another until I'm standing between Wade and Ry. We're all quiet as we watch the Duskers' disciplined columns approach the fortress.

"Maybe Dellin's with them, and they aren't here to fight us," I say.

The words sound as weak as the sentiment feels.

"Yeah," Ry scoffs. "And maybe the Halves and Banished will stop hating each other, and we'll all live happily ever after."

"It could happen," Wade says, his mouth twisting into a humorless smirk.

I watch the oncoming army without the slightest hint of fear. Maybe it's the fact that I faced down an army of reptors and Zeroes, or that I bested my father. Maybe it's the fact that I faced death, and I'm still standing on my own two feet. Whatever the case, I don't feel hopeless or afraid.

I just feel drained.

I hear the clanking of armor and weapons as the Halves and Banished assemble behind us. There are gasps and exclamations as they catch sight of the Dusker army.

There were hundreds of Zeroes, but there are thousands of Duskers. Their gray cloaks stand out stark against the vibrant colors of Tanguro, which are just starting to reemerge after so many months of Darkness.

The Jadem tree saplings Wokee and the Halves planted all around the Wild Lands are growing at a fast pace. Even though it's only a few hours before Dark, a pale orange glow warms the horizon.

If the Duskers kill us, they'll destroy the Jadem trees, and it'll be like we were never here. The Darkness will spread with no one to stop it.

The thought shouldn't concern me since I'd be dead, but still, it just seems like a sickening waste.

"Hold your fire," Ry commands the archers who have lined up on either side of us.

Even though the Duskers are in range, Ry doesn't give the order to shoot. I wonder if she's scanning the sea of gray cloaks for Dellin the way I am. I wonder if she's holding out hope that this confrontation won't end in bloodshed.

Out of the corner of my eye, I catch sight of Dayne coming to join our small group. It's a startling revelation that I hadn't felt his presence before I saw him. I had gotten so used to feeling him as a part of myself, much the same way someone would be aware of their own arm or leg. Now, that place where our connection used to sit nestled inside me is gone.

I know I have no right to grieve for that bond. After all, the bond was responsible for stealing away Dayne's free will. But there was something familiar and comforting about the connection that I'll never have again.

It's a loss no one else can understand, and it's not one I could ever talk about, anyway.

Dayne hands me my sling, which he somehow miraculously recovered after the fight with my father. I bend to the ground and pick up a stone. Even that small movement takes every ounce of strength I possess. I'm breathless when I straighten back up, and stars dance in my vision from the pain in my chest.

Will this weakness ever go away? I wonder. Or is this just what life will be like now that I'm not a Bisecter?

Now that I'm ordinary.

The Duskers stop moving in unison. Their crossbow bolts could reach us at this distance, but none of them raise their weapons. Instead, a single figure continues forward.

The person is wearing a gray cloak and is indistinguishable from the other Duskers, except for the fact that she isn't taking deliberate, controlled steps like any normal Dusker. She's running.

The white-blonde hair streaming out behind her and Ry's intake of breath tells me it's Dellin long before she's close enough for me to see her face. Ry goes forward to meet her.

"Ry," Wade says, but she pulls her arm free when he tries to stop her.

"Don't do anything until I get back," she orders as she breaks into a jog.

Wade, Dayne, and I exchange a look. And then we follow her. We stay a little behind, but I keep a stone in the pouch of my sling just in case.

Dellin isn't bound to the Duskers the way my father and I were to the Zeroes, but I know firsthand the way that being in charge of a powerful army can change a person. In spite of everything Dellin did for me at the

Battle of the Iron Gate, I don't know her well enough to guess at how so much power might have changed her. Besides, I can only imagine what kinds of compromises she must have needed to make to get the Duskers to agree to follow her.

I don't know if the person in the gray cloak and crown heading toward us is the same girl who told Ry she loved her.

I don't think Dellin would ever hurt Ry intentionally, but I also know what the Duskers are like. Only a few days have passed since Dellin became the Dusker Supreme, and yet, a lot has happened in that short time. The sun has come out in Tanguro—for a few hours of the day, at least. The Zeroes transformed back into the humans they once were. And the only two Bisecters in the world ceased to exist.

Another sharp jab of pain goes through me, and I have to force myself to keep my attention on what's happening right in front of me.

"We received word the Zeroes were coming to attack," Dellin calls as soon as she's near enough for us to make out her words. "We came as fast as we could."

"We're okay," Ry says, her mouth twitching into the beginnings of a hopeful smile. "Mer saved us."

"So, the Zeroes aren't a threat anymore?" Dellin glances around uncertainly, like she expects the Zeroes to appear and start attacking.

"We can tell you the whole story later, but no, they aren't a threat." Ry is bouncing on the balls of her feet, looking both anxious and hopeful at the same time.

"Oh, well in that case, I do have another reason for being here," Dellin says, returning Ry's smile.

She whispers something to Ry. Then, she strides over to where Dayne, Wade, and I are standing.

Dellin pushes back her hood. With the weak sunlight behind her, her Dusker-pale skin looks almost translucent. She clears her throat.

"Wade, I would like to suggest a truce."

"A truce?" Wade echoes, looking a little puzzled and a lot like he suspects he's walking into a trap.

"Yes." Dellin holds out a scroll of script tree bark. "As the Dusker Supreme, I would like to make a peace agreement with the Solguards, and if Ekil and the other leaders are willing, with the Halves and Banished, as well."

Still eyeing Dellin with suspicion, Wade takes the scroll. Instead of the tight, condensed writing I expect to be covering the page, there are only a few short, concise sentences. There are no special terms…no extraneous agreements. There's only simple language detailing that the Duskers will not instigate any confrontations with the Solguards under any circumstances. And in return, the Solguards will agree to the same.

In the space at the bottom, Dellin's signature is already written out in blood, which is the indication of an unbreakable oath.

"This contract details the agreement that there will be no more fighting between our people," Dellin says while Wade re-reads those few sentences for what must be the tenth time at this point.

"Why?" Wade asks, his voice husky. He looks up from the scroll and studies Dellin. "You could rid yourself of all of us within a few hours, and then all of this would be yours."

"I don't want what's yours," Dellin says, her gaze sliding to Ry. "I want what should have been achieved many generations ago—peace for my people."

When Wade still doesn't move to do anything with the scroll, Dellin says, "I know the Duskers have a great deal of making up to do before we can earn your trust and goodwill, but it's my hope that this contract will be the first step in that direction."

Wade is still staring at the words on the script tree bark, seeming unable to move or say a word.

What are you waiting for? I want to yell at him. *Sign the damn thing before she changes her mind!*

Since Wade's silence persists, Dellin continues, "I know the animosity between our people goes back farther than any of us have been alive, but I hope that maybe someday, there will be a reason for our people to be something more to each other than non-enemies." Her gaze shifts to Ry again, and there's no mistaking the hope in her voice.

I feel like an intruder as I glimpse their intense and silent exchange, and I look away.

"I support this agreement," Wade says, finally looking up from the contract. "But I'm not going to sign it."

All our eyes turn on him in that instant. I'm stunned. Dellin is offering us a priceless gift, and Wade is turning it down?

"Wade," I begin, at the same time that Ry's cheeks redden in fury. She opens her mouth, but Wade puts out a hand to stop both of us.

"I'm not going to sign the agreement because I don't think I'm the right person to lead the Solguards anymore." He turns to me. "What you did with the Zeroes has given me the courage to make a decision I should have made months ago."

I don't know what to say. I stand there, dumbfounded, as Wade turns his attention on Ry.

"Ry, you have always been the leader the Solguards deserve. I don't know why I didn't see it sooner. You're a natural leader, you've got good instincts, and you can separate your emotions from the tough decisions in a way I'll never be able to. If you'll accept it, I want to officially name you as the new Solguard leader."

Ry lets out a shuddering breath. "Is this your way of getting out of all those boring meetings with the other leaders?" she asks, laughing a little.

Wade smiles at her. "My cover is blown."

She nods, her red curls bobbing. "I want this," she whispers.

"I know," Wade replies. "I'm only sorry I didn't give it to you sooner."

Ry throws her arms around Wade. He stumbles back a step and winces at the pressure on his ribs, but he laughs as he wraps his arms around her and hugs her back.

Once they've separated, Ry takes the knife Dellin holds out to her. She pricks her finger, waits for her red blood to bead up, and then presses it to the contract.

I hold my breath as she completes her signature. Once it's done, I look down at the two names beside each other.

"Do you think Ekil and the Banished leaders will sign it, too?" Dellin asks.

"I'm sure they will," I say, speaking for them. "It's in everyone's best interest, and I think we're all sick of fighting. It will be nice not to have enemies on all sides for once."

"There is a great deal of bad blood between the Solguards and Duskers," Dayne says to Dellin. "And while I have no doubt your intentions are as pure as they seem, there are many now under your rule who are used to a different sort of leadership. It will take time and effort to change their way of thinking."

"There might be a way to speed along that process," Ry says, her lips quirking into a grin.

Ry steps away from our little group and closer to Dellin. She takes Dellin's hand in hers, and then tugs the other girl over to the crumbled remains of the stone wall. Ry climbs up onto a section that wasn't destroyed by the reptors. There seems to be some kind of short argument between them, and then Ry is pulling Dellin up onto the stone wall with her. The two of them are facing each other—the new Dusker Supreme and the Solguard leader. I expect them to begin some kind of speech to announce the peace they've just ratified.

Instead of turning to address either of their armies, though, Ry and Dellin continue to face each other. Ry takes Dellin's hands in both of her own. When Ry begins to speak, her voice is loud and clear enough that those of us standing nearby can hear her.

"Dellin Methuin, Dusker Supreme, Solguard ally, and love of my life, will you marry me?"

I cover my mouth to stifle my gasp of delight. Wade lets out a surprised laugh. Dayne's blue eyes twinkle in amusement. And Dellin....

Dellin throws herself into Ry's arms. Ry lifts her off her feet and spins her around. And then they're kissing in front of everyone. They're both laughing and crying. My vision blurs too much for me to see anything else because I'm crying happy tears, too.

Their joy makes my injured heart hurt a little less.

CHAPTER 46

It takes longer for Dellin and Ry to separate themselves than it takes Ekil, Valior, and Tut to add their signatures to Dellin's contract. Once it's done, Ry's ascension to the position of Solguard leader is officially announced, along with the news that the Solguard leader and Dusker Supreme will be married.

I can feel the crushing weight that's been lifted off all of us. Even the sun seems to shine a little brighter over Tanguro.

The Duskers build their camp a short distance from the stone wall marking the edge of our fortress. They seem well-supplied, but Ry, followed by a group of wary Solguards, bring over fruit from the first harvest of our newly-revived orchards. I can see the tension in every Solguard and Dusker—with the exceptions of Ry and Dellin. Still, the sight of the two groups within fighting distance and sharing food is something I never expected to see. I know that with Ry and Dellin's marriage, and with time, the trust and goodwill Dellin talked about might really come to pass.

It would seem many of the Duskers were as sick of fighting as the rest of us.

Tut, Valior, and I sit outside and eat our own meal as the sun recedes behind a blanket of dark clouds. We watch the unlikely sight of Duskers and Solguards mingling as I bite into a juicy blue fruit I thought I might never taste again.

"Maybe the Halves and Banished could create a similar agreement," I say, wiping away the juice trickling down my chin.

"Don't push your luck, girl," Tut growls.

"I'm afraid that wouldn't be possible," Valior says. "There's too much hatred between us to overcome."

I cross my arms. "If you can find it in yourselves to sign a peace agreement with the Duskers, then why not with the Halves?"

"Because the Duskers are human, and the Halves aren't," Tut retorts.

To my dismay, Valior agrees with him.

Once again, I find myself wishing Liglette were here. She would have wanted peace with the Halves. She would have understood.

I look over to where Ekil and Brogut are explaining the nature of their new agreement with the Duskers to the rest of the Halves. There are some angry faces, and more than a few suspicious ones, but none of them dispute Ekil's decision.

"The Duskers have mostly left us alone since our expulsion to the Banished lands," Valior says. "Our battles with the Halves were more personal."

"They killed your people, and you killed theirs," I say, my frustration mounting. "Can't you move past all of it?"

"We have nothing in common," Valior tells me with a pat on my arm. "There will never be anything stronger than our history of violence."

"Face it, Hemera," Tut says, taking a huge bite out of his fruit. "Some enemies will stay enemies. End of story."

I want to argue more, but my fatigue is catching up with me. Since it doesn't seem like a battle between the Halves and humans is too imminent, I don't push the matter further.

Dellin and Ry come to get Ekil and the Banished leaders to hash out details like territory ownership, distribution of the Jadem trees, and even trade agreements. Jarosh offers to translate for Ekil, so I leave them to it and head back to the building.

The sun is entirely gone by now, and Dark is starting to roll in. The cold isn't as bone-deep as it was before, though. It seems like the ground soaked up the sun during the daylight hours and is holding onto its warmth now that Dark has come.

The constant push and pull between the Jadem trees and darkness trees has resulted in a curious balance between sunlight and Dark. Wokee and the team of Banished and Halves distributing the saplings are still trying to work out the right numbers of each. It seems like the Jadem trees are more potent during the hours of what used to be high day, when the sun is strongest, and the darkness trees are more powerful during low day.

If there are too many Jadem saplings and too few darkness logs, then the Jadem trees die and Darkness comes back. It's a complicated harmony, but it's one I know Wokee will find the answer to in time.

I wave to a few Solguards as I make my way across the short distance between the courtyard and the building. It takes effort not to hunch over to ease the pain of my wound. Sweat trickles down my back from the simple act of putting one foot in front of the other.

My chest is aching, and I feel the heavy weight of exhaustion in a way I've never felt it before. I briefly consider just curling up on a patch of dirt and falling asleep.

I wonder whether I'll ever get used to living without the strength and stamina I took for granted when I was a Bisecter.

The sight of Wade, hobbling toward me on his crutch, is enough to banish my self-pity and replace it with humor.

"Quite the pair we make," I say, motioning to his crutch and the bandages around my chest.

The serious look in Wade's eyes immediately puts me on my guard.

"I wanted to talk to you," he says.

"Well, here I am."

Most of the people and Halves milling around the courtyard have gone inside. In the distance, I can see the twinkling of the Duskers' bonfires. The darkening sky throws shadows over Wade's face, making it impossible for me to tell what he's thinking.

"I have a confession to make." He takes a step closer to me. He reaches out a hand like he's about to take mine, but then he pulls it back at the last moment.

"I knew that, eventually, you'd have to choose between us and the Zeroes. For the past few months, I've been preparing myself for you to choose them." Wade looks down at me, his eyes full of pain and regret. "I was prepared for you to abandon us and become like your father." His voice is so low I barely hear him when he says, "I was prepared for you to become our enemy."

The fact that I very nearly had become my father doesn't stop the sting of betrayal from coursing through me.

Wade continues, "I was distancing myself from you because, in my mind, I'd already lost you." He stares unblinking at me. "I doubted you, and I know that's not something you—we—can easily recover from."

I let out a shuddering breath.

"I shouldn't have given up so easily," Wade says, his distress plain in his voice. "It was wrong of me not to have more faith in you. I know that now."

It takes me a few moments to recover myself enough to speak.

"I guess I can understand why you would expect the worst from me." I let a bitter smile hide the hurt I'm feeling, but I don't think Wade is fooled. "You tried to tell me before, but I couldn't see it then. I was so obsessed with the Zeroes and the power they lent me that I couldn't see the truth in what you were saying. And," I take a deep breath, forcing out the words, "I wasn't myself. Their emotions…their rage…made me into someone even I didn't recognize."

Wade lets his crutch drop to the ground so he can take both of my hands in his. There's a warmth in his eyes I haven't seen in so long I thought I might never see it again.

"I pushed you away," I tell him, speaking a truth that has gone unsaid between us for too long. "I gave you every reason to believe I'd abandon all of you the first chance I got to reclaim the Zeroes."

Wade nods slowly. "I guess there's no going back to the way things were before all of this, is there?"

I shake my head. "We're different people now."

Wade lets out a humorless chuckle. "That's for sure."

"I have a lot to figure out," I tell him, motioning to my eyes, which I still haven't had the courage to glimpse for myself. "I think it's going to be…difficult to get used to being ordinary."

Wade laughs at that. He reaches up and touches my cheek with his fingertips.

"Hemera Harkibel, there will never be anything ordinary about you."

He leans forward, and our lips meet. It's a soft kiss, and I can sense Wade's tenderness and hope mirroring my own. The pain in my chest doesn't stop me from reaching up and winding my hands around his neck.

We stay holding each other even after we've broken the kiss.

"I feel like a part of me has died," I admit.

As soon as the words are out of my mouth, a rush of emotions takes hold of me. I wasn't prepared, and it takes me several moments to catch my breath.

"I know." Wade lets his forehead rest gently against mine. "And it's going to take me a long time to come to terms with all of the Solguards who died because of orders I gave them." He holds my gaze. "I know everyone says there's nothing I could have done to prevent those deaths, but I don't know if I'll ever completely stop blaming myself." His gaze moves to the group of Solguards who brought food to the Duskers and are now returning. "It's weird, but a part of me misses it already. It was the right decision to make Ry the Solguard leader, but now I feel cut off from the action in a way I'm not quite sure what to do with."

I almost laugh at how well we understand each other. "That's exactly how I feel about the Zeroes. I miss their connection and the power they leant me, even though I know they were poison for me."

"So, we're just two broken former-leaders trying to figure out where we fit in a world where we aren't the center of everything?" Wade grins, but there's genuine uncertainty in his question.

I nod at where Dellin and Ry are sitting side-by-side as they watch Vlaz, Wokee, and Everlyn playing. "Maybe we can't be what we were before. Everyone else is moving forward, though. Maybe we can, too?"

"Together?" he asks, raising an eyebrow at me. The hint of his old playfulness makes him more handsome than I've ever seen him.

I take the hand he offers me. He lifts our joined hands and kisses my fingers. Together, we limp back to the building.

CHAPTER 47

Whatever plans Wade and I might have had for stealing a few quiet hours evaporate the moment we step inside the building. A tremendous wailing cuts above the usual noises. Wade and I take one look at each other, and then we hobble in the direction of the cry as fast as our injured bodies will let us.

I stop short as a wall of Halves and Banished blocks my view.

"What's happened?" I ask, breathless.

The Halves part enough for me to slip between them and get a look at what has captured everyone else's attention. A surprised laugh comes out of my throat. Wade, steadying himself with his hands around my waist, leans around me.

Jarosh, happy tears in his eyes, holds up a wrapped bundle. Camike is lying underneath a pile of blankets beside him, looking exhausted but happy.

Jarosh strides forward and holds up the wrinkled, wailing, black-eyed baby.

"It's a girl!" he announces with all the pride of a new father.

Everyone in the crowd begins to clap and whoop. The Halves stamp the ground with their bare feet. Everyone is smiling, even the Halves. Aside from Camike, I hadn't known the Halves could express so much emotion.

"Let's just hope the baby has his mother's disposition instead of his father's," someone in the crowd calls out, "ey, Jarosh?"

Jarosh's smile is so big I think his face might split apart. He cuddles the wailing infant to his chest.

"She has her mama's eyes and her papa's smile," a Westerner observes.

"What are you naming her?" a Halve in the crowd asks.

Jarosh looks at Camike, who gives him a smile and a nod.

"Milia-Jadem," he says.

My breath catches on my aunt's name. I feel Wade's hands tighten around my waist. Morey, who is standing nearby, covers his mouth with a trembling hand. I can see the tears streaming down his face, but when his hand drops, I also see that he's smiling.

"Milia was Camike's grandmother," Jarosh explains in the human language. "And Jadem is the one who built Solis and gave us the tree that brought everything back to life. Jadem gave us hope and the possibility of a new future." He looks at Camike. "Just like our daughter."

"All this hope and optimism doesn't sound like you at all, Jarosh!" a heckler calls. "Who are you, and what have you done with our loveable ass?"

"Hey, I'm a father now," Jarosh replies, "so watch your language!"

Everyone laughs at that.

Beside me, one of the Northerners holds out his hand to the Halve standing beside him. "Looks like we're going to have to share credit for the first baby born in the new era."

The Halve doesn't understand a word the man said, but he takes the Northerner's hand and shakes it anyway.

As I look around, I realize Halves and humans are intermingling. They're standing beside one another and smiling. It's a sight that might be even more surprising than Duskers and Solguards being in the same territory without trying to kill each other. It fills me with hope.

Carefully, like he's afraid his daughter might break, Jarosh hands the baby over to the Halve reaching out for her. After a few seconds of cooing and sniffing the baby, the Halve passes little Milia-Jadem to the Westerner standing beside him. Jarosh hovers over each human and Halve as they take their turn holding the baby.

"Milia-Jadem is going to be the most spoiled baby ever to grace our world," Valior says, looking down at the little girl as one of his people rocks her in his arms and hums a lullaby.

"Damn straight," Jarosh says, and then, at a frown from Camike, amends, "*Darn* straight."

"Seems to me the two of you found a way to bring peace between humans and Halves, after all," Valior says, taking his turn at holding the baby.

"I know." Jarosh lifts a shoulder in what I think is supposed to be his attempt at humbleness. "That's why I'm already trying to convince my mate to try for a second one. You know, all for the sake of peace."

"The purity of your intentions is all-too clear," Tut drawls.

Jarosh winks at him.

Tut continues to frown and mutter to himself. But when the infant reaches him, the surly leader of the Northerners leans down and kisses the baby's wrinkled forehead. The baby reaches up her tiny fingers to grasp at the gold threads woven into Tut's goatee.

"Ah hell," he says, leaning closer to give the baby better access, "I'll sign a peace agreement with the Halves if you'll name me an honorary uncle."

"As will I," Valior says. "Although I'd prefer the title of esteemed grandfather, if it's all the same to the happy couple."

"We'd be honored," Camike tells them, watching Jarosh and their baby with such adoration it brings tears to my eyes.

Within minutes, the contract has been written up, and Ekil and all of the Banished leaders have added their signatures in blood. A giggling Milia-Jadem serves as chief witness.

"Liglette would have approved," Valior says to Tut.

"She always was the heart of our little group," Tut agrees, a reminiscent smile on his lips.

There's a minor ruckus when Wokee and Everlyn come racing through the crowd, clambering for their turn to hold the baby.

"I'm going to teach her to be a bot-i-nist like me," Wokee announces while Jarosh shows him how to support the baby's weight without dropping her.

"Nuh-uh," Everlyn argues, reaching out her hands for the baby. "She's going to be a chemist like me. I can already tell she's going to be too smart for gardening." She gives Wokee a wicked grin as he huffs and stutters.

"My *gardening* keeps everyone in this fortress alive. If you don't watch out, I'm gonna—"

Brogut, who is standing next to Wokee, plucks Milia-Jadem out of Wokee's arms with a gentleness I never would have expected from the enormous Halve. Brogut wraps his arms protectively around the infant and glares at Vlaz, who is panting and wagging his long tail as he sniffs the baby.

"Keep safe," Brogut announces in the human language, giving the hyenair another glare for good measure.

CHAPTER 48

Even with the peace accords signed, there are logistics that need to be worked out. Darkness still reigns in many of the territories, and there is a significant number of rogue Duskers who are still fervently burning darkness logs in their effort to bring about total Dark. They refuse to accept Dellin as their new leader, and they're continuing to terrorize the weak and cut down the Jadem tree saplings the Halves and Banished planted.

Even though Wade and I are no longer in charge of any army, we join the other leaders as they discuss the situation. Wokee comes to the meeting, too, since he understands the delicate interplay between the Jadem and darkness trees better than anyone.

"If there aren't enough darkness logs nearby, the Jadem trees go dormant," Wokee explains. "We'll never be able to turn back Darkness completely, because without the gas and sap given off by the darkness trees, the Jadem trees can't survive."

His eyes light up as another thought occurs to him. "Oh yeah, I almost forgot. Everlyn and I developed a new plant. It's a kind of algae that grows super fast, and it lives in water and feeds off the toxins from the darkness logs."

"You almost forgot to tell us you have a way to purify all of our rivers?" Tut demands.

"Slipped my mind," Wokee says with a shrug. "We've got all the seedlings. Should I start giving them out to the Halves?"

"Yes!" we all say at once.

Dayne ruffles Wokee's hair in the affectionate way he did before he was changed into a Zero. Wokee looks at my brother, his adoration and worshipping glance saying more than any words ever could.

After that, we move on to the non-weather-related issues still plaguing the other territories.

"I've sent a group of Solguards to hunt down the last of the reptors in the Subterrane territory," Ry says.

"The Duskers are working on the remaining wormkill," Dellin adds, "although most of them have retreated back underground now that the Darkness is thinning out."

"We'll need to rebuild all of our settlements so they're above ground instead of below," Tut says, twisting his goatee around his finger. "That way, we'll have less risk of encountering the wormkill that have made their homes closer to the surface."

"That sounds like a job for our Northerner friends," Valior says to Tut.

"Indeed it does," Tut replies. "No rest for the weary, I suppose."

In spite of his irritated tone, I can tell from Tut's posture that he's proud to have so much of our future dependent on the skills of his people.

"What's going to happen with the Duskers who refuse to acknowledge you as Supreme?" I ask Dellin.

Dellin glances at Ry before answering. "The Solguards and Duskers are hunting them down as we speak. Once they're found, they'll be given the choice to either submit to our rule, or they will become the sole occupants of Malarusk."

"You mean the dungeon?" Valior asks, his distaste plain.

Valior's brother died in the Malarusk dungeon, and no matter how good of a leader Dellin is, I imagine that's all Valior will ever be able to think about whenever there's mention of the dungeon.

"No," Dellin replies, surprising everyone except for Ry. "I won't be living in Malarusk, and neither will any Duskers who accept me as their leader. There's too much bad history there, so I'm going to give it to the Duskers who wish to govern themselves." She looks around at all of us. "So long as they don't leave the boundaries of Malarusk, we won't bother them."

"And if they do," Ry adds, "they'll face the wrath of the newly-allied Duskers, Solguards, and Halves."

"Where will you and the rest of the Duskers be living, then?" Valior asks Dellin, looking at her with newfound respect.

"I'll be sending some of the Duskers to the Subterrane territory." Dellin nods at Tut. "They'll be there to help your people with rebuilding the Subterranes, since the wormkill and reptors have made them uninhabitable. The Dwellers were affected by the Darkness more than anyone else, and they're used to the Duskers being their source of authority." She looks around at all of us. "But you have my word that the Duskers will be there to help and guide, rather than to persecute and punish. I have selected a group of my most trustworthy people to help with the building and assist the Dwellers in making a new life for themselves."

"That's honorable of you," Valior tells Dellin, giving her a nod of approval.

Dellin smiles at him before continuing. "The rest of the Duskers will take up residence here, along with the Solguards. We're going to help plant more Jadem trees. We'll also distribute goods to the Dwellers and Banished, at least until their plant and animal life has been renewed."

"Solguards and Duskers living under one roof," Valior muses with a chuckle. "And I thought I'd seen it all."

Ry and Dellin exchange a look full of love and hope. I know if anyone can pull off this unlikely alliance, it's the two of them.

"What's going to happen to Solis?" Tut asks. "Seems like a waste for that whole fortress to sit empty."

"I might have a use for it."

We all turn to look at Dayne, who has been quiet until now.

He clears his throat. "The men and women who were Zeroes are haunted by what happened when they were under Zeidan's control, and the fact that they have no memories of that time. They need a place where they can feel safe, first and foremost."

Dayne has been careful not to blame me for any of it—not what happened to those men and women, or what I did to him. But the truth is that it's as much my fault as my father's, and the guilt of it eats at me.

I look at my brother. Although he is mostly himself again, I can see the weight of the heavy burden he carries, even though he tries to hide it. There's a sadness lurking in his blue eyes that wasn't there before.

"Then, I guess that's all we have to talk about." Valior groans a little as he gets to his feet.

"There's one other thing," Ry says.

When everyone looks at her, she breaks into a smile. She laces her fingers through Dellin's and holds up their interlocking hands. "We'd like to invite all of you to our wedding."

Valior claps his hands together. "The Easterners will provide the drinks!"

CHAPTER 49

I stare at my reflection in the basin. The water is glassy-smooth, allowing me a clear view of my blue eyes. Ordinary eyes.

It's what I wanted every day of my life for as long as I can remember. And yet, now that I look like everyone else, I want nothing more than to go back to the way I was before.

I know I made the right choice with my father. I know it's a miracle I'm alive at all. I know that by giving up everything that made me a Bisecter, I saved countless lives and got back the people I'd lost.

Still, grief at what I've sacrificed hits me at strange times.

Earlier this morning, I was out in the orchards helping to plant new seeds, and a boulder was in the way of a row of root vegetables. In days past, I would have lifted up the boulder, thrown it out of the courtyard, and not given it a second thought. But when I tried to lift it, an unfamiliar burning sensation went through my shoulders and back. No matter how hard I strained, the rock didn't move. I pulled and heaved until fresh blood dotted the bandages still wrapped around my chest, and I realized it was pointless.

The reminder of what I'd lost took my breath away. I would never be what I was, and such abilities would never exist again.

The knowledge of how to create a Bisecter was only ever held by my mother and father, and now that they're both dead, there will never be another like me.

But as I sat hunched over a handful of seeds, Wokee had come looking for me. He saw me staring at the boulder and looking bereft. So, he'd beckoned Brogut, Ekil, and Everlyn over. Together, we heaved and groaned and eventually rolled the stone out of the way.

Afterward, Wokee linked his arm through mine and led me to the outdoor space the Northerners transformed into an eating area. As we sat at one of the freshly-constructed wooden tables, Everlyn served up the first batch of berry tarts since Darkness. I didn't actually get to eat mine, since Wokee scarfed it before I even finished offering it to him.

As a consolation, Vlaz dropped a still-wriggling fish at my feet.

I'm not the only one trying to make sense of everything that's happened. Every one of the people who were turned into Zeroes, including my brother, is dealing with the ramifications of being made into something inhuman and unnatural, and then being returned to their former bodies. They're all experiencing muscle pains and working through the emotional toll of losing and regaining their free will. I don't know if it's better or worse for Dayne, since unlike the others, he retained some shreds of his humanity during the time he was a Zero.

Even though Dayne keeps telling me there's nothing to forgive, I know he hasn't entirely come to terms with the way his freedom was stolen from him. I often find him sitting on the newly-repaired stone wall alone during the time of day when the sun starts to fade and the curtain of Dark comes across the sky.

Dark doesn't feel so foul anymore, now that the hours of sunlight are enough to balance it out. Similarly, the sunlight is no longer harsh and painful to withstand. We still wear cloaks to protect our skin from red, painful rashes that come from prolonged exposure, but the deadly Burn blisters are no longer a problem.

I have to keep reminding myself that, in spite of all the ways I'm weaker now, there are benefits, too. Now that no vestiges of the Zeroes remain inside me, Vlaz has taken to following me around and begging for scratches and food scraps. I hadn't realized how much I missed the hyenair's company. His presence is a constant source of comfort and amusement.

My life is simple in a way it's never been before, and it's more than a little unsettling.

I'm heading toward my own small bedroom, contemplating a short nap, when Wokee catches up with me.

"Mer, come on." He grabs hold of my hand and yanks me toward the nearest set of stairs.

"Where are we going?" I ask, breaking into a jog to keep up before Wokee pulls my arm out of its socket.

"I have something for you and Dayne," he replies.

When we make it up to the third level, I'm slightly out of breath. I lost my natural stamina, and I'll need to build it back up the way normal people do…through training. Wade has promised me that as soon as we're both fully healed, we're going to start back up on our training sessions like when I first came to Solis.

At the sight of Dayne, who is already waiting for us, Wokee's playful mood sobers. While Dayne assured Wokee what happened in Malarusk wasn't his fault and that he shouldn't feel responsible, Wokee hasn't completely let go of his guilt. Like so much around here, I know it will just take more time.

I catch sight of my blue cloak hanging over a wooden rack. It's free of blood and the slash marks from my father's blade.

"You fixed my cloak!" I say, pulling it over my head.

"I would hope that now that there aren't going to be any more battles, you won't get this one all bloody and torn up like the last five I made you."

The bossy affront in Wokee's voice makes me laugh.

"I'm sorry I didn't get you a present," I tell Wokee, feeling a little guilty.

"That's okay." He grins. "You can make it up to me the next time we have some kind of celebration."

"Um, as in the wedding in a few weeks?" I ask.

"Oh, sure, I guess that is our next celebration." Wokee gives me a sly look. "You better hurry up and think of something fast in that case."

I roll my eyes but don't try to hold back my smile.

"I have something for you, too," Dayne tells me.

"Well, now I really feel bad," I say, but I don't hesitate before plucking the small, cloth pouch from his hand.

When I overturn the pouch's contents onto the palm of my hand, my vision mists over.

"How did you even find this?" I ask, looking down at my mother's necklace.

The key is still strung on its same silver chain. The only difference is that the clasp has been mended.

"I found it on the ground right after I killed Zeidan, and I knew you'd be missing it."

"Thank you." My voice comes out as a croak. My hands are shaking, so it takes me a few tries to secure the necklace.

I look down at the tiny silver key, which rests next to Wade's Solguard pendant. The sight and feel of both of them around my neck fills me with a sense of rightness.

"Thank you," I say again.

"Your turn," Wokee announces to Dayne as he bends and picks up a wooden box in the corner.

Dayne takes the box and lifts the lid. I'm watching my brother's face, so I see the moment when the lines on his forehead smooth out and his gaze softens. Gently, he puts the box on the ground and takes out the lute that is nestled on a mound of fabric.

"I made it a while back, when you were still a—" he trails off and then clears his throat. "Anyway, you didn't really seem to like it at the time, so I saved it."

Wokee watches as Dayne runs a hand along the smooth wood and plucks one of the strings.

"Some of the Northerners helped me make it," Wokee continues, "but it was my idea, and I sanded the wood myself."

Unable to contain his impatience, Wokee asks, "Do you like it?" Anxiety and expectation fill his voice.

"I do believe this might be the very thing I was missing to remind me of who I was before." Dayne puts the lute under one arm and uses the other to give Wokee a hug.

Wokee doesn't protest the physical contact the way he normally would with anyone else.

Wokee looks at Dayne and me. "Are we still family?" he asks, as blunt as ever.

"We will always be family," Dayne says without a moment's hesitation. "The three of us."

"And Vlaz," Wokee reminds Dayne.

"And Vlaz," Dayne agrees.

As if he's heard his name, a low growl comes from outside the large window. Vlaz, his black wings fluttering to keep him hovering in place, sticks his nose through the opening. His purple tongue lolls out of his mouth, and when I reach through the window to scratch his flopped ear, a trickle of drool lands on the floor by my feet.

"I'm sorry about what happened in Malarusk during the battle," Wokee tells Dayne, while I continue to scratch Vlaz.

"You have nothing to be sorry for," my brother tells him. "If it weren't for you, every one of us would be dead."

I can hear the brightness in Wokee's voice even though I don't turn around. "Did you notice how I made all the plants in Tanguro come back?" he asks my brother.

"Alright," I tell him, laughing. "Enough bragging. You'll get too big for your britches."

Wokee points down at his newest pair of pants, which are already an inch too short.

"Too late," he informs me.

Shaking his head, Dayne reached over and ruffles Wokee's hair.

Dayne holds out an arm to me, and I join them for a three-way hug.

"I like our family," Wokee says, sighing in contentment.

Dayne's blue eyes, the ones that remind me of everything I loved about our mother, sparkle.

"So do I," Dayne says. "So do I."

EPILOGUE

I smooth a hand self-consciously down the dress I'm wearing for the occasion. It turns out some of the Halves are quite gifted with sewing, and they've been hard at work for the last few weeks making celebration clothes for everyone in the fortress. Mine is Solguard blue, not so different from the dress Jadem once made me wear to one of her feasts.

I stand in the crowd of Halves and Banished that has gathered in front of the raised pedestal the Northerners built in the courtyard. Wokee has been growing flowers for today's celebration, and an intoxicating perfume wafts from the delicate blossoms. Solguard blue, Dusker gray, and white *for contrast*, as Everlyn explained to me earlier.

The sun is just beginning to fade behind the pedestal, and the encroaching Dark is throwing shadows over everything. The torches circling the courtyard have the same effect. Instead of it being ominous, the shadows seem to make everything brighter, especially the four people standing on the podium—five, if baby Milia-Jadem is to be counted. And since she immediately became the most popular person in the entire fortress, she definitely counts.

It had been Wokee and Everlyn's idea to have a double-wedding, and both couples had happily agreed.

On one side of the pedestal, Dellin are Ry are facing each other with their hands clasped. Ry's red curls are loose and wild, and she's wearing a floor-length dress in Dusker gray. It's skin-tight, and I can't help but smile at the outline of the daggers strapped to her thighs. Even though there's no chance of an attack at this celebration, Ry is the Solguard leader now, and she's never unprepared. Dellin's dress is Solguard blue like mine, only hers is far more elaborate.

Camike and Jarosh are standing on the other side of the pedestal, with Mila-Jadem cuddled in her mother's arms. As Jarosh explained—at great length and multiple times—weddings aren't a Halve convention. The mating ceremony is a private one that takes place only between the two who are being mated. But since weddings are a human tradition, and Jarosh is still human, Wokee and Everlyn were insistent that he and Camike should have one. Besides, in Jarosh's words, *there's never a reason to say no to a party, especially when it's being held in your honor.*

We watch and applaud as Dellin and Ry exchange rings and share their first kiss as a married couple. When it's Jarosh and Camike's turn, Camike hands a squirming Milia-Jadem to Brogut.

The giant Halve has appointed himself as Milia-Jadem's personal guard, despite the fact that everyone in the fortress—human and Halve—would lay down their lives without a moment's hesitation for the baby. These days, there aren't any real threats…aside from the plants that grow wild in Tanguro. In all fairness, though, the Tanguro plants can be fatal if one isn't careful.

There's another round of cheering when Jarosh sweeps Camike off her feet and kisses her for far longer than is appropriate. Still, no one seems to mind.

A short distance in front of me, I see Everlyn in a dress she's been spinning around in ever since she put it on. She isn't spinning now, though. She's standing next to Wokee, and their hands are intertwined.

My eyes are still on the happy couples on the platform when I feel Wade's presence next to me. His shoulder brushes against me, and the air around us grows warmer. His hand finds mine, and our fingers lace together. I turn to look at him. His golden eyes are bright with mischief.

"Save me a dance later?" he asks, his lip quirking in that confident, self-assured way I wasn't sure I'd ever seen again.

"At least one," I grin back.

✳ ✳ ✳

After the ceremony, we all gather in the courtyard for the real celebration. It's one thing the Easterners never lost their knack for, no matter how difficult life became…they never forgot how to throw a party.

The sky is dark, but thanks to the Jadem trees, and Wokee and Everlyn's cleaner algae, the air feels pure. The Dark isn't impenetrable like it was before; it's more of a quiet sort of darkness that promises comfort and rest. Except there's nothing restful about the courtyard now.

The Easterners outdid themselves with the decorations. Little glass lanterns have been hung from the branches of the rose-gold Jadem trees. Arrangements of budding branches and new flowers have been placed on every available surface.

The Northerners' wooden tables are covered with the meat hunted by the Westerners, the fruits and vegetables harvested from our own orchards, and flagons of liquid sun…courtesy of Valior.

In the center of everything, people are dancing. I stand with my back to one of the trees as I watch the couples twirl.

My gaze shifts to the musicians, who are playing a lively jig. The dancers laugh and trip over each other as they try to keep up with the beat. Dayne is in the midst of them, his fingers flying over the strings of his lute. There's a look of serene concentration on his face.

It's the first time I've seen him truly relaxed and happy, and the sight warms me to my core. It gives me hope not only for him, but for the rest of the former Zeroes, as well.

There are number of dancing pairs that are made up of a Halve and human, and it seems both impossible and completely natural at the same time. Only a short time ago, the Halves and humans were at each other's throats, even when they were supposed to be on the same side. Now, with one baby, the hatred and distrust are firmly in the past where they belong.

Everyone else is becoming accustomed to how everything has changed. Sometimes, I think I'm the only one who still hasn't come to terms with who and what I've become.

No matter how many times I see my blue eyes, the sight startles me.

There's loud cheering, and I look over in time to see Ry dip Dellin over her arm and give her a kiss that makes Dellin's pale cheeks turn as red as Ry's hair. I smile and shake my head.

"If memory serves," says a deep, rich voice, "you promised me a dance."

I turn to find Wade standing behind me. His eyes sparkle in the firelight, giving them an almost inhuman glow.

"At least one." I take the hand he offers and let him lead me to the dance floor.

The jig ends, and a slower song begins. Wade raises his eyebrows at me, making me wonder whether he somehow arranged for the suspicious timing of this more romantic dance. Wade wraps his arms around my waist, pulling me all the way against him.

I lean in, taking in his earthy, clean smell. I let my fingers slide through his soft hair before wrapping my arm around the back of his neck. The rapid pulse of his heart against my own answers any question I might have had about whether he's as affected by our closeness as I am.

There are others dancing around us, but they fade into the background as I meet Wade's gaze. He brushes his fingers across the Solguard pendant hanging from my neck, and then he leans in for a kiss.

There was a time when I thought I might never get to be with Wade like this again. As Wade deepens the kiss, I live in the moment, wishing it would never end.

The music changes to a raucous beat that is almost deafening. We break apart, both breathless from the kiss and with our ears ringing from the jarring music.

"Well, I guess some things never change," Wade says, sounding amused and a little annoyed.

I follow the direction of his gaze to where my brother is glaring at Wade. Dayne drags a finger across his throat in warning in between plucking the strings of his lute.

"Since Camike wouldn't be pleased about a murder at our wedding, I think you better let me cut in." Jarosh, with Camike and Milia-Jadem beside him, holds out a hand to me.

Wade lets me go, but not before leaning in for another kiss and giving me a look that makes my cheeks heat.

The baby holds out her tiny hands to Wade, and Camike gives him the infant while I take Jarosh's hand.

"Come on, Bisecter," Jarosh says, steering me into the fray of dancers. "You can have your boyfriend back after this dance."

"I'm not a Bisecter anymore," I remind him.

Even saying the words makes a strange pang go through me. I try to bury my reaction so Jarosh won't see anything on my face except for the happiness I want him to see. But my friend knows me better than that.

"You miss it, don't you?" he asks.

I shrug one shoulder, but at the skeptical look he gives me, I admit, "As ironic as it is for me to miss something I resented for my entire life, yeah, I miss it."

"Camike always says grief is a process. In a way, you're grieving for your entire species, even if there were only ever two of you."

I nod, a little surprised at how deeply he's understood my feelings.

"Camike has been a good influence on you," I tell him. "Really smoothed out the jagged edges."

"Don't I know it." Jarosh's gaze softens as he seeks out his mate in the crowd.

She's trying to help Wade contain a wriggling Milia-Jadem. Finally, the baby wins out, and Wade gently sets her down on the ground. All the dancers make way for the baby as she crawls toward us, one tiny index finger pointing at her father.

The baby pauses before she reaches us. She's distracted by Wokee, who is telling Everlyn and the growing crowd surrounding them about the first time he met me.

"Well, I was trapped under a huge boulder," Wokee explains. He looks around and, finding a large boulder on the ground nearby, trots over to it.

Everyone has stopped dancing to watch the dramatic rendition of our first encounter. Much to my amusement, Wokee lies down on the ground, pretending to be stuck beneath the boulder. Everlyn's eye rolls only encourage him. Milia-Jadem crawls closer to investigate, Brogut trailing her like a faithful shadow to make sure no one accidentally steps on her.

"I was trying and trying to get out, but I couldn't."

Wokee pretends to heave against the stone.

"You're exaggerating," I say, loud enough for everyone to hear me. "It wasn't *that* big of a rock."

Wokee ignores me.

"I was shouting *help, help,* and then all of a sudden, the boulder was being lifted right off me."

Chuckling, I turn back to Jarosh to suggest we continue our dance before Wokee's ego explodes from so much attention. But then, out of the corner of my eye, I see movement.

The giant boulder sails over everyone's heads. There's a dull thud as it lands outside the courtyard.

What the—

I look back at the shallow crater where the boulder had once rested. Little Milia-Jadem sits in the center, giggling to herself.

Everyone is staring open-mouthed at the baby, who is now crawling toward us with her gleeful expression trained on her father.

The silence shatters when Jarosh starts to laugh.

"Well looky here," he says as he bends down to scoop up his daughter. His mirth-filled eyes meet mine. "My daughter is a Bisecter."

THE END

Because reviews are so important for a book to be successful, please consider leaving a brief review on your favorite retailer if you enjoyed *Captain Harkibel*. Many thanks!

* * *

Sign up for Stephanie Fazio's e-Newsletter to learn about upcoming books at:
https://StephanieFazio.com/subscribe/

Acknowledgements

I am so grateful to everyone who helped bring the entire *Bisecter* series to life. It was a long and exciting road, and I wouldn't have made it without all of the people who believed in me and this series.

To my editor, Ellen Schaeffer. Thank you for helping me to ruthlessly cut run-on sentences…among other things.

To the rest of my team: Teodora Chinde, Sebastian Lacle, Gia Nikoleishvili, and Whitney Dorr. You're all fantastic.

To Bob Brodsky and the rest of my ARC team for your early feedback, amazing suggestions, and kind words. Thanks also to Linda Thompson and Kathrina Galang for spreading the word about the *Bisecter* series.

To Julie Gibbons for being my bestie, and Rachel Fazio for being my seester.

To my parents, for being the best parents anyone could ever ask for.

To my readers. Thank you for hanging with me to the end of Hemera's journey! I appreciate each and every one of you.

Finally, to Andrew. Thank you for making me happy every single day and for being generally perfect.

About the Author:

Stephanie Fazio is a fantasy author. She grew up in Syracuse, New York, and prior to writing full time, she worked in the fields of journalism, secondary education, and higher education. She has an undergraduate degree in English from Colgate University and a Master's degree in Reading, Writing, and Literacy from the University of Pennsylvania. Stephanie lives in Austin with her husband and crazy rescue dog. When she isn't writing, she's getting lost in parks, hosting taco nights, or ironically and miserably losing at word games, but having fun while she does it.

Connect with Stephanie Fazio:

Visit her Website: https://www.StephanieFazio.com
Sign up for her newsletter: https://StephanieFazio.com/subscribe/